SOMETHING
CLOSE
TO
NOTHING

A NOVEL

TOM PYUN

AMBLE
PRESS
2024

Praise for
Something Close to Nothing

"Tom Pyun's *Something Close to Nothing* is a bold proposition. At a time when the pull toward family and normalcy (and thinking those two are one and the same) is stronger than ever, Pyun's novel wades instead into thornier (and much richer) territory to paint a portrait of contemporary gay male life that refuses neat narratives and tidier still endings. Written with wounding candor and biting humor, *Something Close to Nothing* is a nail-biter of a ride about what it means to break yourself apart to build out who you always thought you could be—for better and for worse."

—Manuel Betancourt, author of *The Male Gazed*

"This is a mesmerizing debut novel. *Something Close to Nothing* is a candid, funny, and shocking dissection of the relationship between one of those gay couples who look perfect in their social media posts. Tom Pyun is writing about contemporary queer life with an honesty and depth that is astounding and welcomed. He has a talent for hitting us with gut punches that turn into belly laughs."

—Rasheed Newson, author of *My Government Means to Kill Me*

"The story is delightfully unpredictable, sophisticated about the complexities of race and class, and a thoroughly entertaining read. Pyun is a gifted writer with a flair for balancing pathos and humor. His characters are flawed in interesting ways that simultaneously engender anger and the urge to root for them. It's a fantastic debut."

—Toni Ann Johnson, author of *Light Skin Gone to Waste* and winner of the Flannery O' Connor Award for Short Fiction

"Cringe, laugh, repeat: Tom Pyun has written a hilarious satire of a late-capitalist couple trying to have it all while resolutely never learning a damned thing about themselves. Infuriating, selfish, and totally lovable, Wynn and Jared trot around the globe in search of love while worrying if their crushes violate semiotics, and if their dancing is a form of cultural theft, all the while trying to convince themselves they aren't so terrible (while often being *so* terrible). I saw myself in there more than I'd like to admit—what a wonderful ride!"

—Glen David Gold, author of *Carter Beats the Dev*

"An engaging, globetrotting debut that captures the many highs and lows of creating the family of one's dreams. Full of warmth, insight, and attention to complicated truths."

—Jung Yun, author of *Shelter* and *O Beautiful*

"*Something Close to Nothing* is outrageous, exhilarating, funny, upsetting, and open-hearted—I cried, I laughed, I cringed, I gasped. Tom Pyun writes with pitch-perfect wit and insight, upending the very contemporary pressures on young gay male couples to settle down and raise kids. As his yearning young heroes travel the globe searching for happiness and meaning, the reader rides an emotional roller coaster with them. This is a book you're going to want to pass on to a friend so you can have someone to dish with when you're done."

—K.M. Soehnlein, author of *The World of Normal Boys* and *Army of Lovers*

"Written with a contagious, full-throttle energy that hooked me from the first page, *Something Close to Nothing* is a fresh and spirited debut. Spanning decades and continents, this tale is equal parts intimate and comic, deftly shifting between character perspectives to insightfully unpack the buildup and breakdown of the love between two men in gripping detail. Tom Pyun infuses each twist and turn with wit and wisdom."

—Genevieve Hudson, author of *Boys of Alabama* and *Pretend We Live Here*

"Get ready for the drama and the humor, the sexiness and the sadness, some bad choices as well as some moments of kindness. Tom Pyun has created characters we come to care for despite their foibles and follies. *Something Close to Nothing* is a rich tapestry of family: how we make it and break it and re-create it."

—Tomas Moniz, author of *All Friends Are Necessa*

Amble Press
Copyright © 2024 Tom Pyun

Amble Press First Edition: November 2024

Print ISBN: 978-1-61294-299-5

Cover Design by TreeHouse Studio

Amble Press
PO Box 3671
Ann Arbor MI 48106-3671
www.amblepressbooks.com

To my beautiful and loving sisters and to H.

PART I

Chapter 1

Wynn
San Francisco, CA
Summer 2015

PART OF ME never wanted to believe the baby was coming. I attributed this ability to live in deep denial to my growing up gay and closeted. It was as if my body housed a vestigial muscle—no longer needed yet remaining toned from decades of hoping that no one noticed I happened to be a flaming homosexual.

In any case, I did notice something was amiss at my last rehearsal before taking a leave of absence from the dance company. We had just finished, and we all sat on the dirty vinyl floor, stretching our limbs and allowing our muscles to cool. I was absolutely glowing, covered in sweat that had turned sticky. It was the most beautiful feeling, that moment you know you've given everything—physically, emotionally, and spiritually—to the rehearsal, and you're almost too tuckered out to go on when suddenly, it's over, and you've finally earned a respite before moving on with the day. Because who can afford to dance all day? We must also work, eat, sleep, and shit.

While I leaned forward in pigeon pose, Elias rehearsed a

new solo piece with Autumn. It was hard-hitting from the waist up—lots of pounding air fists into the chest and thighs, but light in the feet with balletic leaps and turns and even a few martial arts kicks. Not much time passed before I realized this solo was created with me in mind; it considered my strengths as a dancer. Since I'd abruptly announced my leave only a few weeks earlier, Elias had given it to someone else, and this someone else, Autumn, one of the new dancers, struggled to learn the relatively simple choreography. His unibrow furrowed as he muddled through the movements. A curly man-bun flopped about from not holding his head appropriately still.

My face burned with jealousy—I could've killed this routine, really made it my own. I found myself bargaining, willing to give up a finger or even a hand to stay on for one more season. Then the studio lights dimmed, and the intro to "Once in a Lifetime" by Talking Heads blasted on the stereo. Elias and Autumn stopped rehearsal and walked toward me with huge grins. One of the teaching assistants appeared with a pink, frosted cake that spelled out, "It's a Girl!" in bubble letters.

At first, I was confused, unsure of what was happening, until it dawned on me that this was my going away, a sad attempt at throwing me a baby shower. I blew the candle out. Everyone clapped. Then David Byrne's warbly voice rapped, "And you may ask yourself . . ." I started crying, and not the dainty, misty-eyed kind. My outburst was the ugly kind of bawling, where the face collapses into a mushy, red-hot ball of tears and snot. I must've looked like a histrionic widow at a funeral. Someone had the decency to cut the music, and I wiped my face with the collar of my sweaty T-shirt. It was so awkward—everyone's eyes focused on me, wondering what was wrong. Eventually, I managed to cough up a few words: I would miss them, and this was all too sweet.

My attempt didn't work because everyone looked at each other silently, saying, *What should we do?"* There was a heaviness in the air until Autumn passed me a slice of cake. I couldn't bear to look at him. My eyes remained glued to the plate of frosting and fluffy yellow layers.

"It's gluten-free and vegan," he said.

I took a bite. It was awful. The texture was cake-like, yet it tasted like bland applesauce, which was probably used instead of sugar. I pretended to blow my nose so I could spit into a napkin.

"Guys, you really didn't need to do this," I said. "I'll be back next season. It's only six months."

Everyone in the company nodded. Some grinned back at me, while others looked away or down at their feet. I was like a patient in a psych ward who walked around trying to convince everyone I hadn't just tried to jump off the Golden Gate Bridge before a team of nurses strapped me down to inject me with a sedative. Besides, we all knew what happened to Marisa last year. She got knocked up, took leave, and the last time we saw her was after our spring show, rounder and rosy-cheeked with a half-sleeping baby suckling under a nursing poncho. Everyone cooed over the baby, told her she looked amazing, and asked, "How are you doing?" barely waiting for her response before they moved on. Poor Marisa looked so lost, like a ghost who'd been granted a brief visit among the living.

"I'm not giving birth or breastfeeding, guys. I'll be back in six months," I said. "There's something called childcare."

"Of course," someone said.

"It's only six months," I repeated.

"Yes, and sometimes priorities change," said Elias with a smugness that irked me. "Life happens."

"Not this time," I replied with an edge. Elias was undeniably sexy, but he could also be a total bitch.

I hugged everyone in the company and thanked them before heading out, except Autumn. I cupped his shoulder and spoke to his belly button. "Good luck. You're going to be great in the winter workshop."

When I arrived home with half a cake and a $100 gift certificate to Babies 'R' Us, Jared sat on the living room couch with his laptop. A middle-aged Asian woman stared back at me from the screen. Her friendly, open face glowed from the sunshine beaming through the window behind her.

"You remember Bopha? She owns the agency in Cambodia. It's morning there," said Jared.

"Hi, looking forward to meeting you, Winston," she replied cheerily.

"Looking forward to meeting you, too," I said before turning to Jared. "The dance company threw me a surprise baby shower. Isn't that nice? They got me a cake. Have some. Warning, it's not that good." I set the box down on the coffee table.

"Thanks." He turned to Bopha and signaled that he needed a minute. "So, I put your suitcase on the bed and started packing for you, but can you please finish?" There was a familiar impatience in his voice.

"Yes, I will," I said like an obedient child who was all too aware that we were in mixed company. "Nice meeting you again, Bopha. As you can see, I need to pack."

In our bedroom, I moved in slow-motion, packing with the utmost care, as if I had control over time and could delay tomorrow from happening. Then I found myself leaving my body. I have this innate ability—an inherited gift— to disassociate and go through the motions when needed. Within a few hours, though, I quickened my pace and finished packing. I showered and ate a late dinner with Jared. We moved forward with the plan because that is what you do when life happens.

Later that night, I couldn't fall asleep, and it wasn't because I was thinking about the baby. The actual thought of her was too scary, so my mind wandered back to my college days. For some reason, I went there whenever I reminisced about a simpler time. By no means was this period of my youth idyllic. I was deeply closeted for most of undergrad, and the professors notoriously assigned an ungodly amount of reading and term papers. Looking back, though, I missed the lack of foresight into the monotony of adult life that was to come: the 8 to 8 job—the term 9 to 5 was so outdated—the mortgage, and more recently, the heaviness of family-making. There was an idealism then that was missing now. My resolutions at the time were emblematic of this naivete. Around the time of college graduation, right after I finally did come out, I'd made two promises to myself:

1. I wouldn't wind up some corporate bitch
2. I wouldn't end up with a white man

In hindsight, the fatal flaw of this contract was its rooting in the negative. As they say, "If you don't build your dream, someone will hire you to build theirs." Ten years later, here I was, both promises broken, struggling to figure out what I'd been building toward in the first place, only to realize I wanted something completely different.

My first instinct was to blame capitalism—it was the laziest of excuses. Still, I was tired of overanalyzing why I felt so empty in a midnight bed with a lovely man who loved me, too. I was sure of this. We'd been together for years. I'd met his family, and he'd met mine. He had stood by me when my father died. We weren't just planning to go on a major trip tomorrow: we'd been planning a future lifetime together—one that no longer suited me. Inhaling deeply, I made up my mind: I would break up with him.

Right now.

I shook the white man sleeping beside me. Alanis Morissette's nasal, speak-sing echoed in my head—and yes, it was ironic.

Jared rolled onto his side and snapped his tongue twice against the roof of his mouth before falling back asleep. The way the moonlight glowed against his chin and nose—features both delicate and strong—reminded me how much I actually adored the barely noticeable bump on the bridge of his nose and the stubborn pimple on the square edge of his chin that was always in some phase of erupting, healing, or scarring. Where in the world would I find someone this lovely who also loved me? Someone who tolerated my bullshit, whether it be my lateness, my tendency to procrastinate, or my all-around selfishness?

Jared's chest rose and fell. Trapped by my own indecision, panic gurgled up my throat. I needed Jared—my life would be a complete wreck without him. That's when the bathroom down the hall beckoned, and I slipped out of bed. I shut the bathroom door quietly behind me, turned the lock, and reached under the sink for a wrinkled brown paper bag hidden behind the pipes. With shaking hands, I unsheathed the vodka bottle, unscrewed the top, and took greedy swigs that burned on the way down until I was somehow splayed on the floor, still drinking. Still thirsty. The bottle was empty.

Like me.

Less than drunk and more than a little buzzed, I stood unsteadily on my feet and stared at my reflection, admiring my dancer's physique. I swiveled my hips and whipped my head about, admiring my chest and abs, their power and definition, how they allowed me to control my limbs with such quickness and flexibility. And then I kicked the empty bottle over, breaking it into shards.

Cursing inwardly, I turned the lock and cracked open the door to see if I'd woken the man I loved. No. He was still fast asleep. Carefully, using some bathroom reading and too much toilet paper, I cleaned up the mess. I cut myself a tiny bit, not enough to care, and hardly any blood. The minor pain somehow lifted my mood. Tomorrow, I would be content with the gifts bestowed upon me that I'd never done much to deserve: good health, enough money, a loving partner, and a growing family. We would fly to Cambodia the following morning. I would finally get to see Angkor Wat, and, yes, I would finally become a dad. Wasn't that every gay boy's dream? I carefully inserted myself under the covers. Still sleeping, Jared had a sweet little smile on his face. I would be a better version of myself in the morning.

In the morning, Jared was still a semi-clueless white guy, and I was still me, but with a headache—way too sick to say what I needed. During the Uber ride to the airport, I let him babble about taking so much time off work but couldn't bring myself to listen, even if I'd tried. Every aspect of the ride—the smooth suspension of the SUV, the pair of cardboard trees clapping beneath the rearview mirror, the pine scent cloying the air— made me queasy. My usual obsession didn't even appeal to me. I couldn't think about dancing without getting the spins. Curbside at the airport, Jared and the driver unloaded the car, and I raced to the closest men's room, sick to my stomach.

While the cold tile stuck to my knees, I spat the last of breakfast into the toilet. The whoosh of flushes from the other stalls echoed along with the lathering of hands until the dryer's roar overtook them. And though I tried to conjure images of palm trees and cheap smoothie bowls, the latter just made me nauseous again. If I could just get past this hangover, I knew

I could get on the plane and be a better person. I could be grateful. I could feel excited about this child, and I knew I could eventually love her—just like I'd loved him once.

Chapter 2

Jared
San Francisco, CA
Summer 2015

WHEN WYNN BARGED into the house at eight thirty at night, I was on an important video call with the surrogacy agency. By then, I had been in so many work meetings and calls that my voice rasped. Even my vision had started to blur. At first, I wondered if Wynn was drunk. When he kissed me on the cheek, I hunted for the scent of alcohol and was relieved when I couldn't detect anything. My shoulders fell from my ears, and my scapular muscles loosened as if someone had snipped a string holding them together. But then I remembered all I had to do before our flight and that Wynn hadn't packed. My shoulders rose to their previous setting, and the invisible trussing string attached to my shoulder blades pulled tight.

Of course, I'd already packed and had all the essentials in my bags: cash, credit cards, the surrogacy paperwork, and photos for our visas. After the call with the agency—the last of the day, thankfully—a frightening scenario flashed before me: we were at the ticket counter at the airport, Wynn couldn't find his passport, and we missed our flight. I shut down my nightmare and made a mental note to double-check that I'd packed our passports. Over the last few months, I had felt less like a first-time father and more like I was about to have a second kid.

Speaking of which, maybe we weren't ready for a second kid. We'd moved so fast, maybe too fast. We had bought the house last year and taken on a lot with the first baby coming. Yes, I had to accept that we—or instead, he—was not ready. It hurt just thinking about having an only child. Let's face it: only children like Wynn ended up weird. Of course, we would have to wait until Wynn got a new job and could afford to go through this again. Maybe a year or two? Three tops? Four years was unthinkable. I would be almost thirty-eight by then. Also, I wasn't ever doing this Cambodian surrogacy thing again; it was just too risky and too much of a hassle. All the flying and getting the baby a passport at an American consulate in a foreign country was crazymaking.

Part of me still hoped that our kids would be close in age—maybe a year or two apart. That way, we wouldn't be too old if we decided to have a third or fourth later down the line. The big news was that I'd found Wynn's future egg donor, though I still hadn't told him about her. Of course, we didn't know anything about his sperm count since we agreed I would go first, but I was sure he was fine, and this young woman sounded perfect. Like me, she was half Irish-Catholic and half German, with dark blonde hair and hazel green eyes. She was a first-generation college student like me, which was probably why she needed the money. At Stanford, her major was American Studies, and she was also finishing her premed requirements, which made her seem well-rounded. And get this, she played Division I basketball her freshman—I mean first—year, until a career-ending injury, meaning she was very tall, which was a bonus given Wynn's stature. When she came up on the list, I had to whip out my credit card and put a deposit on her.

I'd always wanted a big family, but supporting four or even three people on a single income in the Bay Area made me stress eat. I opened the box and grabbed a piece of cake with my bare hands. It looked beautiful, like a stock photo or a magazine ad, and I took a huge bite. The cake wasn't half as good as it looked, but it wasn't bad nor too sweet; it tasted like apple bread with bland frosting. I scarfed the whole piece down like a hot mess before I realized we hadn't eaten dinner yet.

When I checked on Wynn, he was folding all his clothes methodically like he worked at Abercrombie and Fitch. Usually, he would hastily roll his clothes and stuff them into the suitcase in a haphazard Wynn kind of way.

"Have you eaten?" I asked. "I was going to order Thai. Shrimp and mixed veggie noodles for you?" He looked like a little boy whose dog had gone missing. It was just dance! He would have to get over it. Besides, it was only for a year or two. "You okay?" I asked while scrolling on my phone to order.

"I'm good, just tired." If I had a dollar for every time he said he was "tired." The actual cause of this exhaustion, I never knew since he hadn't had a job in almost a year.

"Damn. King Thai Noodle's closed. It's late. Should we try someplace else?" I asked.

I pressed the order button for a different restaurant. I still needed to double-check our passports and finish online check-in—the earlier, the better, as it increased the likelihood of an upgrade. It was a twenty-plus hour flight with connections, and the possibility of more legroom enticed me. I raced back to my computer.

We ate in silence, eyes glued to our screens. I could hear Wynn's dance videos across the table as I finished our travel logistics. I looked up occasionally to remind myself he was still there. Yes, a total pain in the butt, yet somehow worth all the trouble. I needed to stop giving him a hard time about finding a job. Years earlier, when we moved from Boston to San Francisco, he floated me for more than a few months.

After admiring my loving partner, my eye caught the glint of the shiny new cabinets and stainless-steel appliances, then moved to the custom-built highchair that sat empty between us. I imagined two Brazilian hardwood highchairs filled with Hapa babies—a toddler girl and a newborn boy—pounding their trays, demanding to be fed. Wynn and I were no longer on our phones but instead scraping the bottom of a jar and *choo-choo-ing* mush into their gummy mouths. Just the thought of it warmed my heart, and I let out a chuckle, then waited for him to ask me why I was laughing. He didn't. But it wasn't a problem. I was too busy wondering what I'd done to deserve this life. If my younger self had seen me, he would've asked, "How did you get all of this?" I would have told this little boy it was one part luck, another part hard work. *Very* hard work. Also, I'd add something about picking the right partner and sticking it out.

It's tempting to think there's someone better out there— someone who doesn't need reminding to pack his bags and is gainfully employed with sterling credentials. You just have to put one foot in front of the other, young Jared. Adulthood isn't a fairy tale; long-term relationships don't play out like a Hallmark movie. Relationships are primarily about having shared goals, like creating a family. You have to be in it for the long haul. Right when I was about to open my mouth and say all of this, Wynn let a monster fart rip. Instead of rolling my eyes and getting annoyed as I usually did, I looked straight at him. I kept my face neutral. He looked up from his phone like a kid caught drawing on the wall with a crayon, waiting for me to react. He then shot me a wicked smile, and we burst out laughing like it was the best thing that had ever happened to us.

Chapter 3

Wynn
San Francisco, CA
Summer 2015

BY THE TIME I cleaned up and exited the men's room, I'd already made my final decision: I would stay and make it work. Jared waited for me right outside the bathroom exit, standing next to our bags, his head half bowed over his phone. Looking up, he pulled me in to rub his nose against mine. We'd been together so long that I wasn't even self-conscious of my vomit breath, but he suddenly jerked away and tried to hide it by stroking my damp hair from a distance.

"I'm sorry you're sick, babe," he said.

How could I have thought to leave these lovely, suffocating hugs and his oniony aroma? When we first met, I admit I disliked his pungent musk that even the most potent sports deodorants couldn't entirely mask. Still, over the years, I'd grown accustomed to it. His scent now summoned a familiar coziness, like home.

Then Jared started babbling again and talking with his hands, which he only did when upset. "It was probably food poisoning. These takeout places use farmed shrimp imported from China. You know, there's no regulation there," he said. "Babies in utero are much more sensitive to toxins. Do you think she's been eating organic? Wait, maybe everything is organic in Cambodia?"

Right there, I knew I could've picked a fight and told him I could hear the trill of a dog whistle between his words. I could've also reminded him of my background and what my ancestors had been known to eat that was far worse than imported farmed shrimp. But I was hungover, and besides, he'd heard it before. I was tired.

In any case, I should've interrupted because we did need to talk, like really *talk*. Over the past nine months, I'd avoided the topic and instead prayed the surrogate might've changed her mind or, God forbid, miscarried. When that didn't happen, I'd hoped to magically transform into a normal, thirty-six-year-old man eager to be a first-time father. Although I wasn't quite there yet, I would eventually get there. Jared was sure I could, and he tended to be right about these things. Nobody ever felt truly ready to become a parent, did they? Except maybe Jared, who couldn't wait to become a dad. He was prepared for all of it.

At the airline counter, he smiled at the ticket agent who took our passports, and the two of them exchanged greetings before chatting about the warm weather. I'd learned to let him take the lead in these situations since people usually talked only to him anyway, and ultimately, we got better treatment. Sometimes, I left these interactions wondering if the other person thought I didn't speak English—or worse, if I was a pet or an accessory, like a shih tzu or an iPhone case. Then one day, it hit me that I was wrong on all counts. Next to him, I was invisible. Our country was blinded by a unicorn: a tall, good-looking white man with decent manners and a limited but effective set of social skills. Since then, I had tried not to think about it much. It made me too angry, yet somehow, the world never allowed me to forget it.

"Joni," he said, glancing at her nametag. "Can you tell us where we are on the upgrade list?"

"Let me see." Her red nails clicked on the keyboard, and her eyes flicked to me. "Mr. Winston Kang, you are number one, and you, my dear,"—she twitched a professional smile in Jared's direction—"are number three." Her lips moved as she read the screen. "Oh no," she exclaimed in a tone of mild dismay, "there are only two seats available in business class."

"It's yours," I told Jared, happy I could finally do something nice for him. "You've been working your ass off and did the planning for the trip. Just send me your champagne." I had to give him credit where credit was due. Jared was one of the most organized, hard-working, and generous people I'd ever known—the boy deserved the upgrade.

"No, then we won't sit together," he said.

"Take it, I insist. It's wasteful not to take it." Was he putting on a performance for Joni? Jared lived for flight upgrades, while I could care less about them—weekly travel as a brand consultant for so many years had sucked the joy out of such perks.

"You sure?"

I nodded. Jared smiled at me, then at her, and said, "I have the best partner."

"You boys are adorable," said Joni, who slid our tickets across the counter. "I'm so happy that marriage is legal for you guys."

I cringed while Jared's smile pursed into a grimace. Marriage was a sensitive topic because he wholeheartedly believed in it and whined that our child would be a "bastard." At the same time, I argued it was an antiquated institution created to reinforce the notion of women as property. Instead of a big wedding, I surrendered to a kitchen and bathroom renovation. Who knew that one ceramic tile could cost as much as a tuxedo rental?

We strolled past a dim sum place, a wine bar, a cafe that served only matcha, and some yoga and meditation rooms, then stopped to refill our hydro-flasks at a water station. When he walked ahead of me toward security, I noticed his dishwater blonde hair had thinned more. A quarter-sized spot of pink scalp was visible on the back of his head. It made him kind of dad-hot, and I had to stop myself from running over to caress his bald spot. To kiss it. We were in a public setting, and I'd never been comfortable with PDA. On the other hand, I wondered if it might be the last time I ever touched him.

Once we reached the back of the line, his head dipped back into his phone. His brow wrinkled, signaling concern.

"What's wrong?" I asked, peering over his shoulder.

"That nanny service emailed to say they don't have anyone bilingual available."

"Why are you even worried about that?" I said. "She won't start talking for at least a year."

"True. Plus, you speak a little."

"Don't depend on me. You know my Korean is terrible." One of the childhood benefits of growing up in Connecticut was the lack of a Korean-language school close by. However, with age, I had come to regret not knowing my mother tongue.

"Yeah, but you can teach her the basics," he said. "Besides, since you're not working, you might want to stay home longer."

"I don't know about that. I think we can find an even better nanny. Spanish is actually more useful," I said. My chest tightened. Why was he trying to turn me into a housewife? "You know, my schedule is going to pick up—"

"Babe, I'm nervous about leaving Mare with a stranger while she's so young." He chuckled. "I just gave her a nickname."

My hands shook. The bitter aftertaste of vomit caked my tongue. I was beginning to freak the fuck out. "Can we talk about this when I'm feeling better?"

"Of course."

Great. Meryl, or now Mare, wasn't born yet, and I already resented her. The signs were there: *I was going to be an amazing dad.*

He dropped his carryon in a bin, and I followed suit, depositing my backpack. The conveyor belt rolled through the X-ray machine, shuddering in fits and starts that matched the awful feeling in the pit of my stomach. *Was it too late to stop all of this? Change my mind again? Stop the bins?*

I had to say something, but when I summoned the courage to squeak the word "we—," he was about to march through the X-ray machine. Like Superman in the Agony Booth, right before he loses all his powers.

The last trip we took had been to Maui a year ago. At the time, I had just been accepted into the hip-hop dance company *Full Force*. I couldn't relax the entire vacation because I felt I should've been keeping up with classes and drilling choreography. Jared made me read a business book a coworker had recommended to keep me still. It laid out a concept called the "four burners of life": family, friends, health, and work. To become successful, the book said, one had to cut off one of the burners. To become *very* successful, one had to cut off at least two, so I quit my job.

"Sir, wake up!" the TSA security man said, his voice cutting through my muddled head. "Come in."

I walked through the booth to the other side. If I got on this flight, I had a vision of what my life might look like in a month: I would be stuck at home from 7 a.m. to 5 p.m., five days a week, the hostage of a crying, pooping terrorist.

A conversation about why I was so emphatic about protecting my time was long overdue. Hip-hop dance kept me alive, and though it sounded melodramatic, I knew part of me might die if I didn't even *try* to pursue a dance career—or at least harbor bitter regret on my deathbed. Both my parents were already gone, so the prospect of an early demise didn't seem farfetched. If we weren't following our dreams, what were we doing? Playing it safe. Something close to nothing. Was I afraid of failure? Of course, I was afraid, deathly afraid, which was probably the answer I was looking for. Besides, I'd been so good—too good—all these years. I'd never cheated on a test or Jared. I'd stayed away from drugs and toiled for years at a corporate job I hated. I played by all the rules, and it was time to do something for myself for once. In any case, wasn't I too talented not to pursue dance seriously? Too privileged, as well? Of course, Jared had a point. I could do both: babysitting—I mean, raising a child—during the day and rehearsing at night. Since the beginning of humanity, parents had managed to hold down jobs and take care of their children simultaneously. Why did I have to be all or nothing, so extreme in my ways? Going forward, I vowed to be more balanced because this new life chapter would be hard. I knew I could do it. I could be better. I could be more grateful. Kids *are* great!

A woman tapped me impatiently on the shoulder, nudging me to get out of her way. "Sorry," I muttered before grabbing my bag off the conveyor.

Jared playfully nudged me with his shoulder. "Wake up! Are you going through a routine in your head? How are you ever going to go back to a *real* job when your mind is so laser-focused on dance?"

His voice had a familiar edge, a tone just paternalistic enough to kindle my rage—as if I were someone or something that needed to be managed. Who was I kidding anymore? I was trapped in this relationship, miserable as hell, and so tired of hiding it.

"I can't do it," I said quietly, amazed the words had finally slipped between my front teeth. "I just can't."

Jared stared at me; incomprehension etched on every feature of his face. "What?" he said, looking disoriented as if I'd just shaken him awake.

"I don't want to be a father. I'm sorry." Stomach acid gushed into my mouth. I swallowed and spoke louder over the echoing flight announcements and the crowd's din. "I don't want to be a father; I can't do any of this"—my hands waved aimlessly. "I'm not going. I'm staying here."

His eyes widened, and his lips parted into an *O*.

And instead of telling him that he was better off with someone who genuinely wanted a family, and that Meryl was better off without an asshole like me around—instead of waiting for an answer—instead of trying to have a conversation about just what was troubling me so badly—I ran. I ran toward the exit doors, my half-open pack bouncing on my neck, the straps too loose around my shoulders. About ten feet from the exit, I tripped on one of my flip-flops, which propelled me into a long jump across the ticketing area carpet. My legs split mid-air, and it was as if I were part of an impromptu public dance performance: the airport, my stage, the travelers, my audience. At last, I was free.

A few steps later, I kicked off the remaining flip-flop and found myself on the other side of the terminal doors, the sidewalk cooling the bottoms of my feet. My phone buzzed in my pocket. An index finger silenced it. I didn't even bother to look both ways when I ambled toward the taxi stand.

Chapter 4

Jared
Siem Reap, Cambodia
Summer 2015

THE SUN ROSE amber over Angkor Wat. I watched the shadow gradually brighten before us until, like a camera flash, the massive temple was bathed in the softest of morning light. A droplet of sweat beaded down my face slowly, then accelerated before resting on my lower jaw. I couldn't bring myself to wipe it away—it was like I was under hypnosis. I could only stare at the temple until the incessant clicking of camera phones and growing chatter reminded me to blink. Then I remembered that Wynn and I were supposed to see this site together. My screwed-up head shook in disbelief that he was missing this. And for what? Hip-hop!!

A large pond separated me from the world's largest religious monument. Lily pads covered most of the surface, yet one spikey pink flower floated near the edge. I squatted and reached, hoping its simple beauty might cheer me up, but it was too far away. I was too hot and lightheaded to keep trying without falling in, so I gave up and wiped my face with the hem of my polo.

The crowd inched toward the temple while the sun blazed. Even with sunglasses, I needed to shade my eyes to gain a clear picture of the turrets that looked like pinecones. Once, in second grade, I squeezed glue along pinecone scales before shaking bronze and silver glitter over them. It was messy, glitter everywhere, even though I'd spread newspapers across the table and floor. When Mare's old enough, I imagined us doing this project together in the backyard. We would hang them as ornaments on our Christmas tree.

A young woman, maybe college-aged, asked me to take her and a friend's picture. With touching trust, she handed over her phone. The girls beamed as they posed cheek-to-cheek, arms draping over narrow shoulders. They ran back to me with broad smiles, and I showed them the photo. *Oohing* and *ahhing,* they giggled and politely asked me to take more. This time, they made goofy faces, stretching their mouths with their fingers and rolling and crossing their eyes. I shot a series of pictures and found myself cracking a smile, my lips dry and stiff from frowning for so long. They were the first people I'd spoken to in days whom I hadn't paid to serve me food or drive me places. Part of me hoped for a longer conversation so I could invite myself to whatever they were doing, except, after thanking me, they walked ahead, negotiating breakfast in their clever Irish accents. I let them go, not wanting to give them the wrong idea. Then again, under the circumstances, I wasn't entirely sure what the right idea would be.

Last night, after checking into the hotel, I set out to find this highly rated Asian-fusion restaurant for dinner. The sky hung low and black, and there were so few streetlights I worried I would trip on a sidewalk crack. Just around the corner from the hotel, a man followed me, clucking, "You want girl. I have nice girl. Pretty girl."

I quickened my pace, but he wouldn't relent. Finally, under a string of lights, I said in a pleading yet firm tone, "No, I don't want anyone. Leave me alone. Please."

The man said, "You like very young? Just twelve years old. Fresh." He then looked me in the eye and squinted. "You want boy?" He cackled. "Yes, I have a very young boy, too."

I ran away before circling back to the hotel. When I complained to the concierge, he said he would call the police, though he didn't think they could do much.

"Master Jared, I'm sorry. Cambodia is a very poor country."

"Just Jared, please."

The concierge handed me an educational pamphlet on NGOs working to end child trafficking. I donated to all of them online while slurping ketchup-covered "spaghetti" in my room.

I forced myself to do the Angkor Wat tour because I thought being with others might cure my loneliness, but I only wanted to head to my hotel room. Still, I couldn't help but scan the crowd for the happy Irish girls. I headed toward the temple's unpaved parking lot when I was sure they were nowhere to be found. Clouds of sand-colored dust curled around me. Tourists queued in front of luxury buses that sparkled through the haze. My driver from the hotel, an elderly Cambodian man with a shock of cotton-white hair, recognized me and waved.

After we drove off, he asked, "Where you from?"

I couldn't answer because another crying jag was about to bubble up. Luckily, I had nothing left. After Wynn had left me at security, I sat on a bench in shock for close to an hour, staring into space. It was only after I had boarded the plane that the actual bawling started, and I spent fourteen hours in business with a blanket over my head. When the steward came by with champagne flutes, I'd collapsed into an utter heap of tears. Upon exiting the plane, I had left behind a trail of used Kleenex.

"Where you from?" the driver repeated.

"California."

A strand of wooden beads with a matching brown tassel hung from the rearview mirror. Instead of looking at him, I watched them swing.

"First time, Cambodia?"

"Yes, my first time. It's beautiful."

"Alone?"

"Yes, just me. For now."

I stuck my earbuds in. The driver's mouth moved, probably telling me about some relative he had in California.

A meditation app played while I took deep breaths, manifesting positive vibes through my improvised mantra: I'm on vacation in an exotic land. I'm joyously awaiting the birth of my daughter, my legacy.

Wynn would change. He had to. Nigel, my British psychic, had said so. Just last week, he had shuffled and flipped tarot cards, the stones from his rings and bracelets reflecting a glare onto the computer screen and said, "Ace of Swords, short-term challenges. You need to set an intention to be patient with him and yourself. Wynn will come around after the baby is born. Ah! The Empress card—abundance. Wow, the Ace of Cups, new family connections, beautiful energy here. Yes, I see you both with more than one child in the future." He added that the next few months would be challenging, and I needed to trust that things would work out.

So, Wynn would return, and this was a tiny blip in our life together. I imagined telling the story at a dinner party in the distant future. Our guests—a well-to-do, racially diverse mix of middle-aged, straight, and gay professional couples—would laugh uncomfortably at the thought of a younger version of Wynn running through the airport in flip-flops. The incident would lose its power after two and a half decades full of diapers, family vacations, ballet recitals, and school graduations. Then everyone, including Wynn, would glance at the empty chair where Meryl would've sat if she wasn't across the country in the middle of her sophomore year at Wellesley, Williams, or Wesleyan. Nigel was right—he had to be right.

Mostly, I just wanted Wynn to call. We needed to talk. Why didn't he say anything beforehand? Why was I always last to know? Anger rose within me. I imagined what I would say when he came to his senses. On my phone, I opened the Notes app and created a new document titled "Terms and Conditions."

- Must limit hip-hop to one class a week.
- Must get a new job or go back to old job at Synergy Consulting Group.
- Must stop the not-so-secret drinking.
- Must have sex at least once a week.

I crossed out the last item since making it happen would likely entail doing it *that* way, which I was *almost* ready to start trying. We'd done oral twice since January, yet nothing in the last month or two because he was too tired from class—too sweaty, sore, drunk, and everything to be close to me. True, I'd been stressed about work, but still, two times in eight months? That wasn't normal.

Back in my hotel room, the airport scene played over in my head. I couldn't stop seeing the back of Wynn's head fly away from me in the terminal, the lone flip-flop abandoned in the scuttle. I had never seen him run so fast, making me wonder whether he was running away from me, from us, or from something else.

I did everything to make him happy. I ground away at my tech job, clocking in fourteen-hour days at Reverie, and that work meant that I earned enough so he could quit his job and dance—and drink, which at least he had the decency to do in private. I sacrificed to make this relationship work because that is what adults do. All Wynn had to do now was try to be an adult too, but instead, he decided to be a boy.

After wasting most of the afternoon waiting for a text from him, I threw my phone over the bed, where it bounced on a chair cushion before landing on the floor. Any day now, Wynn would realize what he'd lost: he would see that he was too old for this nonsense.

Nigel had encouraged us to have the baby as soon as possible. He said it would result in the healthiest of babies, despite that we'd just bought the house and were cash strapped—"house poor" was the proper term for it. Nigel muttered something about the lunar moon crossing Mercury rising—I could never keep track—and to be wary of sudden changes and setbacks. Then again, Nigel told me to support Wynn's dancing and look at what that brought me. I did the only reasonable thing: I picked up my phone and called Nigel, eventually leaving a voicemail saying that Wynn had left me and that it was partially his fault. The girls at work all swore by him. Lara, my longtime admin, said Nigel had predicted the exact number of online first dates she'd have to go on before she met her match—seventeen—but missed the number of dates they would have to go on before he popped the question. Nigel said 121, while her fiancé proposed on 149. Served me right to trust a psychic.

Exhausted from thinking about my problems, I searched my room for the remote, but when I found it tucked inside a cabinet, the sight of the black screen depressed me. The hotel room could've been in Charlotte or even Duluth. Heavy, colonial mahogany furniture with brass handles pushed against the walls; club chairs and drapery upholstered in matching rose, beige, and mint green stripes. It was the highest-rated hotel on RevTravel, which I found hard to believe. Sitting on the edge of the bed, I stared out the window onto a manicured lawn of bougainvillea and palm fronds. I watched the golf carts sail by in the distance.

To kill time, I unfolded and refolded all seven of Meryl's onesies, tracing my finger along the embroidered lace necklines, tugging at the pink satin bows on the sleeves, in awe of how someone could be tiny enough to wear them. They were imported from France, cost a small fortune, and even I, "spendy Jared," felt ridiculous buying them. Even I knew that expensive baby clothes were for the parents and that I was probably making up for some childhood deprivation issues. That said, there was a small chance she would be an only child, and if that was the case, why shouldn't I spoil her? What parent didn't want the best for their kids? And even though Mare wasn't born yet, I wanted her to have everything. Yes, I knew "everything" wasn't necessarily good for her, but I considered it a consolation prize. I couldn't afford the hundreds of thousands of dollars to give her a California-based surrogate, but a $78 Egyptian cotton onesie? That I could do.

"Why would you go through all that trouble just to save a few bucks?" Lois had yelled over the phone.

"More like low six-figures kind of bucks, but who's counting?" I'd wanted to say. Talking about that kind of money with her always felt awkward.

My mother had never cared for Wynn, and over the years, I got used to defending him. I was sure she would throw it back in my face, though I couldn't let it get to me. I needed her. Dear God, if I'd known this was going to happen, I would never have moved forward with it all: the sperm testing, the deposits, the freezing and shipping of my genes across the world. Not to mention selecting the egg donor, coordinating the in vitro, and finding a legit surrogacy agency. I did everything all by myself. And yes, Wynn said a few times that he was nervous and unsure if he was ready to be a father, but he never stopped me, never put his foot down, never said no. After he quit his job—without telling me, of course—I'd thought we'd struck an unspoken bargain. I would be the breadwinner while he could dance to his heart's content and *help* with the baby for a finite period. It wasn't like I ordered him to stay home full-time forever. Once he eventually got a new job and we had more money, we could hire a full-time nanny or do daycare. I was sure I'd said all this, but alas, he wasn't listening.

There was no point in rehashing any of this because, like it or not, Meryl was coming into this world. So, I called Lois, who answered on the first ring. I said hello and immediately hit the mute button. My voice trailed off into the most guttural moan I'd ever heard coming from anyone in my life.

"It's after midnight, Jarey. This better be important."

"Mom—" My face collapsed, and I wailed like a dying animal into the phone.

Chapter 5

Wynn
San Francisco, CA
Summer 2015

ANYWAY, I WAS on autopilot, set on manic. When I arrived at the house from the airport, I stuffed as many of my clothes as I could into trash bags and unhooked two framed photos off a wall. The first was of my parents in front of our Cape-style house in Westport, holding me as a newborn. The other was the last photo I'd taken with them. I stood beaming in cap and gown. My head rested on my mother's bird-boned shoulder, while my arm wrapped around my father's sturdy waist. I carefully wrapped both pictures in kitchen towels and shoved them to the bottom of a bag.

When I roamed the elegant beige rooms for what I thought might be the last time, a weight lifted—the relief from unburdening myself of the 2,000-square-foot hungry mouth that had swallowed my money, my life. How I could've talked myself into staying longer seemed out of the question in retrospect. Only after I'd left Jared at the airport did the truth finally ring painfully clear in my ears. A "white picket fence" life might be for some. It had worked for my parents when they were alive, but it wasn't for me. True, maybe I didn't want to grow up. Yet, there had to be an alternative beyond corporate servitude and the inevitable move to the suburbs. In any case, I wouldn't have been doing Jared and Meryl any favors by continuing to lie to myself.

There were only facts now: I wanted to dance. I wanted to feel alive. I wanted to travel. I wanted anal sex. I wanted to fuck other men and get fucked. I didn't want to be someone's partner or someone's father. I didn't want to feel empty anymore and was sure I never wanted to work as a brand management consultant again. All these truths were unpopular, so unpopular in fact that I'd suppressed them until I couldn't any longer, after which I hid them from Jared and even myself. The reason wasn't apparent to me, so I relied on my default explanation for how I live now: capitalism. Specifically, the American varietal, the kind that promoted greed and abject materialism as a moral creed.

Everything I needed was packed. Finally, I could leave all of this behind. And yet, I paused. Hesitated. Waited to change my own mind. To my surprise, I faced the baby room's door, one hand clutching the rose-tinted, crystal knob. Jared and the interior decorator had finished the nursery a few days earlier. I hadn't yet stepped inside to inspect their work. In retrospect, it was probably a sign.

I opened the door to an explosion of pink and white bunnies adorning the walls, floor, and crib. Jared had heard somewhere that bunnies symbolized fertility, so he did his usual thing and went overboard. A giant stuffed white rabbit sat slumped over in the far corner, and I pushed back its floppy ears, revealing cartoonish blue eyes and two oblong felt teeth. There was something judgmental about its expression. I flipped the ears back. A soft felted mobile hung over the crib: more bunnies, each the same shade of Pepto-Bismol pink but wearing different outfits—an office worker, a ballet dancer, a rock star with a guitar, a schoolgirl. I tapped the mobile, and the bunnies rotated. After a few circles, the mobile fell from the ceiling and crashed into the crib—my cue to leave.

I was an only child. Not only were my parents gone, but I'd also abandoned my remaining family—I didn't have anywhere to be or go. All I knew was that there was no way I could spend another night at the house. It belonged, now, to Jared and the baby.

I didn't call Jared or text him back. There was nothing to say. He left messages on my voicemail; I didn't listen to them. He sent texts; I didn't open them. Childish, perhaps, to cut off all communication just like that, but leaving this relationship was the first adult decision I'd made all on my own. I needed a clean break because turning back and reinserting myself into his orbit was too easy.

For the past decade, Jared had controlled everything: he'd chosen the house, picked the takeout restaurants we frequented, selected most of the movies and TV shows we watched, and planned our vacations. Before him, my mom ruled. Although she'd always said she didn't want to be anything like her own parents—Evangelical Christian physicians with exacting standards who'd emigrated from South Korea in the '50s—she was also dismayed by my lack of ambition and had reacted to it by (gently) dictating the terms of my life, while somehow making everything seem like my idea. Mom had gone to Bryn Mawr, so I would go to Swarthmore, just a few towns over. Her favorite uncle in Toronto had played the cello, and so would I, until I quit my senior year of high school, and so on. I was a total cliché: a well-behaved Korean boy with an overbearing mother and emotionally distant father. The only possible surprise—for them, at least—was that I didn't turn out to be straight. But they never knew or wanted to know I was gay. Not officially, at least.

Then there was the time after Mom died and before Jared when I'd felt so lost that I blindly followed my best friend Nicole to Boston to avoid being alone in the house with my father. We became roommates, and I eventually applied to a similar program at the same university even though I didn't particularly like Boston or have an interest in graduate school or policy studies. I'd only done so because I'd had no strong wants of my own.

But that was then. I had a calling now and couldn't waste it. All my hesitation at the airport earlier had been rooted in a deep fear of failure, and for the first time in as long as I could remember, I felt strangely calm.

At the dance studio, everyone was in the middle of warm-up. Soul II Soul's "Back to Life" blared from the studio speakers, and the dancers were on their backs, ab-crunching to the bass line. I elbowed my way to the front row and squeezed between two high school-aged girls in matching zebra leggings. Elias remained cross-legged on the floor, filing his nails. He looked up briefly and made eye contact through the studio mirrors. "What are you doing here?" he mouthed silently, then smiled, his sharp incisors peeking through his thick mustache.

I waved, then shrugged.

"Let's talk after," Elias mouthed through the mirror before lowering the music's volume to teach the first eight counts through a headset mic.

I focused on the routine so intensely that I slipped into a fever state. My movements—head ticks, booty swirls, body rolls— were so aggressive and big, one of the teenagers in zebra tights changed lines. Usually, I was a conscientious dancer, minding other people's personal space and keeping my movements small in crowded classes. Yet, this time, I couldn't help myself from hogging every inch of the floor. At the end of class, Elias patted me on the back.

"You were on fire today. Now walk me out."

From behind, he looked more like a rugby player than a dancer. He stood at least half a foot taller than me, his shoulders twice my width, his deep olive, bald pate glowing under the studio's lights.

When we reached the sidewalk in front of the studio, I said, "I left him, my partner, the baby, everything—so I can dance. I feel horrible, but it's what I want. I need to see this through."

Elias smiled as if he'd known all along, his eyes locking with mine. "You're brave," he replied. "I didn't know you were this serious about dance. I wish you'd talked to me about it beforehand. The life of a dancer is tough. Your body will betray you."

It hadn't crossed my mind to consult him. There was an unspoken teacher-student divide.

"I know," I said. "I'm well aware I don't have many good years left in me, and I want to make the most of them."

We stood on the sidewalk and stared at each other. I tuned out Mission Street's police sirens, ignored the homeless woman asking for money, and paid no attention to the faint stink of urine. Elias even dismissed his students' waves and greetings as they walked past. My old self would've looked away to hide my flushed cheeks, but now, I was determined to win this staring contest. My groin boiled. The air shifted between us.

"Let me know if you need to talk," he said, stepping closer before leaning in. I hugged him like Jared had done to me at the airport, squeezing him tight. Then I inched my lower half toward him, eventually into him. With a playful shove, Elias broke our embrace. "And to think I pegged you as a good boy."

After a lingering goodbye, I floated toward my car and called Federico, my only friend in the city. I knew him from Synergy Consulting, where we'd worked side by side until I quit, and he stayed, the company dangling a mirage of partnership that kept him on the road and well-fed.

"Wynn!" he barked in surprise. "What do you mean, 'you're in the city and sleeping in your car'? Aren't you supposed to be living the gay version of *The Handmaid's Tale* right now?"

"I left Jared at the airport," I said.

"No shit! Really?"

"No shit. Really."

He let out a surprised, ironic laugh. "Always the procrastinator, Special K," he said with dark admiration. At Synergy, I had developed a reputation for putting together fifty-slide PowerPoint decks (outlining Very Important tiers of credit card reward programs to be sent out to millions of customers explaining that you and you alone qualify for these marvelous perks!) mere hours before client meetings. Much to the chagrin of some of the firm's partners, I always managed to pull it off.

"I know!" I said, suddenly self-conscious of how impulsively I'd acted. On the spur of the moment, I'd blown up my life, thrown away a sure thing, and for what?

"Do you think I did the right thing?" I asked Freddie, who never had the answers.

"You'll work it out, but for now, you're free. No job, no family, no place to live. The digital nomad lifestyle is on-trend," he replied. "Hey man, I'd love to shoot the shit, but I'm in Vancouver. About to head to a work thing—"

I spoke fast. It would only be for a few days, and I would look after his stuff. "Sure, sure," he agreed. I figured he wouldn't mind if I crashed at his place; he was rarely home, and his plastic plants could do with a dusting. Freddie usually stayed with his girlfriend in Berkeley when he wasn't on the road for the firm. "Pick up the keys from the super!" he barked. "Talk later! Gotta go!" Abruptly, he hung up.

I was a bit taken aback. I'd just ended a ten-year relationship and abandoned an unborn child, and all Freddie could do was tell me that "I'd work it out" before giving directions to his Uber driver? And here I was, killing it in dance class, flirting with my teacher. Was I a monster? A sociopath? In any case, Freddie was right. I was free, but this was maybe because I wasn't worth shit.

Freddie's loft building in the Bayview was only a mile from my old house. Instead of heading inside, I cranked the volume on my car stereo. I sang along to the hip-hop station, miming and choreographing routines to songs buzzing and scratching through the car's blown-out speakers. I wasn't ready to drag my garbage bags into the apartment and settle in for the night.

The sun went down, and still I sat in the dark car, missing my parents. They would've called me spoiled if they were alive and maybe even blamed themselves. During one of his few lucid moments, my father might've said, "Winston, time to grow up. Time to be a man." Giving up a lucrative career in consulting for a life in the arts would've made his head explode. Dad had worked as a computer engineer at the same helicopter manufacturer his entire career, and he and Jared had bonded over "techie" things. And though he'd never uttered the words "gay" or "your boyfriend" before his passing, I knew he'd liked Jared and thought him responsible and of good character. He would've begged me to stay in the relationship and work it out.

My mother had been an amateur painter and might've understood my decision better. Yet, I could see her chalking this up to a brief phase, an itch I needed to scratch before taking the inevitable leap that resulted in what she'd had and what Jared wanted. If she were here, she might've yelled, "Ay ghu, Uri eorin wangjanim." Our little prince. Unlike my dad, she was second-generation, and her Korean wasn't that good. Still, she sometimes would throw around a few phrases when feeling playful, probably hoping I would pick up some of it.

When Mom had plated my white rice with an ice cream scooper the way I'd liked, she always placed it in front of me while singing my Korean nickname, Uri eorin wangjanim. Only now did the grim significance of "our little prince" seem obvious: the classic tale by Saint Exupéry about a lost boy who floated through space on an asteroid in search of meaning.

Mom had passed a month after I graduated from college and before I'd had the chance to come out to her. It killed me to think she had never really known me and who I'd become as an adult. Although I would never know if she would've supported my being gay and my relationship with Jared initially, she would've eventually gotten there. I knew this in my heart, which was why it remained my biggest regret.

Feeling sorry for myself got boring after a while, so I gave in and texted Elias. In that surprise embrace, there was confirmation on the sidewalk—our bodies saying, "Yaasss!" I didn't want to seem overeager, but I couldn't stand any more time alone.

> Me: Thanx for offering to listen. Are u free tonight?

> Elias: I can be for you

An hour later, we were on Freddie's bed, shirts off, kissing and suckling on each other's nipples. Despite my nervousness, I couldn't get enough of Elias: his polished skin, the curly black fur covering his thick, ropey muscles, and the lush, overgrown mustache that sloughed off layers of my face. It had been years since I'd kissed a man besides Jared, and though I'd been tempted to stray, I'd fought it. This was also my first time with a man of color, which somehow sanctioned it in my mind—making it seem less like a sexual conquest and more like an affirmation of my identity. I'd always wondered what it would be like to connect with another man who moved through the world in similar footwear as mine, someone who doubly knew what it felt like not to belong or fit the rigid standard of beauty established

37

by society and the media.

Soon Elias and I were on our sides, me spooning him from behind. Elias pulled his mesh shorts down and pushed his hairy ass against me. The bed frame squeaked.

"No need for a condom," he said. "I'm on PrEP." Elias reached for my cock, sliding it inside before I could say anything or resist. "I pre-lubed in the car."

"Wait—" I didn't stop him. My first thought was, why *wasn't* I on PrEP? It dawned on me that there would be no reason to take a daily HIV prevention drug if I was in a decade-long monogamous relationship where we never had penetrative sex. So much had changed so quickly since the last time I was single. After years of repetition—the same white man, the same positions, the same hand jobs and blowjobs—I was finally doing something about it.

Elias turned his head toward me and whispered. "Call me The Diva."

"What?" I said, softening. I gazed at the gigantic television hanging from a brick wall to gather my bearings. Our shadows reflected on the blank screen, which unnerved me, so I focused on the back of Elias's head.

"Call me The Diva. Call me The Queen."

I did as I was told. My hard-on returned, and I thrust with enthusiasm and huffed in Elias's ear. "You're The Diva. You're The Queen."

Six thrusts later: finished.

"Sorry," I said, embarrassed. "I don't have a lot of experience with—"

"Oh, you're a bottom, too. That's OK, honey," said Elias, wiping himself with Freddie's white duvet.

"No, I mean, maybe I am? I don't know for sure—I've never really done much of either. I know it sounds crazy, but my partner, I mean my ex, wouldn't allow me to touch his ass. I mean, I did touch it sometimes. But he didn't like it."

"Did he touch yours?"

I looked down, feeling ashamed.

"You're a virgin? How old are you?" Elias asked, his hand propping up his head, an expression of ridicule on his face.

"Thirty-six. I'm not a virgin. I did it both ways back in grad school," I said, yanking the soiled duvet up to my neck. "Jared and I tried a few times in the beginning. He was just so miserable during it."

Elias asked how long we'd been together, and I told him over ten years. "Why did you stay together so long if you weren't getting your needs met?" he asked.

I was too stumped and embarrassed to answer him. After an awkward silence, I finally said, "We met when we were young. We were once very in love. Then it became . . . safe. I was also probably scared."

"Scared of what?" he asked.

"Of being alone," I replied. "Also, of other men, you know, the gay community. It looks like fun and parties from a distance, especially to straight people, but when you're in it, it's kind of a protracted nightmare, like a grown-up version of high school."

Elias rubbed the top of my head condescendingly, even though we were the same age. "You poor thing. Well, now is better than ever to make up for lost time. Get some practice in." He then popped to his feet and headed to the bathroom.

While he showered, I wondered if I was somehow different or changed—more experienced or mature in some small way. I certainly felt more relaxed, as if all the clenched muscles in my body had released their grip. Part of me also felt soiled, just like the duvet—we had both perspired a lot, and what we'd done had been somewhat transactional, a naughty little workout session of sorts—no dinner, no drinks, no long walks filled with get-to-know-you conversation beforehand. But I knew Elias already. He was my teacher, right? We could skip those niceties, couldn't we? Or had we broached an unspoken code?

After Elias showered and dressed, I asked if he wanted to spend the night. I hadn't slept alone for so long. "We can order a pizza," I said. "There's also this new app that delivers craft cocktails. I have a promo code for it."

Cocking his head to one side, he gave me a pitying look and put his hand on the small of my back. "You need to be alone for a while."

I looked away. A knot tightened in my stomach.

"See you in class?" he added.

"Yeah, of course."

Our encounter had become a test, and I'd failed miserably, all within twenty-four hours.

I shut the door behind him, knowing I couldn't return to class or rejoin the company for a long time, if ever.

Chapter 6

Wynn
San Francisco, CA
Summer 2013

WHO WOULD THINK that one silly *So You Think You Can Dance* video clip would convince me to take a dance class?

While the receptionist checked in students and took their payment, I sat in the studio's lobby on the verge of losing my shit. Many other students seemed to already know each other—they exchanged hugs, chatted, and nonchalantly stretched each other's legs and arms. Their utter relaxation somehow made me even more nervous. A film of shame coated my skin's surface—a tell-tale sign in my mind that I was a total fraud. The dancing I'd done in college and the clubs years ago wasn't real or any good, for that matter. It was a joke. I was a joke. I was way too old. Who was I to start formal dance classes in my mid-thirties?

Yet the *SYTYCD* clip I'd stumbled upon on my phone while waiting in the airport lounge earlier that week had awakened something in me. It nudged me to show up to class fifteen minutes early and kept me in the waiting room, helping me defy my flight instinct. In the video, two smoking hot Asian guys popped and locked in-synch to a bass line before spring-boarding off couches, tables, and chairs. They did handstands, carried each other's legs wheelbarrow-style, twirled, and leaped in succession with frenetic energy for one minute and forty-eight seconds. When the song cut, the pair dove past each other across the stage into somersaults and collapsed on the floor to play dead—only their chests heaved from exertion. The live audience roared so loudly that I had to turn down the volume to protect my ears. The TV announcer said, "That was Tommy Lin and Steve Nishimoto dancing to 'Turn Down for What' by DJ Snake and Little Jon. Can you believe that Steve is a ballet dancer by training? Before this, he'd never danced hip-hop before. What a performance!"

It was the first time I'd felt anything since my dad had died from a stroke a year earlier. I repeatedly watched the video for so long that I missed my flight. After, I lied to my boss in a flurry of emails about the flight being canceled, and for the next two days, I played sick so I could stay in bed to watch the clip on repeat.

Outside of a K-Pop music video or two, I'd never seen Asian men, let alone Asian-American men—men like me—dance with such supernatural athleticism. And although the two dancers in the clip were at least a decade younger, I believed that someday I could dance like them and that my infatuation and unrelenting drive might carry me through. I cultivated a hope that somewhere hidden inside me was an untapped gift for hip-hop dance. Indeed, if Steve Nishimoto, the ballet dancer who had never danced hip-hop, could pull off such an exceptional performance, I could come close with some formal training and practice.

In time, I moved on to other videos on RevTube. The more I watched, the more I hungered for what these dancers had: bravado, grace, a fit body, ownership and command of a fit body and the space around them. So, I forced myself to wait in the studio's lobby, hoping to get what the RevTube stars already had.

Never in my life had I been more eager to work hard and earn this.

The other students and I bided our time for almost a half hour when a Dominican man built like a linebacker pushed the double doors open so hard that one almost ricocheted onto my face.

"My dear students, I would apologize about being late, but Elias *never* says he's sorry." He snapped his fingers above his shiny bald head, evoking laughter.

Like Tommy Kwon and Steve Nishimoto, Elias Gutierrez had also competed on *SYTYCD*. However, the former two moved on to dance in professional companies afterward, while Elias hadn't fared as well. Of course, this was to my benefit since he taught packed classes in the city, only a ten-minute drive from my home. Some internet sleuthing revealed that Elias's thick build and over-the-top personality kept him from reaping the spoils of competing on the hit reality TV show. To my knowledge, he wasn't flooded with offers to choreograph concert tours, lead companies, or dance backup for music videos.

The teaching assistants led the warm-up of sit-ups, push-ups, and stretches, while Elias sat on the floor cross-legged and filed his nails. The calisthenics raised my heart rate and helped alleviate my anxiety. Still, I couldn't stop surveying the room, packed shoulder to shoulder with attractive, stylish women of all ages and races. Not surprisingly, there were only a sprinkling of men, four besides me, who were all younger.

Elias snapped the nail file in two and threw the pieces on the floor. He hollered, "Let's get this started, bitches."

LL Cool J's "Mama Said Knock You Out" blared, and I don't think I ever felt more lost in my life. While muddling through the choreography, my head swiveled back and forth panoramically. I was afraid the others were tallying my screw-ups. Still, to my relief and disappointment, everyone seemed to be focused on themselves.

Elias and his TAs taught boxing-themed choreography, fists on chins, punching, and jabbing in sync with brisk slides from side to side and front and back. I couldn't keep up. I was a beat behind and often punching with the wrong hand. When I slid to the wrong side, I bumped into a young woman next to me who shot me a dirty look. It was then that I decided to escape, but not yet—the class was so crowded that there was no way to leave without drawing attention to myself. All I could do was endure the humiliation—eyes glued on the instructor, my hapless body imitating everything he did.

After repeating the routine a dozen or so times, muscle memory took over, and I punched, kicked, swerved, and twirled with the rest of the class. Clenched fists protected my red-hot, sweaty face, and I entered a trance of sorts, and the next thing I knew, Elias was splitting the class into smaller groups. I panicked—the others would see me, see that I sucked. Nevertheless, once my group was up, endorphins fired throughout my body. I jumped into the center of the room and danced as fiercely as I had when I was a kid in my parents' basement.

During my teenage years, my parents often drove off to meet their friends on weekends—other 1.5 and second-generation Korean Americans in the Tri-State area—at house parties or restaurants while I danced at home alone, in secret. When I was sure my parents had left, I would beeline downstairs, lock the door behind me, and obsessively watch and reenact old MTV and VH-1 videos I'd taped on the VCR. Sometimes I even used the old tweed sofa and La-Z Boy recliner as props, tumbling over them before vogueing with Madonna or hopping and crisscrossing with Kid 'N Play. This would continue until the digital clock on the TV hit eleven, after which I'd shut it off, shower, and make sure I was in bed with a book when my parents got home. I believed if my parents discovered my solo dance parties, it would have been akin to publicly announcing my homosexuality—something I was hardly ready to grapple with at the time.

It wasn't until my first year of college that I first danced in public. Swarthmore's Black Student Union, Poder Latino, and Asian American Alliance pooled their club budgets to throw a joint party called "Intersectional Hip-hop Jam 1999." I was tipsy when the student DJ played "It Takes Two." As soon as I stepped onto the dance floor, I spun into a fever state. When I came to, the center of the floor had cleared for me to showboat my retro dance moves: the Snake, the RoboCop, and my grand finale and best move to date, an extended backspin. When I leaped to my feet and looked around, a blur of Latino, Black, and Asian kids surrounded me, whooping and hollering, "Go, go, go, Wynn. Go, go, go, Wynn." It was like a beautiful, multicultural dream— MLK would have been proud, Malcolm X, maybe less so.

Nevertheless, I not only felt attractive, but it might've been the first time in my life that I was "seen" and accepted for being me. No longer the ugly, foreign, nerdy faggot, I was suddenly the cool and talented, the gorgeous and loveable Wynn—the star of the show, and I was finally part of a community—I *belonged* somewhere. Never in my wildest dreams did any of this seem possible growing up. The cheering from the crowd spurred me to continue dancing until Nicole, who I hadn't officially met yet, joined me. She was an enthusiastic dancer, mirroring my moves and responding with her own improvisation. The rest of the party joined us on the floor, and we all danced into the wee hours of the morning. Despite throwing up in the bushes—I'd indulged in too many tequila sunrises—the event marked the best night of my college career. Nicole and I became fast friends from then on, and we regularly hijacked dance floors at college parties.

This continued when we lived together in graduate school. One night at a Boston club, Nicole and I did our usual schtick on the dance floor—a combo of improvisation and plain goofing around. Afterward, to our surprise, bystanders flooded us with compliments. So, for kicks, we started choreographing routines, mainly as a study break, and the next thing I knew, we were performing at two to three clubs each weekend—gay and straight—which is how I met Jared. Unfortunately, between my new relationship and graduate studies, Nicole and I no longer had time to dance, and I buried that part of me away. Until now.

At the end of Elias's class, the teaching assistants led our euphoric bodies through a final cool-down and stretch. I waded in a puddle of my sweat. Part of me wanted to collapse onto my back, but I remained upright. I was too full-on joy.

A succession of taps on my shoulder broke the spell. When I looked up, Elias towered above me. He offered me his palm, and I took it, rising to my feet.

"If I had a most-improved award during a single class, I'd give it to you," said Elias, who, up close, had a head that was almost perfectly round, like the Pillsbury Doughboy. He poked my chest twice and said, "You have something here. Keep coming," before turning around and sauntering out the double doors, his two teaching assistants a step behind. At that moment, I promised to never give up dancing again.

From then on, I attended his classes with an evangelical fervor before adding other hip-hop classes, different pop styles, jazz, urban contemporary, and the occasional ballet workshop. And while all the other Synergy analysts plugged away in PowerPoint and Excel spreadsheets, I slipped out of the office at 5 p.m. to make a class. In time, I left work earlier and earlier, until one day, I marched brazenly toward the elevators at 4 p.m., tapping a one-line email on my phone to inform my manager that I would finish my work at home.

Around this time, the firm had informed me through an annual performance evaluation that I wasn't on track to make partner, even though I consistently delivered stellar work. They saw me as an individual contributor and stated they might be open to changing their minds if I could show "dramatic and demonstrable gains in emotional intelligence and more leadership potential," which, in my mind, was code for being a better kiss-ass. I had never heard a louder dog whistle directed toward me, and if I hadn't been already done with them in my mind, I might have told them so. Oh, how I wish I had applauded them in that meeting. Of the firm's forty or so partners, there was *already* one East Asian woman, one Black man, and a Puerto Rican lesbian. I would have told them they should pat themselves on the back. They'd done their part. They'd already fulfilled their quota.

After the performance evaluation meeting, I needed air. The elevator opened into the building's lobby, and I pushed open the front doors. A chilled San Francisco gale whipped my face, and with it, my rage dissipated into the late afternoon fog. Usually, at the end of a workday, I felt vacant and anesthetized, as if someone had scraped my insides out and swabbed the crust of my empty vessel with Novocain. But I didn't feel this way on the day of my performance review. I surged with power and life. Questions surrounding why other senior analysts had been promoted ahead of me, even though I'd worked there much longer and done superior work, evaporated into the gray San Francisco sky. I no longer wondered if I would be in the same predicament if I looked more like Jared or his sister. I no longer wondered because none of it mattered anymore. The time was 4:03 p.m., and I was on my way to a class.

At the beginning of my obsession with dance, I tried to share my newfound enthusiasm with Jared. I showed him a video on my laptop during one of our takeout dinners. He'd mumble, "Pretty cool," before returning to his screen. When I suggested he take a class with me, he chuckled.

"That's your thing." He winked at me. "I'd just embarrass you."

We returned to our respective takeout containers to chew and slurp in silence. After we finished our food, I could only hear the clicking of keys on his laptop.

A few months after my first dance class, I performed in Elias's annual review. After the show, Jared showered me with flowers and gave me one of his bear hugs. And maybe it was because Jared had recently started lifting weights and his build had thickened or that he'd recently deepened his side part to conceal thinning hair, but he resembled this kid, a football player from Westport High named Asher Ackermann, who used to bully me. After all these years, I didn't know why I only saw the similarity then. The young man's bullying hadn't been anything serious or even consistent, especially compared to the verbal abuse imposed on me by some of the other kids in the school, just a painful wedgie during a ninth-grade gym class, after which I threatened to fight him, and the coward brushed me off. Asher never touched me again, but he did whisper "chinky faggot"—real creative, I know—when I passed him in the hall a couple of times a year, and it hadn't seemed worth it to confront him again.

In any case, I found myself both repulsed and turned on by the newfound resemblance and looked forward to us having our version of sex that night. And between my epic dance performance and the fact that I'd snagged—and held onto—the star quarterback, I was thrilled, finally deemed worthy by a kaleidoscope mirror that revealed the ways I'd perpetrated my own marginalization. My warped self-image had caused me to seek validation, not from someone who'd assaulted or ignored me, but from someone who mimicked them. Jared wore the same clothes and enjoyed his time in the same hallways of corporate America and CrossFit gyms. He even spoke in the same so-called masculine register and cultivated a Mid-Atlantic accent. Proximity to whiteness was an instinct I'd honed. It was my birthright, the wellspring of my self-hatred.

"Babe, you were great! I love this dance *thing* you have," said Jared.

The show was over, yet the hot stage lights continued to sear me from above, and the audience's applause echoed in my head. I was suddenly and irrationally furious at him—my handsome and athletic-looking partner with the face of a bully, smiling ear to ear with pride at my performance. This dance *thing* wasn't a fucking hobby. It was something bigger.

Chapter 7

Jared
Siem Reap, Cambodia
Summer 2015

BEFORE THIS TRIP, the only time Lois had been out of the country was an all-inclusive in Cancun four years ago. I was worried. I was a worrier. I paced in front of Siem Reap's international terminal, awaiting her flight's arrival. This trip was much farther, almost thirty-four hours of air travel with two connections. I couldn't help but think she might have gotten lost in an airport or fallen asleep during a layover and missed one of her flights. Just when I was about to head to the information desk, I spotted her—golden-bobbed hair neatly brushed, makeup freshly applied. I smoothed the front of my crisp turquoise polo and white linen shorts and waved to her. Like mother, like son. We may have been a mess on the inside, but at least we looked like we were holding it together.

We jogged toward each other and hugged. I relished her familiar scent—hairspray and tobacco.

"I can't believe I'm going to be a grandmother. Why couldn't you have gotten a labradoodle like all the other gays?"

"Ha, ha."

"Seriously," she said, "tell me why you're doing this surrogacy thing all the way out here?" Lois paused to eye the airport's shiny marble floors and the Burger King and Dairy Queen storefronts that were so new blue painter's tape lined the walls.

"I told you already. It's a lot cheaper." We hadn't even left the airport, and I already sounded defensive, even to me.

"When have you ever worried about money? You're fucking loaded."

I ignored her and rolled her suitcase off the curb and into the parking lot in search of the hotel van. A Cambodian man in denim cutoffs rode up on a scooter and offered to give us a tour of the temples.

"I'm not getting on the back of that thing," said Lois. We both said, "No, thank you." He stuck around for a moment before riding away.

"You don't have to ride a motorcycle. We're taking the hotel shuttle," I replied. We marched past a row of wan palm trees in the parking lot.

"Hey, slow down. I've been dying for a smoke." She tapped a long cigarette from a soft pack and flipped it between her rouged lips.

I stomped my foot but said nothing. She'd come all this way. I had to be flexible.

As if she'd read my mind, Lois said, "Don't worry, I won't smoke in front of the baby. Not that it really matters. I smoked the entire time while I was pregnant with you and your sister." She patted her pockets and dug through her purse for a lighter. "You both turned out fine."

The man on the scooter rode over again and lit her cigarette with a brass Zippo. He waited, perhaps hoping she would change her mind about a tour. After four puffs in rapid succession, she waved him away. She exhaled a plume of smoke that was suspended in the humidity. The fine muscles in her forehead slackened, and the grooves in her cheeks smoothed over. As far back as I could remember, I'd begged her to quit in hundreds of notes and Mother's Day cards. She would tack them onto the fridge and say, "You don't want a fat mother, do you?"

Lois stubbed out the cigarette on the bottom of her chunky-heeled sandal and looked around again: idling scooters with entire families aboard, battered taxis, and billboards advertising cheap hotels and Chinese beer. "Tell me again why we're here?" she asked. "Was this Wynn's idea? Typical. Makes you cut corners, and then he bails."

"It was actually mine." I didn't tell her how I'd spent too much on the kitchen and bathroom renovations, and there was nothing left until I could sell my next round of Reverie stock the following year.

"Why are you defending him?" she asked.

"He's gonna come back. He just needs some time," I said, but even I could hear the uncertainty in my voice. Proximity to her had also dredged up the ol' Long Island accent, and I made a mental note to stay on top of it.

Lois rolled her eyes. "Never liked him. He always thought he was better than us."

I didn't reply, but inside, I thought, *no*, you *think you're better than him. I think we're better than us.*

After we dropped our bags at the hotel and Lois had napped and showered, I hired a tuk-tuk to take us to town. We had extra time before our appointment with the surrogacy agency, and I thought it might be fun to do something local.

"This doesn't look safe," she declared when a young man on a scooter pulled up to the hotel lobby with our ride. Still, she hoisted herself into the open carriage with its tattered vinyl tent roof. She gripped the rusty metal poles as we accelerated down the dirt road. A cloud of brown dust mushroomed behind us. Lois squealed when the scooter tugged us out of moon-crater potholes and raced over speed bumps. She sucked in her cheeks until her mouth opened into glee, and since I'd just shown her how big the world really was, I smiled, too.

When we arrived at a glass-front high-rise so new that orange construction tape framed the entrance, we both sported matching sweat stains from our armpits to the bottom of our shirts.

"For fuck's sake, it's hot here," she said, wiping her brow with a handkerchief. The air-conditioned waiting room of Assistive Reproductive Technologies (ART) provided immediate relief. However, once we acclimated, we soon realized that it was chilled to the temperature of a meat locker and began to shiver. I pressed goosebumps into my bare thigh while Lois clutched her chest and rubbed her arms. A few minutes later, Bopha, the Cambodian-Australian agency liaison, whom I'd only spoken to over video, came in wrapped in a knee-length wool sweater with a down vest over it. There were details about her that I'd missed on video: her elfin stature, uneven shoulders, and a birthmark above her right upper lip. She shook our hands, Western-style, and ushered us into a cluttered yet modern office.

"I thought your partner was going to be joining us," she said in her Aussie accent. "Winston, right?"

"Yes, I know. He had a work emergency at the last minute and couldn't make it. He's very disappointed."

"Oh, that's too bad."

Lois sucked her teeth and shot me a look.

"When do we get to meet the surrogate?" I asked, getting straight to the reason for our visit. "We're excited to see Chariya and get to know her."

"Chariya is getting her checkup upstairs. After we wrap up some paperwork, you can meet her and observe her final ultrasound." Bopha slid a thick stack of papers and a pen across the desk. "I know you've already signed so many contracts," she said, "but I promise these are essential. They will allow you to get the baby a passport once she's born."

Each time I signed my name next to a yellow tab, I felt one step closer to holding Meryl in my arms.

Lois asked, "Is there a way for you to induce labor sooner? I hate to cause problems, but I have hair clients at home who need me."

"We want to do what's best for the baby's health, of course," I said, scowling at her. Between Lois and her hair appointments and Wynn and his hip-hop dance classes, it dawned on me that even gay men marry their mothers. Maybe I was predestined to be with someone extremely obsessive.

"She's ready now," said Bopha, her face professionally neutral. "But unfortunately, the hospital does not have the medication we need to induce labor. We import it from Taiwan. It should be here next week, at the latest."

Lois shot me a look that said, *I'm skeptical.*

"Cambodia is still a very poor country," Bopha said. "We don't have many of the supplies you take for granted in the US, but I assure you, we have first-rate staff here. Dr. Geller is my husband, assigned to Chariya's case. He did his training at the top medical school in Australia."

Bopha took the papers from me and filed them in the drawers behind her. "There's one more thing we must discuss before we head upstairs and meet Chariya." Her elbows rested on the desk's glass top, her fists propping up her pointy chin.

"You're not allowed in the delivery room for legal reasons," she said. "I promise to give you timely updates while you're in the waiting room."

I told her I was disappointed and pouted a little for show, although I was relieved. Who wanted to watch all that gore if you didn't have to?

"I believe I've said this to you before," said Bopha, "but

Chariya might not want to hold or even see the baby. When she gives birth, her body will be flooded with hormones. She'll need time to emotionally process both the trauma of childbirth and the fact that for the last nine months, she carried a baby she might not see again." Bopha leaned forward and looked me in the eye as if I wasn't already on the edge of my chair, absorbing every detail. "This is why we ask that you stay in the hospital with her for forty-eight hours after she delivers. We ask that you go into her hospital room and personally thank her for her gift and tell her how much you appreciate her. Even hold her hand if she allows it. I can translate."

Months earlier, during one of our video chats, Bopha said that many surrogates were chiefly motivated by altruism rather than money, which sounds like a pretty lie and all. Still, I didn't know this Chariya girl, and holding her hand for hours seemed way intimate. Like Lois, I was already itching to fly home and imagined that I would be even more eager once the baby was born, but I wanted to do the right thing, so I obliged.

When we headed upstairs to the clinic, Chariya reclined supine in a patient's chair. The doctor leaned over her, waving an ultrasound wand over her bare, distended belly. I recognized her immediately from her online profile. She appeared smaller and thinner than I imagined but healthful nonetheless. The agency mentioned she would be provided a generous food stipend and prenatal vitamins throughout her pregnancy, and it appeared she'd been taking them. Her tawny skin glowed, and her jet-black hair shimmered in a cascade over her shoulders.

We introduced ourselves to Chariya and Dr. Geller. When I shook her cold, limp hand—there was a clamminess and fragility that made me wary of squeezing it. Chariya stared blankly at me with wide-set eyes, her unblinking gaze almost feline, making me uneasy. She wasn't looking *at* me but *through* me, and I got the chills when she released my hand. Anxiously, I awaited a response from her but was met with silence. Even though I probably should've anticipated a language barrier, I couldn't hide my disappointment by her lack of enthusiasm. This must have shown on my face because Bopha said something to her.

Chariya cast her eyes downward and, with an air of repitition of resentment and casual aloofness, said, "Nice meet you."

"Nice to meet you, too," I replied. "Thank you for helping me. Having a baby has been a dream of mine since I was a little boy."

Bopha translated from across the room, but Chariya didn't look up.

"We love to hear that," said Bopha, with an artificial cheeriness to compensate for Chariya's emotional distance. "Oh, it's so wonderful to make dreams come true for nice men like yourself, Mr. Cahill, and your partner."

"We consider it our calling to make this kind of service affordable and accessible," said Dr. Geller. "And we also wouldn't mind if you said exactly that in an online review of us." He laughed at his half-joke.

When we stepped away so Dr. Geller could finish setting up the ultrasound, Lois whispered too loudly in my ear: "She looks so young. Too young."

"She's not twelve. She's a year older than you were when you had me," I said through clenched teeth in her ear.

"What are you waiting for? Come take a look at her," Dr. Geller said.

My eyes locked onto the image on the monitor—a grainy black and white shadow—and I was in awe that this tiny being could be my daughter and that she actually belonged to me. I inched closer and closer until my face almost kissed the screen and proceeded to count her fingers and toes.

"They're all there," said Dr. Geller.

My skin prickled, and more goosebumps erupted along my arms and legs. I had seen a few sonogram images over email, but this one played live, in motion, and appeared more fully formed.

I could almost see my own face in hers.

"Wynn, isn't she—?" I turned toward my mother, who caught my mistake. The dark cloud that had haunted me on the flight returned. Dizziness overcame me and I had to sit down.

Dr. Geller didn't seem to notice and asked, "Do you have a name picked out for her?"

"Yes," I replied. "Meryl. We're thinking Mare for short."

"Lovely." He stroked his white beard. "I'm sure she will be as beautiful and talented as the actress." He belly-laughed like a skinny Santa Claus in a white lab coat.

The thought of Mare growing into an adult woman triggered a sense of the passage of time, the precariousness of our family, and the fact that I hadn't heard from Wynn in almost a week. The idea of her growing up without meeting or knowing him brought on a crying jag. The harder I tried to choke it down, the more it seemed to want to come out. Even if Wynn eventually returned, I would likely still be on my own for the birth. Bopha handed me a tissue and said, "Just about every ART client gets emotional during this part of the process. It's why I love my job. Do you want to feel the baby kick?"

I nodded vigorously, then asked her to give me a minute. Lois rubbed my back and passed me a stack of tissues and a wet wipe to clean my nose and face. After a few deep breaths, I declared that I was ready. Bopha barked at Chariya in Khmer, and she flashed an indignant smile in return, exposing her stained teeth.

I rubbed my palms together, warming them, and then placed both hands on her belly. After a few seconds, I felt a kick through her taut skin. I beamed, and then a terrible thought crossed my mind. I wondered what would happen if she kept this child. I hated myself for thinking it. But I would send her a handsome monthly allowance. Chariya could build a house, start a business, maybe a noodle stand, or even a small restaurant. In the meantime, Lois could return to Long Island and her "oh so urgent" hair appointments, and I could slip back into my old life in San Francisco. Maybe I would sell the house and move into one of those new condos they were building on Market Street with floor-to-ceiling windows?

Without Wynn.

With a new boyfriend.

I couldn't believe I was already considering meeting someone new, but it made sense. Once my new boyfriend and I were settled, we could send for Mare or start over and have another child, but with a California-based surrogate this time. I couldn't believe I was thinking about leaving my baby—I needed to snap out of it and not allow my mind to go there. It was wrong. It was not only wrong, but it was also dangerous. But what if?

"Thank you," I said to Chariya. "Au kun cheraown." I'd been practicing this phrase for weeks.

"You know Khmer," said Bopha with great enthusiasm.

"Just a few phrases," I said, straightening my posture and mentally patting myself on the back for the few hours I had spent on the RevLingo app the previous week.

"You speak so well," she said, "Very impressive."

The old me—the more responsible version—gradually returned, and I reentered reality. I reminded myself of the situation at hand, which wasn't ideal, but at least I wasn't alone. I had Lois. Someone had to be an adult if anything was to be learned from the past week. Unfortunately, that person was always me.

We all shook hands. Bopha said she would call us later in the week to confirm the delivery date and time. We waved goodbye for so long that my wrist ached.

Once outside, Lois and I thawed in the heat, and I hailed one of the zillion taxis circling us. After clicking into our seatbelts, I told Lois I needed her in San Francisco for a while.

"I can't do this alone."

She opened a window and slipped a cigarette in her mouth.

"I'm ignoring you," she said before asking the driver if she could smoke.

"I'm serious. I can open a salon for you. You can run it all on your own—no chair fees. You wouldn't even have to pay rent. I have a third bedroom. Imagine, no expenses." I loved the casual yet confident breeze in my voice and my ability to sell a great idea and a win-win situation for both of us.

"So, you don't have money to pay for an American surrogate but somehow magically have enough to open a hair salon in San Fran for me?" Her lower lip curled, which in my mind meant she was pissed off.

"What are you talking about?" I said, trying to keep the conversation light. "Surrogacy in California costs way more than opening a salon." I was unsure if this was true, but it sounded about right, and besides, it wasn't like she was going to whip out her phone and RevSearch it. She didn't even have a data plan here. I mentioned the Reverie shares vesting at the end of the year and how I could take out a loan in the meantime. My credit score was above 800.

"It's not about the money, is it?" she said. Her voice rang sharper. Smoke billowed out of her mouth, and she stared off coldly. "Here's how I see the situation. You're a fucking control freak, and you have your little fantasy. You got caught up in the idea of you, Wynn, and this little test tube baby living happily ever after. Then you realized you didn't want the messiness of some strange woman laying claim to your baby—too much risk, am I right? So, you get this anonymous egg donor who the baby can't know until she turns eighteen. And then you get some poor girl with black teeth halfway across the world in a country where no one can fucking afford real shoes to carry the baby 'cause you know she'll never fly to Cali and drop by for a visit." Her lower lip quivered.

"That's unfair," I said, feeling queasy. "You're being very cruel, you know that? I'm the victim here." Snot dripped from my nose, and I wiped it away.

"No, you are the one who is unfair," she said.

Her hands shook, and ash fell onto her white cotton blouse. I wished she would just go up in flames. I hated her so much.

"I had two kids before I was barely old enough to drink. I didn't get to go to college, and I certainly didn't get to live the *Sex and the City* life in my twenties. I'm *done* being a mom. It's time for you to be a big boy and wipe your own goddamn ass."

The car became silent except for an intermittent rattle every time we mowed over a pothole or speed bump. I opened the window and watched food stalls with milk crate stools pass by and an old woman walking hand-in-hand with a chubby toddler. I couldn't bear to be near Lois anymore. At an intersection, I asked the driver to stop the car. Before he fully braked, I opened the door and tumbled out.

My mom called out my name in surprise. I yelled back, "I'm fine!" They drove off. I scraped my elbow and knee. Blood trickled down my calf and pooled at the bottom of my suede loafer. The pain, a physical manifestation of what I'd felt internally, was a welcome relief. I limped toward a roundabout where throngs of motorbikes and cars whirred past me. Engines buzzed so loudly that I couldn't hear the words of tuk-tuk drivers offering rides before they gave up and drove off. The exhaust left a diesel aftertaste in my mouth. Traffic had exploded, and I couldn't hear myself think over the orchestra of running motors. An intense game of chicken played out on the road. Trucks and minivans edged out cars, who, in turn, battled the overwhelming throng of scooters and motorcycles. Push-bikes and pedestrians like me were rare. Since I sat at the bottom of the totem pole, I cautiously weaved in and out of traffic in fits and starts until I ultimately trusted that all other vehicles would navigate around me.

The sunset cast a hazy orange glow across the low-hanging sky. It was breathtaking, and I wished I could pause and enjoy the scenery, but all I could think about was Wynn. Could I forgive him? Only a desperate idiot would . . . But who was I kidding? Of course, I would. I couldn't be a failure like my mom. Lois divorced my dad right after I was born, after which he drunkenly crashed his Buick into a cement divider on the Long Island Expressway. I couldn't have my story look anything like hers.

So, I collected myself and brushed the dust off me. While I walked back to the hotel, I tapped out a list of talking points on my phone:

- Meryl needs her grandma. She's only going to be a baby once.
- Come for just a few weeks, only until Wynn comes back.
- Free housing. Forget my guest room. I'll rent an apartment nearby for you or build an in-law unit behind the house.
- I can rent a chair for you at a top salon. There are so many hair places right in the neighborhood.
- Fresh fruits and vegetables year-round.
- ~~California sunshine, year-round.~~ Yes, there's fog, but the winters are mild.

A man's voice pulled me out of my list-making. I looked up and found myself in the middle of an intersection. A young Cambodian man straddled his idling motorbike directly in front of me. He jabbed his index finger at me through the dusty air. I said sorry, repeating myself, all while trying to remember how to say it in Khmer. The man continued to yell, and just as I raised my hands to relinquish blame, a bicycle bell rang, and a young tourist couple on beach cruisers swerved around me. They shouted something in French, and only then did the requisite synapses fire in my brain. My tongue hurled the Khmer phrase forward: "Somtos. Khnhom somtos." I hoped using the local

61

language would buy me some grace and, therefore, a little slack from this man, but he seemed furious. Then, a flash of a different scooter with an older man atop appeared in front of me. Frozen in place, I curled my head into my lower half to shield my face. His front tire crashed into my good leg, and I catapulted.

Chapter 8

Wynn
Westport, CT
Fall 2004

FOR THE FIRST time in my life, I was Andie Walsh in *Pretty in Pink* and Harry Burns in *When Harry Met Sally* all at once. During my childhood, when I wasn't dancing in secret in the basement on weekend nights, my mom and I cycled through old rom-coms in the family room. We watched them weekly from as far back as kindergarten up until I left for college. She called it "our special one-on-one time." And more than a decade later, at age twenty-five, I was finally Patrick Dempsey in *Can't Buy Me Love*—the hopeless nerd turned cool kid— who'd wooed and eventually won over Cindy Mancini, the most popular girl in school.

When in reality, I was a Korean American graduate student born and raised in Connecticut, not a white high school senior living in an Arizona suburb, and instead of a pretty blonde captain of the cheerleading squad, Jared was a twenty-two-year-old IT Coordinator from Long Island. Upon second thought, I was probably more like Molly Ringwald in *Sixteen Candles*, while

Jared was definitely "Jake Ryan." And though I was a grown man and not an angsty girl with puffy, red bangs, I could somehow overlook the fact that *Sixteen Candles* was one of the most racist movies I'd ever seen. I felt terrible about identifying with the protagonist, but that's just where my mind went, especially when I was nervous. It was like my brain intentionally chose the most self-hating and shameful topics. In any case, it wasn't time to debate '80s movies. My task was to introduce Jake Ryan to my dad.

In the living room of my childhood home, Jared and I sat side by side, thighs touching on the sofa. Growing up, we'd only used the living room for special occasions, and it felt strange to be treated like a guest in my own house. I almost apologized for the room's décor, which looked like a color-blind patrician librarian had vomited her furniture all over a Korean yard sale, and no one had bothered to clean up. A checkered forest green and burgundy sofa sat between chipped, black lacquer end tables with faux mother-of-pearl inlay. A turquoise and yellow Oriental rug lay beneath a pair of wing chairs—one blessed with mallard ducks, the other a bright pink Laura Ashley floral print my mom had bought from an actual yard sale. As embarrassed as I was, Jared had told me he'd grown up poor and in an apartment, and I didn't want to sound like a tone-deaf, middle-class kid. When we walked through the front door, Jared's eyes roamed the musty rooms. I couldn't tell if he was impressed, disappointed, or both.

"Wynn never told me your first name, Dr. Kang," Jared said after a long silence. He used "Dr." instead of "Mr." and pronounced our last name with the "ah" sound, just as I'd instructed. First point, Jared.

"It's Chi-won, though everyone at work calls me Chip," Dad said, looking startled as if Jared had just tried to wake him up from a nap. After Dad said his part, he reclined in the mallard-print wing chair. "You can call me either," he added as if he'd just remembered his line. Dad had the slightest of accents because he'd come to the US for college. Still, he also tended to over-articulate every word, making him sound a bit robotic.

Even though Jared and I had only been dating a month and a half, I'd wanted Dad to meet my first boyfriend and see how happy I could be as an openly gay man. My dad was kind and gentle growing up but usually checked out and stuck in his head, his attention wrapped up in work. Since Mom and I were always so close, it was as if he'd given up on a one-on-one relationship with me. With her gone, I hoped we would grow closer. However, seeing him now was like zooming in on an extra on a movie set. He was presentable, seemingly polite, and benevolent, but I was eager to return to my leading man. And although Dad had often seemed distant growing up, it felt like he was barely in the same room with us. When he wasn't sticking to the script, he gazed into the distance as if already with Mom. I was only beginning to acknowledge the sad truth: it was probably too late for the two of us, a fact that would've devastated me if I wasn't so damn excited to have finally snagged a boyfriend.

"Jared is an engineer also," I said, hoping to inject some energy into the conversation.

"Like you."

"I studied computer engineering in college, but now I clean viruses off laptops," Jared said. "Not real engineering, not what you do."

Point two, Jared. Although Jared wasn't as book smart as my friends and me, he was thoughtful, intelligent, and sweet. Sure, he'd been a bit of a mess when we'd first met at the club, prattling on about details inappropriate for a first meeting: a family history of alcoholism, and homesickness, to name two. And yes, Jared had recently come out of the closet. And true, it was his first time at a gay club, and the boy had no relationship experience, but neither did I, for that matter. But the sex, or in this case, the sexual contact, was great—the clawing and kneading of each other's skin, the biting and sucking on each other's necks, and the bruises that checkered our bodies afterward, marking our respective territories. We would eventually get to penetration, and I was willing to wait.

When I rejoined the conversation, Dad apologized for not offering refreshments.

"Wynn's mother was the host of the family," he said. "It's too bad you can't meet her." His eyes watered. I wanted to remind him that Mom took care of everything while he hid at work, but my throat tightened, and a tear formed in my left eye. She'd died three years earlier, and every time I thought I'd moved on, I was reminded that it was something I would never truly heal from.

"Dad, how's work?" I asked, not wanting to think about her anymore. "Is the US government still buying helicopters to bomb Afghani children these days?"

"Be nice. We have company." He shot me a stern look. "Our helicopters are unarmed. You know that."

"I'm kidding," I said. "If that's the case, tell Jared what your copters do."

While he talked about his job as Engineering Manager at a helicopter manufacturing company in nearby Bridgeport, I got up to refresh our water glasses. I observed their conversation through the wall cutout between the living room and kitchen sink.

"How do they attach the propeller on top of the helicopter?"

"Well, the assembly line is in Stratford . . ."

Match point.

Muscles in my neck and back relaxed, and I exhaled audibly. They had a topic to discuss, and well, now I was bored.

Jared did look dapper in his turquoise polo, which accentuated a golden tan that had stuck around through the late days of fall. Upon another look at him, Jared wasn't Jake Ryan. He was too soft and more likely resembled a young Andrew McCarthy—but with a stronger chin.

Maybe my life was better than an '80s movie? Our

relationship so far represented what happened after the story's happy ending. Every weekday after Jared left work and I finished classes, we made out until one of us got hungry. We exchanged minute-by-minute recaps of our days between smooches and cuddles during dinner. Our lovey-doveyness was maddening. Nicole had already banned us from the apartment, complaining that Jared and I were too loud and the wall separating my room and hers too thin.

We'd said "it" last Wednesday morning. Jared handed me my coffee and blurted out the three words, and without pause, I whispered it back. Until then, I'd been cautious, labeling my feelings as "lust with long-term potential." Our epic, forty-eight-hour first date when I learned that Jared didn't know how to use chopsticks had given me pause. I watched with horror as Jared stabbed a piece of salmon roll with a fork before jutting his jaw forward to catch each bite before it slid into his lap. Even though we'd both grown up, give or take one hour, outside of Manhattan, we were from different worlds. When the waitress served dessert, I was in the middle of giving a chopstick lesson, demonstrating how to use one's index finger to provide tension. I winced when one of Jared's chopsticks flew into the lap of one of the diners at the next table. Jared laughed and charmingly explained the situation to the family. I was embarrassed but unsure of the reason. Was it Jared's chopstick blunder or the niggling feeling that we were in a twisted, gay version of *Karate Kid XI* and I'd been relegated to the supporting role of geisha tour guide?

I returned to the living room. "We better get going."

"So soon?" asked Dad. His usual vacant expression turned to disappointment. Maybe he *was* lonely? I should've come down to visit more often.

"We'll be back for dinner," I said, pulling Jared by the wrist off the couch. "I want to show Jared the town and my old high school before it gets dark."

"We can order from Shanghai Gourmet when you get back," he said. There wasn't a Korean restaurant within a twenty-mile radius of our home, so we relied on one of the three Chinese places in town. I imagined Dad couldn't wait to return to his home office to zone out in front of his computer before dinner. "It's nice that you're going to show your friend around."

"Not friend." I looked down at the parquet floor. "Boyfriend," I said with more confidence. Though he already knew I was gay, I wondered if my relationship had somehow made it more vivid and too real for him.

Dad's face turned hollow and sullen, just like the day Mom died. He stood up from his chair, pursed a tight smile, and shook Jared's hand. We wouldn't be a PFLAG family anytime soon, but I couldn't have expected a better outcome.

Right after we arrived at my old high school, I lost interest in showing Jared around. The thrill of a new relationship had made me forget what a shitty time I'd had growing up in this town. One look at the monstrous, two-story brick-and-glass edifice and a flash of sensations and memories hit me all at once: alienation, bitchy girls with daddy's credit card, loneliness, a pair of meatheads in matching argyle sweaters throttling me into a wall of lockers, invisibility, the dread that pitted and churned in my gut on Sunday nights and at the end of holiday breaks and summer vacation. At least high school was better than middle school, where a group of boys called me PF Kang's—a spoof on the chain restaurant PF Chang's. In my case, the PF stood for "pure faggotry."

For the first eighteen years of my life, my hometown never ceased telling me I was ugly and shameful, unworthy and untrustworthy, invisible yet foreign. I was routinely assaulted and ignored, sometimes on the same day. I never complained or talked about it much, maybe due to cultural reasons—"saving and losing face"—whereby placing a spotlight on my shame would undoubtedly magnify it. My parents probably knew on some level. They had to. My father likely experienced his own version at work, so he overcompensated with effort and time. I also imagined Mom and Dad expected this treatment. Their generation had different expectations, and they'd lived in other places with less appealing tradeoffs. This town was safe, attractive, close to work, and hosted some of the best public schools in the state. On the other hand, I was a child who didn't know any better. I was born here and wasn't given a choice to stay or leave.

"I thought you wanted to walk around," Jared said.

"Nah," I shook my head. "Let's go to the beach and watch the sunset." There was a semi-private inlet between two public beaches where kids used to go at night to drink and have sex. I'd never had an excuse to take anyone there before. The shore was empty and almost dark when we arrived, just a sliver of gray light poking out from the horizon. We strolled along the crisp sand. There was an evening chill, and I wrapped my arm around Jared's shoulder for warmth. Immediately, he jerked away before his head swiveled like a submarine periscope in search of imminent danger.

"Calm down. I don't like PDA either, but no one's here."

"You never know," Jared said, reaching for the hood of his parka to cover his head.

"You're safe, I promise." I pulled the hood off his head.

After a few more steps, I hooked my arm onto Jared's, clutching it tight against my chest so he couldn't pull away. Jared scanned the beach for other people, and when it was clear we were alone, his shoulders slackened, and he eventually allowed me to pull him along.

"I think today went well," Jared said. "With your dad."

"He likes you; I can tell."

"Relief!" Jared said, breaking into a giggle. "He took the

news really well, all considering."

"All considering, what?"

"You know," Jared said, pulling me closer.

I silently agreed. I'd come out to my father over the phone only a few weeks earlier, saying I'd met someone special and was in love.

"Dad, this person isn't a girl. I'm seeing another guy." I didn't use the word "gay."

"I think I always knew."

His reply startled me. Although I didn't think I looked gay, whatever that meant, I certainly sounded like I was. For the entirety of my adult life, customer service operators often called me Ma'am or Miss over the phone. Yet I'd always assumed my father lacked gaydar or, even more likely, didn't consider me, his son, a sexual being.

"It's going to take some time for me to adjust to this, but I'm happy you met someone you like," my father had said. "I'd like to meet your friend sometime." Right then and there, Dad and I scheduled a Saturday for us to visit.

I unlatched my arm from Jared's and turned to face him.

"Love you."

"Love you too."

I cupped Jared's stubbly chin, slowly pulling it toward me until he pulled away.

"Not here. What if someone's watching?"

I rolled my eyes. "I guess swapping blowjobs on that bench is out of the question."

"No way!" he said, laughing now. "We could get arrested. This is a high-end town. They don't tolerate that kind of stuff."

"Oh God, lighten up. It's not like you'd be the one arrested. They would probably let you go and then haul me down to the station for lewd behavior."

"Why? You're the one who's from here."

"Because you actually look like you belong here," I said,

stopping myself from sounding bitter. No one felt bad for a kid from Westport, nor should they. Besides, it was supposed to be a romantic moment, so I listened to the tiny waves lapping against the shore and calmed myself down. If it killed me, I would force myself to become more like a plucky character in a sickeningly earnest movie starring Rachel McAdams—someone who wouldn't dare ruin romantic moments.

"I'm getting cold," said Jared. "Should we go downtown, get a coffee or something?"

"Sure." I paused. "Before we go, though, you have to say one thing."

"What?"

"You have to say, 'I'm gay.'"

"Why?"

"Because you've never said it before, and it's weird. You have internal homophobia issues." My little game offered the promise of a thrill, and I was excited to see where it went.

"What does *that* mean?" Jared said, twisting his face.

"You're self-hating."

I had worked up the courage to stand up to my father. I'd told him to call Jared my boyfriend, and now, I imagine I wanted something in return. "How can you say you love me if you don't love yourself?" I asked indignantly. "You have to say 'I'm gay' before we leave. No, you have to yell it and then scream, 'I'm out and proud.' Loudly."

"You said I had to say one thing. That's two."

I dangled the car keys in front of Jared's face. "I'm throwing these in the water unless you say it. Come on, no one's here. It's not a big deal. See, I'll do it first," I said, enjoying the newfound power I wielded. I reached up, both arms in the air. "I'm gay! My name is Wynn, and I'm out and proud!"

Jared slapped my hand, and the keys fell to the sand. He then snatched my keys off the sand and raced down the shoreline. I chased after him laughing and screaming every four-letter word I knew.

When Jared reached the end of the beach, he kicked off his boat shoes and rolled up his pants before wading into the frigid Long Island Sound. Once knee-deep, he bent down to splash frothy water around him like a benediction.

With his head tilted, he shouted into the dark gray sky. "To the good people of Westport, Connecticut, I want to let you know that my name is Jared Cahill, and I am an out and proud gay man!"

I collapsed into a laughing ball, writhing on the wet sandy ground.

"I also want to announce that I'm in love with Winston Kang!"

In shock, I froze. Once I came to, I pinched the top of my hand to make sure I wasn't dreaming. The final scene of *Say Anything* flickered: John Cusack held the boom box playing "In Your Eyes" in front of Ione Skye's window. It was my favorite movie and paled compared to what was happening before me. Never in my wildest dreams did I ever imagine someone making such a bold and romantic gesture. Jared was wading in freezing water in the middle of October for me.

Take that, John and Ione.

Jared walked out of the water and toward me, arms outstretched, eager to drench me in brackish water. I shrieked and pretended to recoil.

We kissed in the dark, the icy water numbing our ankles and feet.

"What made you finally say it?" I asked.

He rubbed his nose against my forehead and kissed it. "Deep down, I have this feeling," he said. "That this is forever. And if that's the case, I have to change. Or at least meet you halfway."

Speechless, I kissed him hard. Our mouths flooded with saltwater from my tears. I waited for Jared to stop and ask why I was crying. Still, he continued to kiss me back and squeezed me even harder, the pressure of his arms holding me steady as I shook from the biting wind and my grief. Our extended kiss was a balm, healing my hatred for this bastion of toxic whiteness and the pain it had caused me that I thought I'd forgotten. At that moment, I knew I couldn't change my childhood. I couldn't bring Mom back. I couldn't help Dad move on from her death or make him emotionally available. But I could change Jared, and he could change me.

Chapter 9

Jared
Coram, NY
Winter 2004

BECAUSE IT WAS my turn to come out, Wynn and I devised a plan where I would break the news during Thanksgiving dinner. There were only the three of us for the holiday—no cousins or friends—just me, Mom, and my older sister, Jenny, and by the time we sat down at the table, my nerves were out of control. I ate frantically, barely chewing the lukewarm chunks of turkey smothered with too-salty gravy and jellied cranberry sauce straight from the can.

"Take human bites," said Mom. Her chuckle was beginning to sound like a smoker's wheeze.

Neither my mom nor I glanced up at Jenny across the small round table, but we could for sure smell her. Jenny was on one of her benders. She reeked of stale beer mixed with skunk weed from hotboxing in her boyfriend's Camaro. I shoveled forkfuls of stuffing and potatoes into my mouth to mask her odor until I scraped the plate clean. It was time for a breath, so I put down my fork to text Wynn a play-by-play update under the table.

I'm going to tell her now.

Without turning, I could feel Jenny's bloodshot eyes sear me as she took swigs from a beer bottle before washing it down with a gulp of whiskey and Coke. Her food remained untouched.

"Stop with the phone," Mom said before scooping a second helping of mashed potatoes on my plate. "Who are you talking to, by the way?"

"Just a friend."

"He's texting his homo lover," said Jenny, her eyelids heavy. "Does he play baseball? Your homo lover? Do you go to Mets games together?" I ignored her, but the comment stung, and it showed on my face.

"What did we talk about yesterday?" said Mom. "Now that your brother lives far away, I thought you were going to try to be nicer to him. I mean, goddammit, Jenny, you're twenty-six. Start acting like it."

Jenny gave her the finger.

Mom turned to me, smiling, and asked, "So have you made any new friends in Boston?"

I told her I had and then dropped my fork, which clinked against my plate. The question was too ripe of a segue for me to pass up. My heart pounded into my left ear.

"She's right, Mom. I was texting my boyfriend."

"What?" Mom's eyes widened, and her hands gripped the table's edge. "Wait, you're gay?"

To avoid her gaze, I focused on a glob of cranberry sauce dangling off the rim of my plate. It dripped like blood onto the Jack-o'-lantern placemat.

"You're the last to know," said Jenny, and with an arm swing, she swiped everything in her vicinity—the plate, beer bottle, tumbler, and half the tablecloth—onto the floor. "This. Is. The. Best. Fucking. Day. Of. My. Fucking. Life!" Blobs of mashed potatoes lingered on the suede cowboy fringe of her jacket. She craned her neck to taste a morsel before lifting both arms. The fringe whipped about like feathers, splattering potato flecks onto the front of my shirt. "Golden boy falls," she said, between hoots and whistles.

"What the hell," said Mom. "Get the fuck outta here. I am so sick of your shit."

I escaped to the bathroom. As usual, Jenny had stolen my thunder, evoking both relief and annoyance. Even the running faucet and the burr of the old bathroom exhaust fan couldn't drown the crash of dishes and jingle of utensils hitting the floor. While on the toilet, I considered how I would have inserted myself into the fight only a year earlier. I would've stood up to Jenny and defended my mom, who'd put in more than a few hours to prepare a holiday meal. In turn, we would've ganged up on Jenny, who would've behaved the same as she always did. Our family was stuck in the same cycle—repeatedly pushing each other's same buttons, then acting surprised when it resulted in the same outbursts. Both living on my own and my new relationship had provided the necessary distance to see our dysfunction with newfound clarity, which in turn provided the fortitude to safely extricate myself and watch the family drama from afar.

I flipped my phone open and found a text from Wynn.

how's it going?

> I'm so stuffed.
> I feel as though my stomach
> and chest have merged
> into a food baby.

no ur news
how did your mom take it?

> Too soon to tell.
> She knows now and

that's all that
matters.
I'll report more
later.
Love ya!

cant wait to hear more
so proud
good luck
miss u
love u

My relationship with Wynn had given me the courage to come out. Since we'd met, I had never been more hopeful about my future. There was even a silver lining after this dumpster fire of a day. The following morning, I would take the train into Manhattan to meet Wynn in Herald Square for Black Friday shopping, after which we would ride back to Boston together. I would be away from this place forever.

Thankfully, Wynn hadn't come. He had wanted to join to provide moral support. Still, I'd had a bad feeling about it, and he was thankfully at a safe distance in Connecticut, spending the weekend with his father and some family friends. I imagined him in some fancy restaurant, his dad sitting next to him, no one fighting, everyone feasting on lobster and short ribs and conversing like normal people.

"Get off my back, you hag," my sister said. One . . . two . . . three . . . four . . . "I *told* you I'm not gonna drive," she yelled. "Dylan's gonna pick me up!" I could feel the thud of her Doc Martens stomping on the linoleum. On the count of nine, the front door slammed shut.

I waited five minutes before leaving the bathroom—my safe space. A trail of cranberry goo and mashed potatoes meandered from the front door into the small alcove kitchen. I tiptoed around the mess to find my mom on all fours wiping the floor with a rag. She looked up at me wearily and asked, "You still hungry?"

I shook my head and cleared the table, raking leftovers into the garbage and stacking dishes into the sink to soak.

Mom broke our silence and said, "I can't make her go to rehab." Dark shadows formed half-moons under her eyes, and eyeliner smeared from one of her lids past the apple of a cheek. "I've been going to Al-Anon meetings, and they say I have to wait for her to get worse till things get bad enough that she wants to go herself."

I stacked the last dish and dried my hands before sitting at the table. "Isn't rehab expensive?"

"You figure out a way," said Mom. She flicked the switch for the stove's exhaust fan and opened the kitchen window. A gale of frigid air gushed in, cleansing the cooking odors and tobacco smoke. An unlit cigarette dangled from her mouth when she joined me at the table.

"I'm glad you never picked up smoking or drinking," she said. "You know, with our genes on both sides." She lit her cigarette and exhaled out the window. I'd heard her say this too many times to count. My father was a drunk, my grandfathers—both drunks. They all died young: a fatal car crash, cirrhosis, and pancreatic cancer. None of them even celebrated their fortieth birthday. With this family history, was anyone more entitled to a happily ever after than me?

Mom didn't know I had picked up drinking in college. My brief stint ended in the emergency room with a tube rammed down my throat pumping my stomach. Since then, I had sworn I would never touch another drink.

"Dinner was such a bust. I almost forgot about your big news." Mom fanned the smoke away from my face.

"I thought you were mad," I said, feeling timid after exposing myself. Now that my big secret was out in the open, I lived in a new skin, relearning how to talk to and interact with people.

She brushed her hand through her hair before placing the other on my shoulder and squeezing.

"No, honey, I don't care that you're gay," she said, stubbing the cigarette in an amber glass ashtray. "I'm surprised, though. Remember, I'm a hairdresser. I work side by side with gay men all day. You're not like them." Mom lit up another cig and took a deep drag, blowing smoke toward the stove fan. "You don't look like them or sound like them. I mean, you played lacrosse."

I shrugged and looked down at the table. Nothing felt gayer than running around a field in short shorts, death-gripping a long stick.

"I guess the gays nowadays come in all types," she said. She blew smoke rings this time, and I watched them float, then disappear into the ceiling.

"So, you're not disappointed?" I asked, starting to feel ill. Change was scary, and our mother-son relationship had always been an anchor.

"No, not really. Just worried."

"Well, I want you to meet my boyfriend." I smiled, attempting to bring cheer into our abysmal evening.

"What's his name?" asked Mom in a peculiar tone that implied she either didn't want to know or planned to have him investigated, or both.

"Wynn," I said, noticing how smoothly it rolled off my tongue. "It's short for Winston."

"What kind of name is that? Is he a British prince or something?" she asked.

"He's Korean. I mean, Korean American. But he's from Connecticut."

"Exotic," Lois said in a nasal voice.

"Actually, I think they've been here for a few generations. His grandparents came over in the 1950s—"

"You use protection? Rubbers?"

I jumped up from my seat. "Mom, that's private." I'd always hated when she tried to talk about sex and birth control with me. Growing up, she wanted to ensure I wouldn't knock anyone up. Little did she know it was the least of her problems.

"Sit down," she said. "I can only deal with one dramatic outburst today. All I'm saying is that you need to be careful. Remember Denny? He was only twenty-nine."

I did remember Denny. He'd rented the chair next to Mom at the salon in the mall. I only met him once or twice and mostly remember the obscene amount of cologne he wore. Inside a cloud of Drakkar Noir was a short and muscular body that wore a thick gold chain partially obscured by a nest of chest hair. When I was in the fifth grade, Mom came home crying and told me he'd died of pneumonia.

"That was a long time ago. It's 2004. HIV is no longer a death sentence," I said, parroting what Wynn had said our first night together. "There are medications now. Besides, don't worry. We're exclusive." I considered mentioning that we weren't doing anything that would put us at great risk, but that would be TMI.

She asked if we'd been tested.

"Yes." I sighed. This game of twenty questions was getting tedious. Wynn and I had each tested at our own doctor's offices. I insisted on it, just in case. One rainy night, we showed each other the results before tearing each other's wet clothes off.

"What does he do?" she asked.

"He's a grad student at Harvard," I said proudly.

"Fancy. Must be nice."

"He graduates this year, which brings me to more news. Wynn got a job offer in San Francisco, and we're moving next summer." The words tumbled out. I squeezed my eyes shut as if I couldn't believe it was real. I was unsure how she would react. Like Jenny, Mom could be erratic. On the inside, I was beaming in anticipation of starting a new life across the country with him.

After a long silence, she said, "All the way to California? How long have you been dating?"

"Three months," I replied. It had been two and a half, but I rounded up. "Ma, they have been the best months of my life."

This seemed to soften her until she shook her head and said, "Well, it's just too soon. You barely know each other, and now you're talking of moving across the country for this guy."

"I know it seems fast, but when you know, you know."

"And what do you know?" she snapped, flicking ash into the tray. "You're twenty-two. This is your first relationship."

"Exactly," I replied louder. "I'm an adult now. I'm paying my own rent and working a full-time job. I'm doing everything that adults do."

She took a long drag. "But you don't need to marry the first guy you meet," she said. "I'm sure there are lots of good-looking guys in Boston."

Of course, there were, but they weren't Wynn. I wanted to tell her I was smart enough to know a good thing—a sure thing—when I saw it. Not that she would ever understand. When was the last time she was in love?

"I'm moving," I said, losing patience with her naysaying. "You can't stop me." My voice cracked in disappointment. The last time I had had big news to share was when I got a job offer in Boston last summer. She had radiated enthusiasm and helped me pick out work clothes at the outlets. A month later, she drove up to visit with new sheets, cookware, and a houseplant for my apartment. I had hoped she would react similarly, especially since Wynn was more important and brought me much more happiness than my mindless job.

Mom put out her half-smoked cigarette. She looked tired, the parentheses around her lips etched deeper. "Ugh, I'm sorry," she said. "I sound like such a bitch. I can't stand the sound of my own voice anymore." She yawned and stretched her hands above her head. "One question," she added. "Why didn't you tell me sooner? About the gay thing?"

"I wasn't sure until recently." I squirmed in my chair because, in truth, I'd always known. Sure, I hadn't said anything because I didn't want to disappoint her, but even more likely, I didn't want to disappoint myself.

"Meeting someone has changed you," she said.

It wasn't clear whether she approved of the new me. Change was change, and in my case, change was good. Very good. Wynn had opened the door to a new world where the day ahead wouldn't look like today. I foresaw big opportunities out there for us. I imagined us standing side by side, one of our hands holding each other's, the remaining ones ready to grab what was ours.

She covered her face with both hands and pushed her forehead into her fingertips. For a while, we sat together in silence. Though things felt awkward between us, I was comforted that Wynn was just across the Long Island Sound, thinking of me like I was thinking of him.

For lack of anything else better to say, I told her: "I brought *The Sopranos* on DVD like you wanted. Want to watch it?" Mom loved Edie Falco. With each season, she changed her hairstyle and color to match Carmela's—she was her idol.

"No," she shook her head. "I need to go to bed. It's been a long day."

"Sorry, Mom." Part of me was relieved because I could text Wynn since he was all I could think about.

She stood and yawned again. "Since you're so grown up, you know you don't have to call me Mom anymore," she said gently.

"What do you want me to call you?" I asked, surprised by this request. "Lois?"

"Sure, why not?" She kissed me on the forehead and said, "I like the idea that I've graduated from something." Lois walked toward the bathroom, and just as she was about to open the door, she turned and said, "I guess I need to figure out what to do with myself now that I've lost both my kids. One to booze and drugs, the other to California and maybe AIDS."

The bathroom door slammed. Her comment hurt, but she was just jealous. I tried to focus on the positive: a new life awaited me. While my mom and Jenny rotted in this town, I would be living in San Francisco! I remembered what Wynn told me when I said how worried I was about moving so far away from my family: *You can't save them.*

I flipped my phone open.

RU ok?

> Yes, I'm great.
> Mom knows everything
> She's super supportive.
> ☺

yay so glad just finished
dinner prime rib was yum
ate so much
will u still like me if I'm fat

> Prime rib is so much
> better than turkey.
> I doubt you ate that
> much.
> No, I don't like you.
> I LOVE you.

LOVE YOU TOO ☺
ok going to crash
sending love
see you tomorrow
xoxo xoxo

Chapter 10

Wynn
Bern, Switzerland
Summer 2015

I HAD NO reason to stay in San Francisco anymore. I no longer had a relationship. I didn't want to go back to Elias's classes. I couldn't stay at Freddie's apartment forever. Besides, the streets held too many memories. I always seemed to cross paths with old colleagues at an intersection or pass by restaurants Jared and I had once frequented. Worse was when I'd dropped into a dance class where I ran into someone who knew about the baby and had questions.

I spent the following week planning my escape, putting in hours of web research until I stumbled upon *Slay and Groove Urban Dance Camp*, a month-long workshop in Switzerland. Their roster listed all the best hip-hop and street dancers worldwide, and naturally it was sold out. I added myself to the wait list.

After wasting a day mired in self-pity, I said to myself, *fuck it*: wait list or no wait list, I was going to show up unannounced and beg my way in if I had to. Besides, I'd outgrown most of the studios in San Francisco. I bought a one-way ticket to

Switzerland on the spur of the moment. After landing, an email from the workshop director informed me of an open spot.

A sign.

The dance camp was located at an all-girls boarding school that had closed for the summer. When the taxi dropped me off, clusters of enthusiastic young people in baggy hip-hop clothes chatted underneath the yellow lights of lampposts along a walkway. I pulled my suitcase down a cobblestone path toward my dorm room in a Tudor-style chalet. That was when I felt it: someone was following me from behind. Electricity coursed in waves over my skin. I turned my head. It was dusk, and I could only make out the outline of a man with long, muscular limbs sprouting from a tall, lean frame that was all shoulders above a trim waist.

Without any signs of hurry, he followed me into the building. Was he a dance student? When I arrived at my room, I turned around, and there he was, leaning against the wood-paneled corridor wall: an angular face covered in freckles, a short, bleached-blonde afro, East Asian eyes like mine, and more notably, he was young—couldn't have been older than twenty or twenty-one. His grin belied a kind of self-assurance that tended to fade with age.

Staring directly at me, he asked flirtatiously: "Can I come in?"

"I was just about to ask you the same thing." The words tumbled out of my mouth before I could decide if it was a good idea.

The following morning, the young man roused me from our twin bed.

"How about we go again?" he asked hopefully.

His breath was sour, but I liked how his long fingers wrapped around the entirety of my ribs. What was his name? Taylor? Tyler? I couldn't remember. I hoped sex would be more elegant than last night, which had been an awkward and fumbling affair. Limbs and elbows knocked and collided into each other, the walls, and headboard.

We found our way the second time around. Mismatched in height and size, we moved more gracefully on the firm, narrow mattress and arranged our arms so as not to knock each other. Eventually, Taylor/Tyler pushed his ass into my chest. A cue. I tore through the condom wrapper waiting for me on the nightstand and slipped it on deftly using just one hand.

"Can you warm me up?" Taylor/Tyler rolled onto his stomach. Sliding a pillow underneath, he arched his back like the Little Mermaid.

A first for everything. There was no getting out of it. I spread his muscular cheeks and imagined I was about to eat a peach. I snapped my tongue against the roof of my mouth to summon moisture. It wasn't sweet or bad, just musky and bitter with a slight chemical aftertaste, almost tannic. Taylor/Tyler bucked and moaned until there was no longer a need for the condom.

He apologized for his hasty climax, and I reassured him that something similar had happened to me recently.

"When it's good, it's good, am I right?" I said before kissing him.

We giggled about it, and then he tried to make small talk. "Are you Korean?" he asked. After I confirmed, he enthusiastically shared that he was half. "I want to break into K-Pop, but I don't know the language well enough yet."

"I barely speak a word myself," I said.

"One day, I'm going to move to Seoul and become a huge star."

"You can learn the language. You're still young."

"Thank you, I love your energy! You're so positive. Where are you headed after camp?"

He leaned back on the pillows, his eyes mooning at me.

"I'm not making plans," I replied truthfully. "Kind of going through a lot right now." My mind was weary. All I wanted was the bed to myself for a few hours of shut-eye. I didn't want to be a zombie on my first day of workshop. "What about you?" I asked out of politeness.

"I want to travel more since I'm already over here . . ." As he talked, I swung my legs over the side of the bed, wrapping the top sheet around my waist. I stood up and marched to the door. Our rendezvous had been fun but a mistake not worth repeating. Dating this guy wouldn't be too different from raising a child. He would need constant reassurance, maybe even coddling when his K-Pop career didn't immediately take off.

". . . I'm like actually dying to go to Berlin. My parents were stationed at a base there once. I hear it's a pretty cool country since it got all unified and stuff . . ."

Too tired to correct him, I grunted an apology, turned the doorknob, and mumbled something that sounded like "need sleep," "see you later," and "thank you" until he shuffled out of the room.

When I returned to bed, I set my alarm but couldn't fall back asleep. I was too wired; feelings of *guilt—gratitude—elation* pulsed under my skin. I'd had exciting sexual encounters with two different men within days of each other. I couldn't fool myself this time. Our tryst was far from an affirmation of my identity. It had been plain lust, a handsome opportunity that was too good to pass up. However, it did make me wonder if my taste in men had changed. My Connecticut upbringing, coupled with decades of bingeing Hollywood rom-coms, had poisoned my consciousness, warping my definition of sexual attractiveness. The leading men in American movies had established a baseline for male beauty that was undeniably white and masculine, which had turned me against myself. I couldn't help but think that leaving Jared had somehow broadened my racialized perceptions of male desirability—altering my vibe and thereby attracting more men of color into my orbit.

In any case, I couldn't wait to start the workshop. There had been so many adventures over the last few weeks, and my bones were telling me there was more to come. Could I get discovered at camp? If I'd stayed with Jared, I would probably be changing a diaper, gagging at the stench of it, or doing something similarly awful in a supposed state of domestic bliss. But now, anything was possible. Any*one* was possible.

The alarm went off, pushing me out of bed. I showered and dressed, checking myself out in the mirror, the new Wynn, ready for the camp's orientation and faculty performance.

During the opening number, the workshop's B-boy instructor spun with such a dizzying velocity that he gave me motion sickness. The pop-and-lock teachers moved with vibrant precision like they were digitized. The jazz-funk dancer-in-residence leaped so high she almost hit her head on a hanging spotlight. What I'd seen and learned in San Francisco was nothing compared to this—mediocre at best. And while I'd seen many of these same faculty on RevTube, their skill, energy, momentum, and grace had been muted on screen. I'd never before seen dancing that felt this alive.

The audience hollered, whooped, and stomped their feet. I sat in silence, crestfallen. I would never break, boogaloo, uprock, or waack like these men and women. I would never join this group of world-class performers. Even with formal training. Even with hard work. Even with stringent discipline and obsessive practice. Admiration turned to awe, which soon morphed into envy, until I turned into a crumpled ball of despair. A knot had formed in my gut. It was talking to me. I would always be a follower—a teacher of beginners at best.

After the performance, I skipped my first day of classes to drink two bottles of wine alone and feel sorry for myself. I almost booked a flight home until I remembered I had nowhere to go.

For the remainder of the week, I participated in classes with shamefaced, guilty fervor. At 5 a.m., I stretched; at six, I drilled the choreography from the previous day. Taylor/Tyler dropped by my room for more, but I turned him away. I avoided socializing with other students and took my meals to a practice studio or my room. There would be no booze, no sex, no distractions.

During camp's second week, I signed up for a "Basics of Hip-hop Choreography and Instruction" workshop, and of course Taylor/Tyler was part of it. The class was small—only eight people—and the teacher, David, asked us to sign up to teach three minutes of original choreography to a song of our choosing. Each of us would perform the routine twice alone, once half-time and once at tempo. After, we would carefully break down each step for the class before performing it together. When David asked for volunteers to teach later in the week, everyone remained silent. Although I didn't have anything prepared, my hand shot up in the air. If I was going to be a follower, I was going to be the best at it.

The next afternoon, while the rest of the camp attended a lecture from an academic, cultural theorist titled "The Match That Burned Down the Master's House: The History and Politicization of Hip-hop," I choreographed and drilled a new routine in an empty studio to the stereo's loudest setting. I practiced until my face turned maroon, and my hair and clothes dripped in sweat. When I turned off the music to sip water and rest, I heard clapping from behind.

"Looking good, but you're a little behind the beat on the second eight-count," said Taylor/Tyler, who now sported a new hoop through his septum. I wondered if it was fake.

"I'm just tired," I lied.

"We missed you in lecture, by the way. I learned a lot."

"Yeah, not really interested in the polemics behind hip-hop," I said, wiping my face with a towel. "Besides, isn't it the whole point of dance to be out of your head and in your body?"

"What's polemy?"

"It's polemics, and it's basically academic-speak, like today's lecture. Racism, neo-colonialism, appropriation, blah blah blah." I stopped because I was beginning to sound like a Republican asshole. "Sorry, I guess I'm just tired of studying books and ideas. I've done plenty of that already, and where has that gotten me?"

"You can't become a better hip-hop dancer without understanding how you fit within institutionalized systems of oppression and racist power structures."

"No, you're right. Hip-hop is political. Hip-hop is resistance, especially within the white supremacist capitalist patriarchy that we live in," I said before standing up and putting a sweaty hand on the small of his back. "Listen, T—you're a great guy, and I had so much fun the other night. I'm sorry that I haven't been available, and I hope I didn't lead you on. But I'm just out of a relationship and really need to focus on myself right now. Also, I'm pretty sure I'm too old for you. I'm thirty-six."

Horror registered on his face before I said, "Please tell me you're over eighteen."

"I'm twenty-one, but damn, you're almost the same age as my parents. They're thirty-nine and forty-two. Aren't you kind of old for this? This camp is supposed to be pre-professional."

I snickered. There wasn't much to do or say at this point. "Not to be rude, and nothing on you, but I need to get back to choreographing my routine for David's class."

"OK, suit yourself." He made a peace sign with two fingers. "Good luck," he said before walking away.

The morning I was scheduled to teach, I had stress-induced diarrhea and showed up to class a few minutes late.

"We've been waiting," said David. "Life isn't a dress rehearsal, Monsieur Kang."

Unlike the other instructors, who were cheery to the point of condescending, David maintained a stern disposition. I aimed to impress, so I took a cue from Elias and didn't apologize before immediately marching to the sound system to plug in my phone and queue up "Work It" by Missy Elliot. I whispered a silent prayer and reminded myself to keep my knees bent and to stay low.

The intro played. After a deep breath, I rearranged my face and performed my short routine. Every move and pose were on the beat; the footwork was simple, too, just a few box steps and a series of hops.

I taught the routine, count by count, breaking down each move clearly and slowly. I spoke with authority, which meant I basically imitated Elias. The front mirrors allowed me to spot students who missed a beat and correct them. I hollered with enthusiasm between each take, "And a one, two, one, two, three, four." After most of the students had mastered the routine, David shut off the music and instructed us to sit.

"Feedback time, what did y'all think?" he asked the class. "Wynn, this is where you stay silent and listen." I stood off to the side and stopped breathing.

"Awesome," someone said.

"It flowed well, it was easy to follow, and his teaching style was clear," said a young white woman in a hot pink tube top and booty shorts.

"I like that you added different hip-hop elements throughout, like some tutting, some stepping, and then some sassy, lyrical shit," said a Black man in his fifties sporting a purple beret.

"Yeah, a lot was going on, lots of mixing without being too busy."

"I liked it, too," said Taylor/Tyler. "But I also wondered if there was appropriation."

"What do you mean by that?" asked David.

"Well, I noticed a Bollywood move, and there were some moves from Dance Hall, which is Jamaican, and I wondered, what gives you the right to do all that? To take it for yourself?" His tone wasn't defensive but probing; it was also just as clear that he didn't feel slighted that I'd turned him down. As far as he was concerned, I was the same age as his parents and too old to dance. In any case, I did hope it was no harm, all good.

"Well, that's a larger conversation, Taylor," David said lightly. "But, duly noted. Nice job, Wynn." He chuckled to himself. "My favorite part was how your face lit up when Missy spoke, 'Boys, boys, all types of boys. Black, white, Puerto Rican, Chinese boys.'"

The room erupted. I laughed, too.

After class, David asked me to stay behind. "Wynn, my man," he said in a lighter tone than before. "You dance with a lot of heart. It almost makes up for your other deficiencies."

"Thank you," I said, licking my chapped lips. My limbs thrummed with excitement or desire, maybe both. David was a little older and not my usual type, but yeah, I was ready to fuck him though I wasn't feeling particularly clean down there. I wondered if we should do it in the studio.

"The manager of Misty Espinoza's comeback tour is holding auditions on Friday in the auditorium. I'm in charge of recruiting folks for it. It's not an open call. We're only inviting a few people from camp, so if you could be discreet—"

My head bobbed up and down. This was way better than dirty dance-floor sex. "Really? Me? Out of everyone?" My voice lurched up an octave.

"Yeah, it's a specific circumstance. You know, Misty is in her sixties now. She's well-preserved and all, but she doesn't want young dancers that make her look even older."

I was puzzled. I always thought I looked much younger than my age, especially if the lighting was right. "How did you know I'm older?"

"Wearing a baseball cap to cover your gray isn't fooling anyone, buddy." He flipped the cap off my head, and I caught it. "Seriously, we can see it in your movement. There's some great flavor in it, but it's a little slow. You don't have the same explosiveness in your thirties and forties."

I brushed a hand through my hair before putting the cap back on. "What does that mean over the long term?" I asked. "You know, for my dance career?"

"It means this is your big shot. Don't fuck it up."

Chapter 11

Jared
Siem Reap, Cambodia
Summer 2015

A ROW OF hedges cushioned my fall. I was fine, except for a wound on my knee, new cuts on my arms and back, and a dull throb in my thigh. A waitress from a nearby café—an angel really—emerged with a stack of napkins and chilled water to dab my scrapes. She welcomed me to sit at one of the outdoor tables. I ordered a latte and asked if they had almond milk. They didn't, so I settled for soy. When the angel brought it to me, a foam rose floated on top. I uploaded a photo to ReverieSocial with the caption, *Unironically @Hipster coffee shop in Cambodia. #CoffeeholicsAnonymous. #ColonialistCaffeine.* It was my first post on the trip—unlike me to wait so long to share on social media. I felt more than a little guilty for taking so long to promote my employer.

One of my junior account coordinators commented, *Beautiful! Safe travels, boss. Post more when you can.*

I was still shaken, so much so that I couldn't even take a sip of the latte. But when the "likes" rolled in, my God, I felt instantly better.

The Cambodian man who had hit me stood on a patch of sidewalk a few feet away, looking dazed. He and his scooter sported matching road rash: a bloody forearm with brown skin flapping off and one side of his shiny blue bike disfigured by chalky white gashes. Sure, I probably shouldn't have been walking and texting, but he should have watched where he was going. For Chrissake, I was the pedestrian here. But I was too exhausted to stay angry, and because I was a guest in this country, I needed to be the bigger person, so I offered him a stack of napkins. He shot me a side-eye before snatching them out of my hand. White crepey paper bloomed crimson.

A police officer appeared and offered to drive me to a hospital, but I insisted I was fine. Like a nurse, he poured a dribble of cold water on a napkin and gently dabbed one of the scrapes on my forearm. I winced and told him I was fine; I got it. The officer then turned to the scooter driver and scolded him before writing him a ticket. After snatching it from the officer's fingers, the driver mounted his bike and motored off, the wind brushing horse-haired bangs away from his angry face.

After a quick taxi ride to the hotel, the concierge called in a French doctor who informed me of my double luck: minor wounds, and the driver hadn't demanded compensation. He handed me a few packets of ibuprofen and a tube of antibiotic cream. Lois doted on me for the remainder of the evening, our argument forgotten. She spread ointment on my scraped back, arms, and knee, then blew on them like when I was a kid. I was still miffed, but I didn't have a choice. All returned to equilibrium, and we were left to wait for Bopha's phone call.

Lois and I sat in lounge chairs by the pool for three days. Neither of us went for a swim: me because of my bandages, Lois because of her hairdo. Instead, I stared into my phone, scrolling the news, eventually texting Bopha again for an update. In her last text, she had said they were still awaiting delivery of the drug, and I wondered if I should call her but decided that I didn't want to come off as a nag. Beside me, Lois reclined and flipped through a magazine dedicated to celebrity hairstyles. I considered calling a friend but decided that would entail explaining the situation. I didn't want to throw Wynn under the bus, mainly in case he chose to return. This spurred me to open the RevSo app and check if Wynn had updated his profile. In general, he disliked social media, and his most recent post was a photo of us in matching suits at his cousin's wedding over a year ago. His gaze was cast downward while I smiled directly at the camera. I loved weddings, every special occasion, while he, on the other hand, would've rather been at home or in a dance class.

To take my mind off him, I took photos of the pool, of my bandages, of the hotel's grounds, of the back of Lois's head—she hated being photographed—and posted them. I drank up the affirmations on the screen.

A few hours later, I got stir-crazy again and tried to coax Lois to tour Wat Thmey—one of The Killing Fields—just outside of town.

After I explained the site's historical significance, she replied, "Ugh, too depressing," and waved off my suggestion. Then I suggested a Khmer cooking class, to which she said, "I haven't gotten sick yet, and plan on keeping it that way."

Every night, we ate the same thing at the hotel: Lois had a cheeseburger, no lettuce or tomato, with boiled veggies on the side, while I ordered the same Pad Thai (and yes, I know that Thai food is not Khmer or Cambodian) that tasted vaguely like ketchup. If Wynn were here, he would have greedily eaten from outdoor food stalls and suffered zero ill effects while declaring, "We're only one Cipro away from an adventure!" Yet even though I would've scrupulously brushed my teeth with bottled water and refused ice and raw produce, I would have ended up with the runs and spent the remainder of the trip chewing Imodium tablets and guarding my precious packets of toilet paper. So, to put it bluntly, I wasn't taking chances on this trip either. I had to stay healthy for the baby.

"This is kind of nice," Lois said after a long silence. "Us spending quality time together in this beautiful resort. Just you and me till the baby comes."

"Yup," I said. I searched and downloaded online images of Angkor Wat during sunrise. I had been so upset about Wynn during the tour, I forgot to take photos. I uploaded stock images of the temple to my RevSo page to compensate for this oversight.

Lois looked up from a photo of a glamorous Asian woman with a sleek, asymmetric bob and said, "I keep wondering what Merry will look like. I hope she's pretty."

"As long as she's healthy." I did *not* like this new nickname. And although I was being honest about caring primarily about the baby's health, I couldn't remember ever meeting an ugly Korean girl, let alone an ugly half-Korean girl. Sure, maybe plain or chubby, but never objectively unattractive. I wondered if this was racist but decided it wasn't since I was generalizing about a positive attribute. It was positive, wasn't it? Didn't everyone want to be beautiful? Anyway, I had often thought about beauty when choosing the donor since we weren't provided any pictures.

And then we found her—No. ZX14477: Korean American from Orange County, graduated from Berkeley *summa cum laude*, scored perfectly on her SATs, and won numerous awards for her sculpture. The perfect blend of right and left brain. Also, she stipulated in her profile that she only wanted to donate to one couple, which raised the price of her eggs and meant that there was no risk of half-siblings roaming around some other high-income zip code.

Meryl would be the only one. An original.

"You know, there's never a good time to have a baby," said

Lois. "You're never truly ready for it. You think I was ready when I had you and your sister?"

"I don't know. I just want her in my arms and to go home." The heat made me drowsy. My eyelids weighed heavy.

"One step at a time, honey," she said. "You're going to be a great dad."

"I can't sit out here anymore and wait for the delivery. It's too humid," I said.

And then a minute later, my phone vibrated. There was a God.

"Maybe it's Betty Boop telling us that Cher's water broke," Lois said, chuckling. She really needed to stop with *the microaggressions*, as Wynn would've called them, but it was too hot, and I also lacked the right vocabulary to explain it to her. I know it was part of my job as a white person, but I just couldn't deal.

I answered the call, and Lois leaned in as if it would help her to listen in. She tossed the magazine aside, and the pages flipped in the breeze.

"Hello, Mr. Cahill?" said an unfamiliar male voice.

"Yes, this is him."

"My name is Sopheak, and I am driver for Assistive Reproductive Therapies. There is problem. Ministry of Health has shut down all surrogacy in Cambodia. Police have taken Bopha away."

"What? Is this a joke?" My voice cracked.

"No, sorry, sir, I wish it was so. The good news is that I drive Chariya across border to Thailand. She and baby are good."

"I'm glad they're safe—but wait, you're in Thailand?" My heart thumped in my ear, and my mouth and throat lost all moisture.

"Yes, hospital better here. You come now."

I leaped out of my chair to stand, and so did Lois, who shouted, "Put it on speaker. I can't hear." I waved her away.

"Wait, who are you again?" I asked, my concentration broken by Lois's interruption.

"I told you, I work for ART. I take girls to appointments, hospital, to buy food, wherever they need. When Bopha arrested, I drive all pregnant girls to Thailand. I make sure you get baby when she ready to come out."

My stomach lurched—I was so freaked out that I could barely comprehend what he was saying. "Wait, what did Bopha get arrested for?" I covered the phone and told Lois, "Bopha is in jail. Don't worry. Cher and the baby are safe."

Sopheak lowered his voice. "You can read about in newspaper. Don't believe what it says. Bopha and Dr. Geller are good people. Do nothing wrong. Police very corrupt here."

"Wait, where are you? I know you're in Thailand, but where in Thailand?" I was ready to throw myself into the pool just to wake myself up from this nightmare.

"We are at Royal Thai Swedish Hospital in Bangkok, very nice, private hospital. Best care in all Southeast Asia. We have baby here tomorrow. You come."

Chapter 12

Wynn
Bern, Switzerland
Summer 2015

ON AUDITION DAY, we lined up outside the camp's main auditorium. There were about twenty dancers in total—an even gender split—almost all of whom I recognized from workshops and classes. Most were solid to excellent dancers, but I told myself none were markedly better than me—just different. And then I wondered if this was a defense mechanism I'd devised to protect my ego and avoid acknowledging my mediocre talent. My psychological theory ballooned into an "I suck" narrative, and the next thing I knew, I was packing my stuff, about to bail on this once-in-a-lifetime opportunity. That was when I told myself to calm the fuck down and proceeded to take some deep breaths, so I could banish this wastebasket of self-doubt I'd created. My self-sabotage death spiral wasn't serving me, and I wanted to believe that passion and drive would carry me through the audition. I needed to believe in myself. As David had said, this was my one shot. Don't fuck it up.

For the tryout, I wore my best hip-hop clothes: a baseball

cap from Brixton, white high-top sneakers, and a baggy vintage FUBU T-shirt that fell past my hips, paired with drop-crotch sweatpants. The outfit was hip, but not so hip that it would distract the judges from my craft. The other auditioners didn't seem to get this memo. They pranced in animal-print leggings, gold lamé shirts, and bejeweled hats that spelled out "Amay-zing" and "Born To Be A Star." And that was just the men.

Once the doors opened, we crowded into a dressing room that reeked of Axe body spray and Red Bull. I avoided the other dancers and focused on my own stretches. Then, a young woman with a headset, presumably the audition coordinator, checked my name on her list and handed me a bib with the number 008. I pinned it to the front of my shirt. My mother used to say that eight was an auspicious number, and I took it as a signal from the universe.

The woman with the headset then called everyone to the stage. I was so nervous my heart thumped in my stomach. She shushed the crowd and ordered everyone to line up in two rows: girls in front, boys in back.

"Congratulations. You were all hand-selected to audition. We're only looking for two men and two ladies for the tour, so it's competitive. If you don't get picked, please don't take it personally. The tour managers are looking for something *very* specific."

A woman raised her hand and said, "Can you be more specific about what they're looking for?"

Without acknowledging the question, the coordinator walked away. We exchanged puzzled glances, hoping one of us had the answers. Then we scrutinized each other. It didn't take long to figure out what we had in common. None of us were teenagers, and while we weren't old by most standards, we were squarely in our thirties and forties, though we dressed and styled ourselves much younger. We covered our gray with baseball caps and box color. We wore clothes more appropriate for our children—if we'd had any.

The coordinator returned, not with answers this time, but to teach us a short routine to one of Misty's old disco numbers that had tricky timing. Picking up new choreography was my superpower. I had a great memory, always have, which had gotten me through school with minimal studying all those years. A woman in sequin booty shorts in front of me particularly struggled with the choreography. She consistently missed the *pas de bourrée* on the downbeat of three and turned her head late on the half count of six. From her errors, I learned.

Each time we ran the sequence, my confidence grew. I relaxed into my body, putting my unique flavor into my movement. Soon, my stomach unclenched, and I began to enjoy the routine, yet I didn't allow myself to get too comfortable. I kept my movements small and precise—the job was for a backup dancer, not a soloist—and soon, I had a gut feeling the job was mine for the taking. When it was time to audition with the whole group, I decided I needed to stand out and add vibrancy and bounce to my steps just to demonstrate to the judges that I could turn it up when necessary. The song's last few counts entailed lifting a bent leg to the side and humping the air like a dog with arms outstretched like Jesus on the cross. I gyrated with hammy glee, all while eye-fucking the three-person panel of judges in front.

After we performed twice in groups of four, we waited in the stage's wings for announcements. I was sweaty and thirsty but didn't dare touch my water bottle. I couldn't even think of nourishing myself until I'd successfully completed my mission. One of the other dancers, a white guy with dreadlocks, said, "I just wanted everyone to know that whatever happens, it's been an honor to dance with you beautiful, talented people." The syrupy tone of his platitude made me think he probably said this at every audition. We were all there to win, weren't we? So why pretend otherwise? But then I remembered the conversation with Taylor about the politics of hip-hop. "You can't become a better hip-hop dancer without understanding how you fit within institutionalized systems of oppression and racist power structures." Hip-hop was about collaboration, not competition. It was about making art as a collective, a form of resistance. I clapped the guy on the back and said, "Thanks, man, I appreciate your positive vibes. You were really good out there." We exchanged smiles, and the sharpest edges of anxiety melted away.

We waited in anticipation. My surroundings switched gears into high definition, slow motion. I could hear the pulse in my neck racing. Pores along the surface of my body closed, and perspiration evaporated into the room's humidity. I was shivering when the coordinator called us back on stage and shouted through her headset.

"Urrutia 4, Vargas 17."

She paused and squinted at her clipboard. "Kong, 8." Not my last name, but it was close enough, and it matched my number. Not needing to listen further, I pounded my fist in the air and hissed the longest "yessssss" of my life. It was a douchebag move, but I couldn't help myself. Then the coordinator said, "If I called your name, you're invited to stay. If you didn't hear your name, thank you for coming. Remember, keep dancing, keep trying. You're all talented. The tour is looking for something *very* specific, and we can't take everyone." There were tears, howls of pain. The dreadlocked guy waved peace signs to everyone and slumped off stage.

We were down to eight dancers: four men and four women—a fifty percent chance. I sussed out my competition from the corner of my eye and immediately noted we all had dark hair and eyes. The other three guys appeared ethnically ambiguous—white, Latino, Arab, or some combination thereof. I was the *only* East Asian—total kismet. After all these years hating being the only one, it was now my saving grace.

"So, while the ladies are learning their combination inheels, we're going to have you freestyle," the coordinator said. "There are going to be different-sized boxes on the stage. Please incorporate them into your performance."

My own routine flashed before me like a vision. It would be simple: I would swirl my hips in a sassy twerk, mix in up-rock, funk, and pop-and-lock, then close with a long backspin to show that I had a knack for old-school breakdancing.

We pulled numbers from a hat. I was second, another lucky number. Before I could celebrate my fortune, music blared through the auditorium's sound system, and they called the first dancer up. They were moving so fast! He started vogueing with lukewarm energy across the stage. His movement suited his long and loose limbs yet didn't quite match the harder beat of the house remix of the song.

"You got this," I whispered to myself. Then out of nowhere, he performed a backflip off the highest box, landing on the floor at the exact moment when the music cut.

That was when I started to panic. I needed to revise my plan—do something splashier—but drew a blank.

The coordinator called "Wynn King, 8." I shuffled onto the stage, stomach cramping and my mind in a fog. "Belly breaths," I told myself. The music started, and I moved to it, executing my vision even though I couldn't get into a groove or flow. I was too distracted by how I was going to close the routine. When the chorus came on, I cut my backspin short as Misty sang, "Baby, love your body, hate your face," and proceeded to leap onto the black wooden box.

Meanwhile, questions whirled through my head: should I do a center split or a karate kick? I decided on the latter. It felt like a sad attempt to remind the judges of the importance of diverse representation. Was I succumbing to a self-created trap? Was I playing into a racist trope?

When I was about to close the routine by leaping off the box, I changed my mind at the last microsecond and attempted a split. Due to my indecisiveness, one leg bent midair, and I landed harder on the other. There was a crack in my heel before a violent pain shot through my foot, ankle, up my calf, and through my knee. I tumbled onto my back and writhed more intensely than when I'd performed the actual routine. The studio went silent.

"Call an ambulance," I heard someone say. Then I blacked out.

Chapter 13

Jared
Bangkok, Thailand
Summer 2015

ON OUR TAXI ride to the airport, I received a text from
Sopheak asking me to cover his travel expenses, including
petrol, tolls, a flat tire, food, and lodging for their long journey.
They needed to ditch their phones to avoid being tracked by the
police, which sounded like a ploy to get me to buy them new
ones. But I didn't have much choice, did I? So, I obliged. A wad
of cash lined my pockets, and I felt like a victim of extortion.
When I complained to Lois that I was paying twice for this, she
said, "Human trafficking is expensive."

Soon after arriving in Bangkok, we ended up in a posh
yet sterile hospital waiting room. Like before at the pool, Lois
and I sat side by side, in chairs upholstered in glove-soft white
leather that reclined in eight positions and had innumerable
cooling, heating, and massage settings. Despite their sublime
comfort, I couldn't nap. All I could think about was my
misfortune—how I was being punished for no good reason.
First Wynn, and now this debacle? I paid my taxes. I donated

to the Human Rights Campaign.

The late afternoon sun projected a bright glare from the glossy, white marble floors, preventing me from reading the Khmer-English newspaper sitting on my lap. It didn't matter since I'd already read the article dozens of times, wasting the last two hours staring at the photo of Bopha in handcuffs, flanked by two policemen leading her into a car that took her to jail. I'd even memorized the headline: *Head of Surrogacy Agency Charged with Human Trafficking.*

Lois leaned over an end table, wrapping one of the two smartphones I'd bought at the Bangkok airport. Edges of metallic red gift paper pinched squarely around the box's corners. Her craftsmanship was perfect—the detailed handiwork of someone who used her hands for a living.

"They're going to tear them open anyway." I was looking to pick a fight.

"Gives me something to do. I need to keep busy. Can you please stop reading that paper?" she said before carefully dabbing a corner with Scotch Tape.

"What else is there to do?" I snapped. "I can't use social media. You know, it's risky."

"I was joking before," she said in a low whisper. "It's not human trafficking or whatever they call it. No one's holding Cher against her will. She agreed to do this."

I didn't know what or who to believe anymore. All I wanted was to return to my home with Wynn and Mare. Why me? I hadn't broken any laws.

A middle-aged white couple entered the waiting room and sat across from us. I could sense they wanted to make conversation, so I pretended to fall asleep. It was rude, but I'd been through enough.

The man whispered to Lois, "Are you here for—" he cleared his throat and whispered, "—surrogacy?"

"My son is," she said.

"Shhh, be careful," he said. "It's illegal here. I take it you're with ART too?" He asked about the half-wrapped phone in Lois's lap before adding that they had brought their own gifts.

The woman said, "The laptops we bought are top of the line."

"They're both for Sothy," said the man. "What's the name of yours?"

"Cher," Lois said. I snorted before returning to my fake nap. I hoped to pass it off as a snore.

They seemed unfazed by her answer and introduced themselves as William and Charlotte—Australians from Perth.

"Don't mind him," said Lois after telling them her name. She kicked my foot and said, "Jared isn't sleeping well."

"Us neither," Charlotte said. "We were all ready to fly to Cambodia last night when we received the call that they moved the girls over here."

"Next thing you know, we're changing our flights," said William, "and heading to a country where we're scared shitless we'll get thrown in jail. Everyone is a bloody crook out here. They see white skin and think we're walking ATMs. If worse comes to worst, I imagine you can pay a bribe."

The phrase "white skin" sounded slightly off, but I couldn't say I entirely disagreed.

Lois said, "Cher and the driver guy said that Betty Boop and Dr. Geller haven't paid them yet."

William replied, "Bullshit, I don't believe it. But did you know that Dr. Geller isn't in jail? He's in Australia. He was visiting his elderly mother when the whole thing went down. I've tried him hundreds of times. He won't return my calls."

"The paper doesn't even mention him. We've read the same story your son has in his lap," said Charlotte.

"I'm not paying him another dollar," William said. "Especially since surrogacy isn't even allowed here. I mean, the driver said that the hospital here will turn a blind eye, but we still have to get through the paperwork at the embassy once our son is born."

I remembered my own escape plan that Sopheak had concocted over text. To get Mare her passport from the US Embassy, I would say that Chariya and I were ex-lovers, our baby an accident. I planned on taking Mare to America for a better life while Chariya stayed behind. There was something romantic about this fib, more than reminiscent of the plot of *Miss Saigon*, the Broadway musical I had seen with my eighth-grade social studies class.

Maybe Wynn's absence was a blessing in disguise. Together, we would have been a dead giveaway. No one would have ever believed I was Chariya's boyfriend if he were here. I could pass. He could not.

The sound of my name awakened me from my pretend nap. A handsome young doctor stood before me. I tried not to stare.

"My name is Dr. Khanna," he said before asking, "Are you the husband?"

"Boyfriend, I mean, ex-boyfriend." I beamed and fluttered my eyes at him. He didn't seem to notice, which was annoying.

"I'm his mother," Lois interrupted, standing up and smoothing imaginary wrinkles on the front of her blouse. "I know. I had him young."

We bade our goodbyes to Lois's new friends to follow the doctor out of the waiting room and into the elevator, our rolling suitcases behind us.

"I reviewed Chariya's chart," said Dr. Khanna, "and she's doing well and ready to deliver. We're booked for deliveries today but can induce tomorrow morning. So, after you see her—"

"Can we watch the delivery?" asked Lois.

"It's not customary in Thailand."

We thought it had to do with Cambodia and surrogacy rules—"

"Mom!" I shouted.

"Sorry," she said.

109

"I'm going to pretend I didn't hear that," said Dr. Khanna. "We only allow family, and it's not customary in Southeast Asia for expecting fathers to view the delivery."

Once we entered the hospital room, Dr. Khanna left for another appointment. We knocked firmly on the open door, but Chariya didn't look up. She wore a hospital gown and sat upright in bed, peering into a portable TV/DVD player. Sopheak slumped over on a window bench in the far corner of the room until our entrance startled him awake. They both looked exhausted: dark under-eye circles and unwashed lank hair. I scrutinized whatever bare skin was visible on her from afar and suspected she'd lost weight, which made me anxious. However, I had to remind myself to be grateful she'd made it across the border while carrying my baby.

"Suasdey," I said. Sopheak shot to attention. Chariya glanced up briefly before returning to her screen.

"Two days, we stopped at border," said Sopheak. "Usually takes a few hours. I bribe border guards to let us through."

I could take a hint. Lois passed out the gifts, and I slipped them their envelopes, after which my hands hovered over Chariya's stomach. She begrudgingly nodded her head. Just like at the clinic, her belly emanated warmth through the thin fabric of her gown. A minute after, the baby kicked, which made me smile ear to ear and giggle. This little bundle of life underneath this skin would soon be in my arms. All my resentments toward Sopheak and Chariya evaporated, and I was even ready to pay them more if necessary.

"Can you ask her how she's feeling?" I asked Sopheak. "Is she nervous?"

"I speak English," Chariya said in a confident alto.

I took my hands off her stomach and stepped backward. "Oh, sorry, I thought—"

"Bopha thinks foreigners prefer us to speak as little as possible, so I pretend I don't speak English." She unwrapped her gift box and held the shiny phone up to her face. The overhead fluorescents refracted light off the device's smooth obsidian surface.

"You speak English so well," said Lois.

"I learn from American television."

"So, are you nervous about tomorrow?" Lois asked.

"No, not at all. I've done this four times before. I give birth to baby last September. Japanese couple. They still send me gifts. They send me this," she said, pointing to the portable TV on her lap.

"I didn't know that you've done it so many times before," I said, barely concealing my disappointment.

"Every Westerner is like you. Wants to feel special." She smiled tightly.

"Well, that's very entrepreneurial," I said. "It's good money, too, I'm sure. Are you saving for something in particular?"

"I want to start a tour company. We ride Vespa motos all around Siem Reap." Now she pantomimed the revving of the engine with the curl of her wrists. "Westerners like you will pay lot to see the real Cambodia."

"That's a great business idea," said Lois.

"Yes, but now I look at you and see you tall and have big head. Maybe this one will be bad? Baby head get stuck. Is egg mommy big, American like you?"

"No," I replied, stifling a giggle. The words *egg mommy* sounded funny. "She's American but of Korean descent."

"Oh, that is relief. I hope baby is smaller. I don't like Korean drama so much. All Cambodians love Korean drama. Too much crying. All sad. I like American TV. Everyone happy. Always smile."

"Once this is done, maybe we can visit Cambodia every few years and have the baby visit you. Her name is Meryl. Do you know who Meryl Streep is? She's my favorite actress. She is more of a movie star than a TV person, though." I pulled up photos

111

of Ms. Streep when she was young, more *Kramer vs. Kramer* and *Sophie's Choice*, less *Mamma Mia* and *Devil Wears Prada*.

Chariya twisted her face and said, "She is kind of strange-looking, no? Not beautiful, not like Jennifer Aniston. You like *Friends?* It is my favorite television show."

Sopheak said, "She watched the discs many times over and over on the car trip from Siem Reap. So many of them."

"Oh, I love *Friends,* too," said Lois. "You know, I could do your hair like Jennifer Aniston. I have my scissors and blow dryer with me. Even the color and everything. I do hair professionally."

I shot Lois a look that said, *Have you lost your mind?*

She glared back at me. "What? She crossed borders and escaped the police to give you a baby. It's the least we can do." Lois pulled up photos of Jennifer Aniston on her phone and showed them to Chariya. "Which do you like better?" she asked. "Her hair in seasons one and two, when it's short with volume, or do you like it sleeker and long like it was in the later seasons?"

"I want famous one from early in show," said Chariya. She flipped her long hair behind her and clapped her hands in delight. "Yes, I am a surrogate like Phoebe. It's where I get idea to do this. Except she do it for brother for free. I get money. I am like Phoebe but smarter. I will soon have Rachel hair. Best of both worlds."

Lois reached over and gave her a hug. "Thank you," she said. "You're giving my son the greatest gift. You're a hero, just like Phoebe." The next thing I knew, she had pulled a pair of scissors and a blow-dryer out of her suitcase and filled a spray bottle from the room's sink.

"I want to put some caramel strands in the front," she said. "I'm thinking not too blonde. I don't want to wash out your beautiful skin." Lois dug into her bag for a hand mirror and held it before Chariya. "No need to freak out, Jarey," she said. "They say it's safe to color hair after the first trimester."

"No chemicals," I said firmly. "She's giving birth."

Lois made a fart noise with her tongue. "Fine," she said. "Let's go to the bathroom and wash your hair, honey."

I turned to Sopheak for an ally, but he was too busy playing with his new phone.

When they returned from the bathroom, Chariya sat in a chair, and Lois snipped. Chunks of wet hair plopped onto pages of a disassembled celebrity hairstyle magazine spread across the floor.

"Don't you worry," said Lois. "I've done this haircut a thousand times. I still do it. Hairstyles don't really change where I come from."

"I trust you," said Chariya. On her lap TV, Chandler and Joey reclined in matching La-Z-Boy chairs.

When Lois finished the cut, the room smelled of burnt hair and fruity hairspray. She held up the hand mirror again. Chariya squealed with delight, fussing with the layers around her face and admiring how they swayed back and forth across her cheekbone and chin.

"I love this part," said Chariya. She tugged a tendril in the back that curled upward like a fishhook. "I don't know how you do this. This is the best day."

Chariya stood, and Lois hugged her tight. Watching them act like besties made my heart drop. For the past week, I'd bent over backward to charm her, given Chariya enough money to live on for over a year, and my mom's twenty-minute haircut ended up winning her over. I felt like a total jackass, but I also knew when to concede, not that it was ever a competition in the first place.

"You did an incredible job," I said. "And Chariya, you look great. This cut really flatters you. Well, I don't know about you guys, but I'm hungry. Why don't I order us dinner? Celebrate Chariya's new hair?"

"Great idea," said Lois, her arm wrapped around Chariya's shoulders.

While I searched for a food delivery app, a chair squeaked loudly against the floor. I looked up to find Lois helping Chariya up. Then I heard a pitter-patter on the magazine pages on the floor. My first thought was, *Oh my God, why is she peeing in front of us?* Then Lois said, "Holy shit. Her water broke!" I ran into the hallway, yelling for Dr. Khanna.

Chapter 14

Wynn
San Francisco, CA
Summer 2015

I WAS A morning person on days I wasn't drinking. My body naturally roused me, eyes bursting open between 5:45 and 6:03 a.m. Yet after the injury, I couldn't get out of bed at any time of day. The painkillers put me in a stupor and weighed my muscles down. On the bright side, the drugs also numbed me to the point where the audition stopped replaying in my head. The surgeon who'd sewn my tendons back together had been smart enough to write me only a five-day prescription. An OxyContin addiction was the last thing I needed in my life. I muscled the last two pills down my dry throat. I waited for them to kick in so I could fall back asleep, but a sharp and familiar pain in my heel needled me awake. Then I heard a rattle from the front door and sat up in bed.

Of course, it was only Freddie with two bags of groceries in his arms. "Good morning, sunshine! How are you feeling?" he said in a campy voice.

"Better, now that I'm medicated," I said.

Freddie dropped the bags on the kitchen counter, slamming Formica doors and cabinets so that there was no mistaking it as unintentional.

"Feeling good enough to eat? Got you some staples," he declared in a particularly booming voice. The meds had dulled my appetite, and food no longer appealed to me, but I was touched by his thoughtfulness.

"Thanks," I croaked. "How much do I owe you?"

"This one's on me."

"No, don't do that—" I said, rubbing sleep crust out of my eyes.

"I insist." He gritted his teeth into a half smile.

Despite Freddie's passive-aggressiveness, his presence buoyed me—I was *that* lonely. When we'd worked together at Synergy, I'd felt the stirring of a crush but never allowed it to bloom for obvious reasons. Nevertheless, he'd proved to be a good friend, and I was grateful to have him around the last few weeks. Freddie had picked me up at the San Francisco airport, brought me to the hospital for surgery, and taken me back to his place for recovery. He'd even moved his bed from the loft to the living room so I wouldn't have to hobble up and down the spiral staircase. In addition to lending me his apartment while he stayed at his girlfriend's, Freddie brought me groceries and picked up my prescriptions on his way to and from work. He was in no way obligated to me, but I suspected he pitied me for my lack of family and close friends.

Freddie plopped on a beanbag chair that faced my makeshift bed. "How's the shower seat treating you?" he asked.

"Clearly, I haven't used it yet," I replied before running my fingers through greasy hair. A flurry of dandruff fell onto the pillow. I couldn't put in the effort to wrap my cast in plastic bags to shower, especially if I had no intention of leaving the apartment.

He nodded absently, not really listening. "OK, good," he said, heaving himself out of the beanbag and standing back up. "Hey, man, I gotta run to work, but wanted to ask you something." He paused. "This is kind of awkward, but I'm going to have to ask you to start paying rent."

He'd caught me off guard. "Sorry, I should've offered." I twisted to hide my embarrassment, fluffed the pillow behind me, and adjusted myself upright. "I never thought I was going to be crashing for this long. So, how much?"

Freddie reached forward under the bed: the fluffy green circle of the Twister game-board rug had been hiding one of his cordovan loafers. Straightening back up, he mumbled an astronomical figure, then added something about a "friends and family" discount.

I whistled. "Money's been tight. There've been doctors' bills, dance camp tuition, and the flight home. And I haven't worked in a while," I said, tallying what was left in my savings account and wondering how I could go about cashing out my 401(k). "How about I pay both this month and the one before? Full price, though, with no friends and family discount. I'll probably move out since my heel will be better by then."

"Sure, that works," said Freddie. "Well, that was easy. Thanks. You can be pretty generous when you want to be."

"No, I suck. Seriously, Freddie, thank you for everything, and I'm sorry I never offered. It's bad manners." I chuckled. "I'm even *more* self-involved than usual."

"No biggie, you're going through a lot," he said. "So, what are you going to do afterward?"

"After what?"

"After next month. When you move out?"

"Oh, I'll be fine. My friend, Nicole, has been bugging me to visit her, so I might do that first. After that, maybe I'll head to New York, maybe LA, or wherever there's a good dance scene."

A silence ensued, and I could feel his disapproval and the flex of his willpower to not say what was on his mind. Our conversation was headed into uncharted territory. We'd never had the kind of friendship where we openly talked about dreams and goals or even displayed emotions other than cheer or jest. There seemed to be a tacit understanding that we'd never discuss anything serious. Freddie was kind and generous but also meticulously organized and highly practical. The son of Colombian garment workers, he wasn't a management consultant for only his job. It was also who he was as a person. Or maybe all friendships with straight men were like this.

"Have you, uh, thought of getting a job?" he asked, standing up to leave as if my indolence had made him more cognizant of his own use of time.

I closed my eyes and scrunched my face tight. "I'm not going back."

"You don't have to go back to Synergy or even consulting. Maybe something with more work-life balance? Like a nonprofit or government? Somewhere they won't mind if you leave early for rehearsals."

"Maybe," I said. "But not now." My chest tightened at the thought of rotting in a dark cubicle, counting the minutes until the clock hit 4:59 p.m.

"So, how are you going to support yourself?" He rested his hands on his hips, making him look matronly.

"I've got some savings," I said.

"And after?"

I shrugged. We'd never discussed my financial situation. I'd barely discussed my inheritance with Jared, for that matter, and I'd already used most of it to pay off my student loans and make the down payment on the house. The truth was, I was waiting for Jared to sell the house or buy me out of my share, which would carry me for a while or at least until my career in the arts—whether it be performing, teaching, or something related—took off. Part of me couldn't say this aloud because I feared I would sound like a trust fund kid or, worse, a delusional and entitled fool.

Freddie walked over to the front door and hovered there, hesitating, as if he wanted to say something he couldn't utter aloud. Then he said, maybe for lack of finding the right words: "Must be nice."

Then, quietly, he left, shutting the door firmly behind him.

It then dawned on me that I had mastered a particular interpersonal skill that entailed ruining every relationship I touched. Maybe I should've added it to my resume? Freddie was too good for me, and we would both be relieved when I was gone.

Our conversation had put me in a sour mood. Freddie was right. I didn't have much cash left and had no serious plan. LA and New York were the places to go if I wanted to dance professionally, yet I had doubts, especially after the accident, about my ability to make it in these markets. Besides, I didn't know anyone in LA or New York and was already so lonely.

A stiff drink called out to me. Alcohol was technically out, and I wasn't quite self-destructive enough to mix it with the painkiller I had popped. Yet I couldn't stop fantasizing about the prospect of floating above my body and forgetting about my worries for the future. Part of me just needed to accept that I was already beginning to pine for Jared—the mindless chatter, the oniony scent, the bear hugs, even the jerk-off sessions seemed enticing now. It was the first time I'd missed him since the breakup, and I couldn't stop thinking about what he might be doing. Was Meryl even born yet? Was she healthy and happy? Had he already met someone else? Would there ever be a day when we could be friends? These questions made me feel guilty, reminding me of what I'd done and how I'd hurt him. If I only had the power to turn back the clock and we could've communicated better . . . but back to when, or what moment? Before he'd contracted with the surrogacy agency? Or earlier, like before we closed on the house? Wasn't a joint mortgage the beginning of the end? Any of these hypothetical conversations would've inevitably led to a breakup earlier, yet likely a more civil one—a "conscious uncoupling." In any case, I would have probably ended up in this same position: alone and a hot mess.

To get my mind off him, I watched porn to little effect. I needed the real thing: skin-on-skin contact, hot breath on my neck, a man's weight on top of me. After powering up my phone, I fell into a trance of tapping and swiping at headless torsos. Text bubbles burst onto my screen—each ping a tiny thrill.

'sup

You looking?

Top or bottom?

Discreet?

The last message tickled me. This was San Francisco. Who needed to be discreet? Eventually, I found a familiar face on the digital chessboard. His name was Kyle, and he was someone I'd met at a party a few years back. It felt safer to connect with someone I'd already met, even if it had only been once. We started chatting, and I was impressed that he typed in almost complete sentences and spelled everything correctly. Within a few minutes of texting, I invited him over, and lo and behold, I finally had an excuse to use the shower seat Freddie had given me.

Within the hour, the door buzzed. I rested my knee on a scooter-like contraption and wheeled to the door to greet Kyle. He looked the same as I remembered, tall and lean like a swimmer, with broad shoulders and posture so vertical, he stood swayback. He'd grown his hair out, which now draped past his ears in wooly, auburn curls. He bent down to kiss me on the cheek. I grabbed the front of his shirt and pulled him toward me. I inhaled him in the hope he might fill the emptiness.

"What happened to your leg?" he asked once we came up for air.

I licked his minty flavor off my lips. "I ruptured my Achilles tendon. I had surgery last week."

"Bummer. How did you do that?"

I pulled him toward me again. Conversation was not on my mind.

I was disappointed we couldn't fuck. The boot made every position awkward. When we finally found one that worked, I became increasingly anxious that I might lean on my ankle the wrong way or that Kyle would sit or fall on it.

So as Jared and I had done all the previous years, we just lay on our sides kissing, our hands clutching each other's cocks. We came within a few seconds of each other, our foreheads locked, noses pressed together.

Still, the familiarity of the act triggered something. Namely, I felt even more empty. Part of me wanted to ask Kyle to leave, but it would mean I would be alone.

"That was exactly what I needed," I said. "Thank you."

"You're welcome." Kyle pecked my cheek innocently like I'd given him a plucked daisy or a shiny green apple on our walk home from school. "So, I have a confession," he said with a wicked grin.

Oh no, I thought, *he has an STD.* I pulled the sheet over my groin as if it could rub away an infection. Thankfully, we hadn't had sex.

"I've had a couple-crush on you guys since Ted and Lucas's party," he said.

"A couple-crush?"

"Yes. It's weird, I had a crush on both of you, but I was jealous too. You guys seemed so happily married with your house and fancy car," he said. "Wait," a recognition that he was breaking social mores showed up on his symmetrical face. "I hope I'm not freaking you out."

"No, not at all," I said. "It's flattering. The fact that you liked both of us seems rare. It means you probably don't have an Asian fetish,"

"No way, I like *all* men, but I get it. I know how it is." Of course, he did. I second-guessed my statement, wondering if non-white men *could* have an Asian fetish since so much of it was about the semiotics of a perceived unequal power dynamic. But Kyle was white-passing, or was it white-presenting? I couldn't remember the correct term. In any case, did this fact change things? Or was it less about appearance and more about one's political and social consciousness? All of it made my head spin, and I just wanted to enjoy the moment, so I rolled closer to him, savoring the warmth of his body and how easy it was to be around him. With a fingertip, I traced the distance between his cheekbone and a beauty mark on the hinge of his jaw. I no longer wanted to talk. I just wanted to admire him. In silence.

"Sorry, I can't deliver on a threesome," I said. "We broke up."

"Yeah, I figured," he said. "I follow him on RevSo. He's like in Asia or something and had a bicycle accident."

I shot up, hitting my head against the headboard. "Wait, an accident? Is he OK?"

"I think he's fine. He posted photos of his band-aids. It looked like a couple of scrapes." Kyle pulled up the photos on his phone and showed them to me: A close-up of scabs on his legs, a bandage on an elbow, and a selfie of Jared making a sad clown face. It made me miss him less.

"That's a relief. I'm glad the accident was minor," I said, in disbelief that Jared would ever ride a bicycle in Cambodia. "Even though we're not together anymore, I still wish the best for him."

Kyle scrolled through his phone. "Cool! Jared just posted. Wait, did he just have a baby? Did you know about that? Aww, she's so cute. You want to see?"

I shook my head.

"Of course," he said. "Are you OK?"

"I'm fine." My throat closed, and I almost choked on my saliva. He placed his hand on my shoulder. I squirmed.

"Can I ask why you broke up?"

"It's complicated." I hesitated. "In a nutshell, he wanted kids. I didn't. Or rather, I thought I wanted kids but changed my mind. No, that's not fair. I think I *liked* the idea of having kids. I wasn't ready, though; honestly, I'm unsure if I will ever be ready or want to take on that kind of responsibility. You would've thought we would've talked about it more before hiring a surrogate, but I told Jared all of this *many times*, and to be frank, he's not the best listener. Not to talk smack about him. He's a great guy. If you ever hung out with him, you would see that. I also think he needs gay friends. I need gay friends, too. You know, gay friends I'm not sleeping with. No offense. Anyway, Jared has a huge heart. Maybe I'm not that good of a communicator. Yeah, it was a bad combo: he was a bad listener, I was a bad communicator." I panted, realizing I hadn't taken a breath. Trying to make light of my outburst, I smiled and laughed at myself. "So, as you can see, it's all very complicated."

"Wow, that's deep," said Kyle. "Sounds like you're going through a lot right now. Have you thought about seeing a therapist?"

"Yes, I have thought of seeing one, but I'm not working now, and my Medi-Cal plan only covers the big stuff like my heel." I took a deep breath and rearranged my face into a smile. "I'm actually pretty good. It worked out for the best. I had my dreams. He had his. They just didn't overlap." I wondered if I should be drawing Kyle a Venn diagram. I preferred this to having to admit that I'd given up my long-term relationship for a failed endeavor. Suddenly, the emptiness I'd attempted to fill returned, and I needed to be alone. "So, this was fun. A big workout for me. I'm really tired," I said limply and swung my legs off the bed.

Kyle searched under the tangle of sheets for his clothes. Once he was dressed, I asked if he needed the bathroom or a glass of water for the road, but he shook his head.

At the door, I gave him a peck on the cheek. He was deliciously handsome, and his face was so smooth, but I couldn't wait for him to be gone. I wasn't worthy. "I had a great time, but clearly, I'm not ready for anything serious right now."

"It's cool. We're on the same page," he said with a sheepish nod.

"But I'm glad we reconnected. I had a lot of fun," I said, opening the door.

"Me too." His voice echoed in the hallway. The boy did have impeccable manners, and for a moment, I considered pulling him back toward me. Still, I didn't have the mobility to do so with my knee scooter in the way.

After shutting the door, I vowed to avoid all social media. I drank Freddie's beer and his entire liquor cabinet for the next two days—vermouth, Frangelico, and Jägermeister included.

Chapter 15

Wynn
San Francisco, CA
Fall 2013

JARED CONSTANTLY REMINDED me that we had no gay friends. On the other hand, I never had a burning need for more friends—gay, straight, or otherwise. And maybe due to my growing up as an only child, I preferred my circle tight: Jared, my best friend Nicole, who had recently moved to Kenya, and my "work husband," Freddie. Three seemed like enough, so why waste time with catty gays when I could otherwise be in a dance class?

"But Ted's so fun," said Jared before pulling out of our garage in his brand-new, leased Audi SUV. "He's a total hub." He would rather die than show up to their party in my beat-up hatchback.

"What's a hub?" I asked.

"A social hub, meaning he knows important people who can help us."

The "us" meaning "him," of course. I was over this new tone in his voice, which implied that he was on top of the latest lingo, and I was not. Since his promotion at Reverie, Jared now saw all people as "potential connections" who could be summed up by their accomplishments or what he called their top-line bio or TLB. Ted's TLB was four words: M&A attorney, Yale Law. Reducing someone to an acronym for their accomplishments represented everything I hated about the professional class. Of course, I was part of the problem. Still, whenever I tried to figure a way out—aka leaving my "career" while also finding a way to support myself—I ended up lost in a tangle of circular logic, where the only possible solution was to euthanize myself.

Ted and his partner, Lucas, had married in Tulum last year. We hadn't been invited. Their wedding happened before we'd met them, but Jared mentioned it almost daily, pushing his phone in my face during dinner. Images of matching tuxedos, Mayan temples, and Ken-and-Ken-doll wedding cake toppers blurred together. The overall aesthetic—basic with a touch of outdated camp—repulsed me.

A succession of cars tailgated us through the winding hills above The Castro until they eventually passed us on the left. Since he'd leased the Audi, Jared drove fifteen miles below the speed limit and signaled ten blocks too early. After the blinker signaled for over a minute, Jared said, "Remember, Ted is short and super skinny, a corporate lawyer and an ultra-marathoner. Lucas is taller and has a more athletic build. He's a family medicine doctor, though I think he attended med school in the Caribbean. Don't bring it up. Aren't we lucky we don't have this gay-twinning problem?" He punched me in the shoulder playfully and laughed.

I'd mixed up their names at our first double date at a French Japanese fusion restaurant. The second time I did it during the same night, Jared kicked me under the table.

The party was full of straight couples—presumably friends from work and school—and their kids. After scanning the patio more than once, I immediately made note that everyone was white. I was tired of being the only one, not just the only Asian, but the sole person of color. "In San Francisco, of all places," I muttered aloud, but Jared had already followed Ted into their new house. I met them in the master suite's gleaming bathroom of slate and chrome.

Ted said, "I wanted it to look exactly like the bathrooms at the W Hotel." When Jared said, "Wow, I love it," four times in a row, I excused myself to sip a beer on a teak bench in the backyard's far corner.

After sunset, the straights packed up their kids and said their goodbyes. The wine and beer were put away. Lucas poured tequila into the blender with a leaden hand while Ted unveiled the hot tub. White lights strung across the cedar fence illuminated the sudsy water.

The hosts passed a round of margaritas for the remaining guests: me, Jared, a redhead named Kyle, and a handsome Arab man who must've arrived late. After fulfilling their bartending duties, Ted and Lucas held hands. They drunkenly flitted around the backyard, margaritas spilling onto the grass, and called each other "Cliff" and "Claire" from *The Cosby Show*.

"We're the gay Huxtables," they sang in unison.

"You know, because one of us is a doctor," said Ted, who pointed to Lucas, "and one of us is a lawyer."

"Sans the five kids, of course," said Lucas.

At that point, I decided to make the most of the situation and chugged my margarita. Alcohol-induced confidence persuaded me to introduce myself to the sexy Arab. We exchanged names, and he had a firm handshake. His name was Youssef, and he also conveniently lived two doors down.

"I'm his partner," said Jared, who moved between us as soon as we released each other's hands. "Nice to meet you."

"A friendly neighbor," I declared. "Well, the water looks great. I'm heading in." I pulled off my sweater and unbuttoned my jeans to reveal a pair of white spandex trunks decorated with green palm trees.

"Come on, get in," I said.

"You go in," said Youssef. "I'll join later. Lucas needs help with the drinks."

"Don't pout," said Jared, "I'm coming." He pulled down his khakis, revealing baggy swim trunks. I disliked his overly preppy, straight-boy fashion choices for all his traditional gay-ish obsessions with cleanliness and perfection. Since his promotion, he'd gained some weight, which honestly didn't bother me, though it was likely the reason he kept his white tee on. As soon as he entered the water, it billowed around him like a parachute.

Soon Kyle, the redhead, and Ted joined us in the tub, while Lucas and Youssef pattered off to the kitchen to prepare another round of margaritas. I leaned my head back against the edge of the tub and gazed at the stars.

"We bought this house because we plan on having kids down the road," said Ted. "The city is just getting more and more expensive, and we thought that if we didn't buy a house now, we would get priced out and have to move—" Ted paused, "to Oakland." He spat out the word as if it were sour milk. "Besides, what else will we do with all our money?"

I imagined this wasn't the best time to go on one of my rants about capitalism and how "winners" like them were ruining our cities. The last time I had done this at dinner, Jared got annoyed. He said criticizing capitalism was a waste of time since even China had given in and adopted free markets. Our debate then spun out of control. I argued that economic systems didn't have to be binary, communist vs. capitalist, and that we needed to re-envision market systems. Jared continued to drive his point home, using Venezuela as an example while ignoring that the economies of one-resource countries tended to tank due to old-fashioned corruption. After thirty minutes the other guests, a straight couple who worked with Jared at Reverie, had complained that they had an early morning and asked for the bill before we finished our main courses.

"I want 'em," said Jared, interrupting my train of thought. His Long Island accent was slipping in. "You need at least one kid, preferably two so that the first one doesn't get lonely, right?" He elbowed me in the ribs before taking a long swig from a can of Diet Coke. "Kids. We want 'em."

I swatted the air in front of Jared's face. "Yeah, but later, much, much later."

"We have a responsibility to show an example," said Jared.

"To whom?" asked Ted.

"To everyone. Straight people need to see that our love is as real as theirs. They need to see that we can build a family that's just as legitimate and loving. It's a form of activism, really. And gay people need to understand that having a family is even more important for us than for straight people. We need to learn there's more to life than circuit parties, orgies, and party drugs. Monogamous, committed relationships, and raising children will save us."

Ted hollered, "Preach, girl."

"Amen," said Lucas, who walked toward us with a tray of drinks.

Everyone whistled and clapped.

I rolled my eyes. "Heteronormative," I said between coughs. "My main issue is that we're too young. We don't have a biological clock ticking in our ears."

"Not that young," said Jared. "My mom was nineteen when she had my sister."

"Let's be real. Your mom is not a shining example of happy motherhood," I blurted. The alcohol had taken effect, and I immediately regretted it and hoped Jared wouldn't kill me after the party.

Ted spit a mouthful of margarita back into his cup. "I like drunk Wynn. He's spicy," he said. "And by the way, Lucas and I feel exactly same way." He hoisted himself out of the tub and sat on the edge. "We've been working our asses off our entire lives. We just want to have fun for a bit." He flutter-kicked water in my face.

"Still, who wants to be an old dad?" asked Jared. "Who knows if we'll have viable sperm in a decade?"

"We're putting our sperm on ice," said Lucas, who passed another round of margaritas. "This is our last soak before we jack off into a cup."

The steaming, bubbly water soothed my tight hamstrings and quads. I leaned my head back to savor it until I started to bang my head against the edge of the tub. What was Jared's rush? Since my dad had died a year earlier, I was only beginning to feel like myself again. And as dull as work was, it had become easy: making rent was no longer a struggle, and best of all, I was dancing.

"I have a virgin margarita coming right up for you," Lucas said to Jared before heading inside.

I pinched my nose and dunked myself. When I returned for air, I scanned the deck for Youssef. He must've stayed inside.

Then, a hand below the water's surface grazed my thigh, lower back, and waistband. Fingertips swayed in and over the crack of my ass, making me tingle. The weight of the touch was too feather-light to be Jared, who usually grabbed, pinched, or squeezed.

"Claire! Are you done making the next batch? We're thirsty," said Ted.

"Just another minute, Cliff," Lucas called through the screen door.

The hand, which I was sure belonged to Kyle, the redhead, crept toward my inner thigh.

Ted stood in the tub. Water beaded down his pale, concave chest. "Claire, honey, what's taking so long? Can you bring the pitcher? We all need a top out here."

Kyle sniggered, though he continued to work on me. I

closed my eyes and turned to face him. He glanced back for a moment before averting eye contact. I detected something I'd missed earlier in that flash of a second. It was subtle, in the texture of his hair, on his cheekbone's curve, and the bridge of his nose. He wasn't white. Kyle was mixed. I was sure of it. This new knowledge made what we did acceptable because Kyle and I were now a team. We weren't cheating. We were imposters together—subversive in our passing—while everyone else in the tub, including Jared (no, *especially* Jared), were separate from us. Or maybe I was just drunk?

Ted hopped out and wrapped a towel around his waist like a sarong. "Lucas. Papa is thirsty," he said, sashaying into the house.

Someone tapped my shoulder and I flinched. The hand inside my trunks released me.

"Did I scare you?" Jared asked. "Are you drinking enough water? Your eyes are red."

I squeezed my eyes shut to activate my tear ducts. So, he wasn't pissed about my comment about his mom?

"You seem to like the hot tub. Can we get one in our new house? Please."

Oh, he wanted something. We heard a loud crash before I could remind him there would never be a new house.

"How could you do this to me?" a voice yelled inside the house. "You fucking asshole." Another crash—this time, it sounded like shattering glass. "You fucking faggots."

Jared and Kyle hopped out of the tub and raced inside. I carefully wrapped a towel around my waist—still hard—and followed reluctantly from behind. When I got to the kitchen, Ted was yelling, his face red with a large vein throbbing down the middle of his forehead. Lucas's shorts hung below his knees, his palms covering his groin. On the floor next to him, Youssef crouched naked, his hands protecting his face.

"Can you believe this shit?" Ted asked me. "I work sixty hours a week, like a slave, so he can go be a do-gooder in the ghetto, and now I catch him giving a hummer to our neighbor?"

Before I could point out the many things wrong in his sentence, Lucas sprinted out of the kitchen and into the living room before curling into a fetal position on the sectional. Jared followed and sat down next to him, patting his back. When I looked back into the kitchen, Youssef and Kyle were nowhere to be found. I'd been so consumed by the chaos I hadn't seen them sneak out of the house.

It was then that Ted followed Lucas into the living room. He was about to lunge at his partner until I grabbed him by the shoulders. Ted turned and pushed me away before saying, "I knew it was a bad idea to open up the relationship. He can't follow the rules because he's a cheating whore."

There was no way to diffuse the situation with both of them in the same room, so I dragged Ted by the hand upstairs to their bedroom. "Let's take a time-out," I said in my most soothing voice.

We sat on their king-size platform bed overlooking a picture window that showcased the downtown skyline and the flickering white lights of the Bay Bridge.

Ted rested his head on my shoulder and bawled. Even though I'd never liked him, I didn't have the heart to leave, so I endured.

"You're so lucky, Wynn," he said, lifting his head from my now-damp shirt. "Jared would never pull a stunt like this on you. He's so solid and hot, even with the extra weight." I wondered how Ted could know much about Jared's fidelity unless he'd tried something himself. "Hey, I've always wondered," he asked. "Does it ever bother you that you guys are a stereotype?"

I pulled away from him immediately and stood up from the bed. "What do you mean?"

"You know," said Ted. "Successful older white guy with a younger Asian."

"I'm actually two years older," I corrected him. *And in*

132

the beginning, I was the more successful one, I almost added but stopped myself.

Listening to Ted prattle on about Jared, it dawned on me that Ted had a crush on him; yet I wasn't jealous. That lack of feeling troubled me. More than anything, I just wanted to be back in the hot tub enjoying the unexpected touch of solid and stealthy hands.

Exhausted by betrayal, Ted eventually slipped under the covers. I tucked him in, and when he fell asleep, I shut the lights and tiptoed out.

When I came downstairs, Jared was cleaning the kitchen while Lucas snoozed on the sofa. Jared and I made eye contact, sharing a look full of strange arousal and need. Without saying a word, we left that house and raced, almost giddily, to the car.

Once home, we hastily undressed. We pumped and grunted for what seemed like hours through lubricated thighs, clenched fists, and puckered lips. When it was over, and we lay drenched in sweat and fluids, Jared attempted to roll out of bed to shower, but I wrestled him and said, "Stay." And so he did until I fell asleep. Later, I awoke to him shaking me. He was swaddled in a fluffy bathrobe and smelled of eucalyptus shampoo.

"Baby, I'm freaked out. Please say we'll never become them."

I squinted. "We will never be like them," I said.

Jared turned on the lights, and I shielded my eyes. "Get up," he said. "I don't want to be middle-aged and throwing hot tub parties."

I propped my head up with an elbow. "I promise we won't ever open up our relationship." This was true. I wanted monogamy. It was my dick that sometimes wanted other men. I still loved Jared. I wanted him, too. Our middle-of-the-night rendezvous fueled by the party's half-naked bodies and the passion-filled fight had proven this, hadn't it?

"But I want more than just faithfulness," he said. "I want a house. I want to get married and have a family. I want kids."

"Of course, one day." None of those options appealed to me, but I assumed that would change. More than anything, I wanted to fit in with the rest of society, who seemed to covet the same things as Jared.

"No, now."

"Right now? I hate to break it to you, but what we just did doesn't lead to babies." I cackled at my own joke. "Can't we talk about this tomorrow? It's four in the morning."

"I need to feel like we're progressing," said Jared. "In case you were wondering, we've been together for almost nine years, and our anniversary is coming up. We're going to end up bored and messy like Ted and Lucas and sleeping with our neighbors."

"Of course, our anniversary. I remember," I lied. In truth, I hadn't given it a thought, which made me feel like a total jerk.

"I need something." Jared tossed a pillow at me. I caught it.

"Like what?"

"I'll even give you a choice," he said with a self-assured smile. "Wedding, house, baby."

"How about—"

"No, none of the above isn't a choice. Whatever you pick, I'll do the work. Don't worry, you can dance."

I was cornered and exhausted. All I wanted was sleep. So, I agreed.

Just to the house.

Chapter 16

Jared
Bangkok, Thailand
Summer 2015

ALL ROADS LED back to the hospital waiting room. I was alone this time: the Australians were long gone, and Lois had gone back to the hotel to catch some much-deserved shuteye. It was late, past midnight, and I was so anxious I couldn't imagine falling asleep. Not even my phone could distract me. I needed to talk to someone more than anything, so I called Nigel, the British psychic in London. It was early evening his time, and he said, "You're just in luck. I just happen to have an opening."

I suspected he said this to everyone, though it didn't stop me from RevPaying his fee before telling him everything. Words spilled out of my mouth so quickly that I almost forgot to breathe. The room started spinning when my story reached the part with Chariya in labor. I hung my head between my legs so I wouldn't pass out.

"Breathe, young man," he said over the phone with the strongest cockney accent I'd ever heard, so strong that there were times I could barely understand him. "I know things may seem hard right now," he said, "but the cards tell me it will all work out, and the cards don't lie. Your partner is coming back, I'm sure of it. Wynn, right? Wynn just needs some space and time right now."

"For how long?"

"Longer than you'd like, I'm sure of that. At least six months, more likely closer to a year or more."

"A year?" My voice cracked. I no longer wanted to talk about Wynn anymore. The thought of waiting for him for an entire year made me sick, and I didn't want to waste any more time thinking of him when he clearly wasn't thinking of our family or me. Instead, I asked, "What about the baby? I'm worried about the surrogate. She's been traveling, and who knows what she's been eating, and she looks thin, and she's kind of nuts and is obsessed with *Friends*, the TV sitcom—"

"The baby will be very healthy," said Nigel. His voice purred a soothing and calm baritone in my ear. I was no longer gasping for air, just panting.

"But what will I do about getting Mare out of the country?" I lowered my voice to a whisper and held the inline mic up to my lips. "Surrogacy is illegal in Thailand, and I need to get her a passport from the embassy. We have a plan, but—"

"It should all work out. Just tell a little fib. I mean, you're a clever young man. An actor, really. The dramatic arts were probably your true calling, but it's too late for that now. And back to the child, well, you don't have to worry. No one at the embassy will give you a hard time."

"What about when I bring her home?" I asked. "I only have one income now and—"

"The cards have always said you're very blessed in that department," said Nigel. "You'll have ups and downs but never have to worry about money for long. Of course, you'll never be satisfied with your wealth, but you'll always have more than enough. My advice is that you hire the best nanny and babysitters you can find. It will be worth the expense. Also, try and get out there and date other people. It might even make Wynn jealous and expedite his return. It will be beneficial for you and your relationship."

"I can't think about other men right now," I said, "I'm having a baby."

"Later then," he replied, "once you're settled. I'm sorry, but our time is up. I have another appointment. Remember, I'm here for you. Cheers!"

Right after he hung up, Lois returned, her face scrubbed clean of makeup, her hair a wet nub atop her head. She handed me a Saran-wrapped plate of scrambled eggs and sausage. I inhaled it in three bites.

"What am I going to do without you?" I said with a mouthful of food.

She shrugged. "You'll survive. Hey, maybe your sister can come help? She's been dry for almost three months."

How many times had I heard that before? I pretended not to hear, and we sat and waited in silence. Lois watched Netflix on her phone while I paced. Although my reading with Nigel had helped me feel more secure about the immediate future, I was also worried about the long term. What would I do when Mare got her period? What about when she needed a bra? Could I fly Lois in for that? Why hadn't I thought about all this gender stuff before? I remembered my first shave and how she instructed me to glide the razor with the grain, and I relaxed a bit. Lois had taught me how to shave. My mom. Not my dad. I could also teach my daughter how to shave when the time came.

When Dr. Khanna entered the waiting room, Lois and I jumped out of our chairs. His scrubs accentuated his biceps, and that five o'clock shadow made him look straight out of central casting for a prime-time medical drama.

"Baby is healthy," he said without preamble. "3.6 kilos. That's almost 8 pounds for you. Apgar score is a 10. A first perfect score of the year."

God, I hoped this Apgar score translated to her SATs. Nigel was hopefully onto something.

"Now, let's meet her," Dr. Khanna chirped, guiding us toward the maternity ward.

When I walked into Chariya's private room, the stench immediately overwhelmed me: raw onion, urine, salt, and cleaning solution. I was relieved to have been spared the delivery. The new mother was asleep, covered in sweat, her bouncy *Aniston* ruined and slick against the sides of her face. I may not have been particularly fond of this young woman, but I was proud and in awe what she had accomplished.

A nurse came forward, cradling my baby in her arms. Upon seeing her, my heart pounded in my eardrums, and an instinct flared. I took off my shirt. The nurse passed her tiny body to me. I nudged her forehead toward my chest and thought, *Damn, I forgot to shave.* I worried my chest hair would irritate her delicate skin, but it didn't seem to bother her. She drooled, and her warm saliva ran down my torso, pooling in my belly button. I stretched my palm to support her warm, downy head while she gurgled. Love wasn't a strong enough word to describe the feeling of her in my arms. This tiny, innocent baby healed a deep emotional wound within.

The nurse escorted us into a private room next door. I sat in a rocking chair and sniffed the top of Mare's head, greedily inhaling that sugary and earthy scent. I couldn't believe Wynn was missing this. Missing her. Missing me.

It finally registered that he wasn't coming back anytime soon, maybe ever, and that Nigel was wrong. From then on, it was going to be just Meryl and me. Overwhelming sadness muddled with transcendent joy, and I began choking back tears of confusion and misery. The tears of an abandoned child suddenly turned into a father.

"Let me take her," Lois said gently. "Whenever you're ready."

Shaking my head, I refused her outstretched arms. I'd worked so hard for her. I couldn't let go because she was all I had in this world. Lois positioned a Kleenex over my drippy nose, and I obediently blew into it before sobbing some more.

Eventually, Mare fussed; she was hungry. Reluctantly, I passed her to Lois to search for formula and a bottle in my baby bag. We spent the next hour taking turns feeding and burping her between naps. Her face appeared almost one-dimensional—mushy, flat, and adorable, and her nest of hair shone jet black and wiry like one of those troll dolls. Lois said her long and skinny frog legs were identical to mine when I was a baby, which was a nice way of saying that she didn't look much like me yet, but I expected that to change. As long as she was healthy, I told myself. If I had believed Nigel anymore, I would have probably asked him about it.

After the feeding, she fell asleep in my arms.

"Meryl is so beautiful, a wonder," said Lois.

"A miracle, she's a miracle."

Lois then nodded toward the next room. "You should go talk to her now." She reached for the baby.

"Cher likes you better." I let Mare go. My body missed her immediately. I found myself craving her warmth.

Lois looked down at the sleeping baby in her arms and beamed with pride before shaking her head at me.

When I entered Chariya's room, a laugh track played through a tinny speaker. She sat up watching her TV/DVD player just like last time. I tiptoed over. Right before she clamped the player shut, I caught a glimpse of Lisa Kudrow in a hospital gown.

"I came over to say thank you," I said. "Do you want to hold the baby? I can bring her over. She's so beautiful." I flashed the most welcoming and sunny California smile I could muster.

"No, no, no," she said. "I don't hold baby. It's my rule."

Her response so relieved me that I reached for her hand, just like Bopha said I should. Chariya pulled away and shielded herself with the TV/DVD player. I wanted to do this right and be a good person, a good client, or whatever, but she was making it so hard. "I'm sorry," I said, "Bopha said that I should stay with you—"

"No," she replied. "That is only to make foreigner feel good, less guilt. Bopha makes it up."

"I thought—"

"You think wrong," she said. "Bopha is a thief. She and Dr. Geller take all the money. I get next to nothing. I hope she rots in jail." She then mumbled something that sounded like French.

"I don't understand," I said, even more exasperated. She was tired, I told myself. She just gave birth. I needed to have more empathy for the young woman.

"Un clou chasse l'autre." She over-articulated every consonant as if I were dumb.

"Is that French?" I asked. "I'm sorry. I actually took Latin in high school."

"It means I speak three languages, and this is the best job I can get."

"I said I was sorry," I said, trying not to sound too defensive. "Is there anything I can do to make you feel better?" This was starting to become an ongoing theme in my life. People who were important to me—my sister, Wynn, my mom, and now this woman who carried my child—always seemed angry with me. I never knew why, after which I was stuck playing guessing games. At this point, I'd lost patience—you would've thought I'd done enough already. I double-paid and gave her the money Bopha would've given her, plus a new smartphone. What else did this girl want from me? I was tired, too.

"You can go now. I do my job," she said dismissively. "You get what you came for."

Chapter 17

Jared
Boston, MA
Fall 2004

PERCHED ON THE ledge of an open window, I crouched on my tippy-toes and looked down at the empty sidewalk. A screen prevented me from jumping. Desperation forced me to strike a bargain with myself: I would stay in Boston for one more week. After that, I would quit my job and move back in with my mom. This imaginary contract made me feel slightly better about my situation until the same questions plagued me: could I break my one-year lease after only three months? If so, would the landlord sue? Could this ruin my credit, keeping me from renting another apartment later? Did this mean I would live with my mother on Long Island for the rest of my life, jobless for the rest of my life? None of it would matter if I jumped. If only I could become someone else: someone who could fall in love with a girl or even a girl who could fall in love with a boy. I wished I were braver, someone who could drop everything, quit his job, give away all worldly possessions, and then backpack alone across Europe. Maybe if I were smarter? Someone with perfect grades who won academic fellowships to study at Oxford or traveled the world researching obscure playwrights or rare infectious diseases. My alarm clock beeped, so I hopped off the ledge. I promised myself I would make a change.

I got ready for the day and headed to work. At my desk, I was in no mood to do my job, so I surfed the web, mostly researching what was troubling me until I landed in an online chat room. An outreach worker pinged me, offering me a free HIV test. All I had to do was make an appointment and come down to the clinic, and if I answered a short survey, they would give me a $20 gift certificate to Tower Records. Though the incentive was tempting, I told him I didn't need one since I had never been with another guy, after which he sent links for two different coming-out groups. One of them met later in the evening. My heart raced, and I remembered my promise earlier in the morning. *Be brave. You need to make a change.*

After watching the clock for the next seven hours, I shut down my computer and caught the T to the South End. I paced the same block outside the Lesbian and Gay Community Center for the next half hour, observing everyone going in and out through the front doors. One guy around my age with a blue mohawk trotted past me in studded motorcycle boots. Something about his style reminded me of my older sister, Jenny, who wore thick eye makeup and an armor of tattoos on her neck and arms. How that guy and Jenny would ever get jobs was beyond me. Those accessories seemed like a one-way ticket to excluding themselves from white-collar employment for the rest of their lives. God, even these thoughts about jobs were making me anxious. Then a cyclist swerved past a row of parked cars, which triggered an alarm, shocking me out of my thought loop. Caught off guard, I jumped and emitted a shriek. A young woman with a shaved head and a hoop piercing her chapped bottom lip looked through me and giggled. I checked my watch and decided I couldn't do it, so I marched back home to my fifth-floor closet and stared out the window, just like I'd done in the morning.

The following week, I showed up at another men's questioning support group in a small brick church in Back Bay. It was for Catholics, and I hoped they might be less judgmental. And though I didn't consider myself religious, I had graduated from a Jesuit college and I attended catechism classes throughout my childhood up until confirmation. The few men who walked through the door wore orthopedic sneakers and dowdy sweater vests with moth holes. A man with a handlebar mustache tottered past me. He leaned on a black cane decorated with white rhinestones that crunched the dry leaves on the front stoop. The man asked me for the time.

"7:02 p.m.," I said.

"The meeting's started already, honey," he said, heaving the church door open. "We'd love to have you." Something about the way he said "honey" spooked me. I ran away, eventually slowing to a jog. I passed seemingly endless rows of brick townhouses and leaf-covered cars. I didn't know where I was headed except that I needed to get as far away as possible from the man who called me "honey." The thought of honey made me suddenly crave something sweet, maybe an ice cream cone, a brownie, or both. When I stumbled upon an ice cream shop, it was closed. I was disappointed and even jiggled the door handle just to make sure.

I eventually gave up and took stock of my surroundings, hoping to spot a nearby café or bakery. Across the street, a rainbow flag flapped in the wind above a neon sign that said, "Chance." A long line snaked out the door. Thumping music pulled me in, and like a weak magnet, it slowly tugged me into the queue. The guys around me were about my age and clean-cut. I felt my nerves acting up again, so I studied the back of the person's T-shirt in front of me to distract myself. It listed the dates and cities of Sheryl Crow's most recent tour. Only then did I realize that someone might recognize me before remembering that no one here knew me. Despite this, my heart pounded louder as I approached the door. Just when I was about to turn around and leave, a man's voice asked for my ID. My hands shook when I pulled a New York State driver's license out of my wallet. The bouncer, a meaty man with thick steel hoops hanging from one ear, looked me in the eye and said, "Goddamn, you're a pretty one." The attention both disgusted and excited me.

The club resembled a dark fortress with a long bar near the entrance and a dance floor in the back with a spinning disco ball. It wasn't crowded—just a few guys standing alone or roaming in pairs—and the place stank of Tommy Hilfiger cologne and beer gone rancid. There were lingering stares. I could feel them coming from every direction, but I couldn't return them because there was already too much information around me to process. The music—some Top 40 hit—was so loud, I couldn't hear myself think. The place had a tropical feel between the fog machine in the corner spewing white mist and the room's warmth. The other guys wore tank tops and skin-tight T-shirts with school names emblazoned on the front, while I boiled in a V-neck merino wool sweater and fleece-lined khakis. Perspiration curled under my flannel boxers, and just as I was about to pull my top off, I remembered the yellow pit stains on this particular undershirt. The buzz in the air made the heat bearable and pulled me out of myself, nudging me into action. I was no longer satisfied to stand in place like a spectator when there was so much erotic excitement around me. And because I couldn't think of anything better to do with all this energy, I marched up to the bartender and asked if they had O'Doul's. "I think we have some in the basement," he said. I ordered a seltzer with bitters. The bartender didn't charge me.

While I sipped my drink, the weirdish disco ball reflected shards of light onto my sweater and a new song faded into the mix. The intro sampled the opening of a daytime soap opera that my mom used to watch, which made me miss her. Between the festive lighting, the graceful melancholy of the tune, and the joy of being lost in an attractive crowd, I was actually beginning to enjoy myself. Over the next few minutes, the club grew more crowded. These guys looked a lot like me yet were seemingly unashamed. It was almost too much, and part of me wanted to bolt again. At least finish your drink, I said to myself. I sipped it until a landslide of crushed ice nipped my nose, after which I watched the disco ball spin until I got dizzy.

My nose felt numb when I noticed a striking, young Black woman with shoulder-length banana curls standing in the dance floor's far corner.

She swayed unselfconsciously to the beat of the music with a presence I wished I had. When the chorus of "No More Drama" began, she lip-synced the words. She pointed to an Asian guy standing on the dance floor's edge—her curled finger mimed for him to come closer. The young man shook his head, but she ran over and pulled him in by his wrists, after which they undulated their hips, bobbed their heads, and rolled their torsos in tandem. During the second chorus, the pair's slim arms floated above their heads, and they each performed spins and turns. Soon after, they mimicked each other's moves until they entirely mirrored one another. The flawless pacing of their choreography—how the routine gradually built and released tension—made me think they had rehearsed the dance beforehand.

My attention returned to the woman's lovely round face, her expression joyful, a counterpoint to her friend, whose features were more severe and angular. And though she had a more spirited facial expression, my eyes were soon pulled toward the man since he was the better dancer. His movements were explosive, a quick succession of energy bursts that I wanted to catch with my hands. Despite his compact frame, he devoured the empty space around him, the arcs of his motion so broad, it was as if his limbs weren't attached to his body. What would it feel like to be so confident and free?

When the song ended, the pair sauntered to the bar. Someone else took over my body, and I walked over to them.

"You guys were incredible," I said with sincerity.

Amazingly, they turned around and introduced themselves. Her name was Nicole, his name was Wynn, and they were college friends who'd moved to the area to attend grad school.

"What are you studying?" I asked.

"I'm in Public Policy. Nicole is in the School of Public Health," Wynn said.

"Wow, where?" I asked this since I wasn't entirely clear on what public policy or public health was, despite having heard the words many times before.

"Nearby, in Cambridge," he said.

Nicole squeezed Wynn's arm and said she was headed to the ladies' room. She winked and swaggered off.

Wynn and I were alone. He was even better-looking up close with gentle eyes, coarse hair neatly parted and smoothed into a gelled pompadour, and a face with a dewey glow. We moved to a table farther from the dance floor to hear each other better.

"Aren't you hot in that sweater?" he asked.

"It's not too bad." I wiped the sweat from my brow, then blotted my hand on my khakis.

"So, Jared, tell me your story."

A mass of words poured out of my mouth, something about how I had just graduated from college and was new in town and didn't know many people here—that sort of thing.

He took a tiny sip of his drink and looked into my eyes.

I pointed to my cup. "Oh, and this is nonalcoholic. I don't drink," I said. I told him my father was an alcoholic before he died, and my sister had a drinking problem too. I couldn't seem

146

to stop myself from talking. His gaze shifted away from me and toward the dance floor. I lost him.

"I work in IT at an investment firm," I said. "It wasn't what I wanted to do, but it got me here, and I needed a change of scenery. What do you do again?" I asked.

"Did you forget already?" he asked flirtatiously. "I'm a grad student at the Kennedy School." He swiveled on his stool, seeming like a wise older man and a restless child all at once.

I apologized and found myself telling him a story from my first week at Hamilton-Adams Investments, where one of the senior vice presidents, an athletic-looking man in his fifties, had stormed into the IT department and scanned the faces of our three-person office before pointing at me. He said to follow him. When we arrived in his corner office overlooking the Charles, his computer screen flashed a video of him naked and face down over the laps of two busty women—one Latina and one Black— taking turns spanking his butt. There were dozens of tabs open behind this video, and every time I tried to close one, a hundred more popped up. A wormhole. After two hours, I managed to fix the computer without losing any of the files. He thanked me, but barely. "I asked for you specifically because the others might not understand." He then rushed me out of his office, already thumb-typing his BlackBerry.

After that, word got out that I was good at fixing these types of problems, code for "ask Jared" to scrub your porn—he was discreet. I received a promotion, a small raise, and a new *Trojan Horse and Anti-Virus Specialist* title. And for all that, I spent the entirety of my workweek cleaning spyware off computers.

"I hate my job," I said, noticing that I had finally captured his attention. Pride suffused my face. Wynn stared back at me, mouth agape.

"What?" I asked.

"That's crazy," he said before erupting into warm laughter. He pounded the table with his fist.

"I'm glad you find my pathetic career entertaining," I said.

He said, "I'm sorry about your job, but it's a funny story."

"It's OK," I said, though my feelings were hurt.

"You know why he really chose you," said Wynn.

I shook my head.

"Let me guess, the VP was a white guy?"

I nodded.

"He picked you because you're white and he assumed you were straight. He thought you might be sympathetic to his situation," Wynn said, as though the answer was obvious. I thought back to who was in the office that day. I had two female colleagues, Fatima and Xiao. "Though I bet this guy wished he looked like you when he was young," he said in a softer tone.

My face got hot. I wasn't sure if I was being hit on or insulted. "Is that a compliment?" I asked.

"It's not a compliment. It's a fact," he said.

For some reason, my eyes began to water. "I'm new to all this."

"Coming out isn't easy. It takes a while," he said. "Be patient with yourself." He gazed frankly and openly at me with those oddly gentle eyes. I looked back at him with the same undisguised interest. I knew I was nice-looking, handsome even. I knew this because girls in college often told me this late in the evening before I either freaked out or slipped away, hoping to avoid the inevitable: an awkward goodnight kiss that made me feel nothing.

Wynn placed his hand on mine, making my head feel like it might pop off. I focused on his eyes and savored the heat emanating from his palm. I sniffed his cranberry-laced breath and took in the curved slope of his graceful neck.

"I think you're cute."

I was stumped. After a beat, I said, "You have the most beautiful Adam's apple."

Wynn erupted into laughter. "No one's ever said that to me

before," he said.

I pointed to his cup and asked if I could buy him another to avoid saying anything even more stupid.

"No, I'm good," he said. "You can give me something else, though."

Wynn scratched his head and leaned in closer. I had never kissed another guy, but his lips landed on mine before I could pull away. My hands moved on their own over his shoulders, then massaged his lean chest and neck before stopping on the small of his trim waist. Part of me wanted to pull away, but I couldn't. There was no will, no fight within me. It felt so good, too good, for it to be wrong. So, I gave in, despite knowing there was no turning back. Wynn grabbed my hand and squeezed.

"I never asked for consent," he said. "Sorry."

"You can kiss me. Again."

"Let's get out of here," he said as if daring me.

Without answering, I took his hand and guided him off his stool. We hurried toward the exit without even saying goodbye to Nicole.

PART II

Chapter 18

Wynn
San Francisco, CA
Winter 2016

THE DOCTOR UNSTRAPPED my boot, rotated my foot, and slipped it into a sneaker. When I stepped onto the floor, I was careful not to place my weight on it. After the appointment, I walked to the BART station and felt some stiffness in my heel. The surgeon had said I could dance again in two to three weeks but to take it easy. Her words gave me hope. While I waited on the BART platform, the wind from the oncoming train blew cold air onto my face, marking a new beginning.

Although my heel felt fine, I took a seat for two stops before abdicating it to a pregnant woman. I stood for a while, one arm grasping the pole, while I whispered along to Drake, blasting through my headphones. My remaining hand mimed improvisational choreography: an index finger hooked, a wrist flicked, a palm flexed to the smooth beat of "Energy."

I rapped along silently with my eyes closed: "I got enemies, got a lotta enemies . . ."

Then the music abruptly stopped. My headphones were

gone, and I looked up to find a man clutching them over his head. He wore ill-fitting gray trousers with white sweat stains and tattered cuffs. An unkempt salt and pepper beard framed his angry face. He was almost undoubtedly unhoused and possibly mentally ill.

"You didn't hear me," he growled, "so I had to rip them off your fucking head."

"Give them back, please," I said quietly, not wanting to make a scene. I reached for them, but he held them above his head as if to throw them. All eyes and phone cameras were on us though no one said a word or leaped to my defense.

"Singing along to that bullshit, using the N-word over and over. No respect," the man said, his overgrown, yellowed fingernails wrapped around the shiny red cord.

"I didn't say it," I said loud enough for everyone to hear. "I skipped that lyric." I swore on my parents' graves that I'd never uttered that ugly word aloud.

"That's what's wrong with this country: everyone loves Black culture, but no one gives a damn about Black people."

The train stopped. When the double doors opened, he threw the headphones at me, slapping me in the chest. They fell onto the train's dingy carpet before I could catch them. I squatted down to grab them, and when I looked up, I found the stranger hovering over me. A hot gob slithered from the apple of my cheek, down my neck, and into my T-shirt's collar. "What's your fucking problem?" I howled. "Why did you do that?" Scrunching my eyes shut, I furiously wiped my face with the sleeve of my hoodie.

When my eyes reopened, he was gone, along with half of the passengers on the train. The remaining faces in the car were full of pity. The pregnant woman I gave my seat to offered me two wet wipes from her purse. A nearby man handed me a packet of Kleenex and a tiny bottle of antibacterial gel.

After a hot shower, I thought about canceling on Jared. For weeks, I'd been asking him to let me come to the house to retrieve some of the belongings I'd forgotten—paperwork, clothes, my mom's jewelry, and my dad's watch. My stomach knotted when I thought about meeting Meryl for the first time. I wished I'd asked Jared to mail my things, but there wasn't time. My flight to Nairobi was the following evening.

Of course, picking up my stuff wasn't my only intention. I had to show Jared that my leaving wasn't due to cold feet, but a rational decision rooted in my professional calling. As such, I wanted to look Jared in the eye, apologize, and get some closure. I assumed Jared would likely have some choice words for me in return, and I genuinely thought I was ready for his ire. And so, I did what I always did before an uncomfortable conversation: I procrastinated and showed up two hours late.

As soon as Jared opened the door, I winced. I anticipated being spit on for a second time that day. After finally opening my eyes, I saw the living room was cluttered with toys, unopened mail, dirty dishes, and stacks of papers.

"Why are you twisting your face weirdly like that?" asked Jared, sounding congested, his nose chapped and bright red. "Come in. I don't have all day." A wad of tissue hung out of his bathrobe pocket. I opened my arms for a hug, but Jared held up both hands. "I'm sick, don't get too close."

The house was even messier than at first glance. Stuffed toys—a white bear and a pink unicorn—lay on the foyer floor, a rainbow of Le Creuset pots was piled in the kitchen sink, and unopened mail covered the surface of the dining room table.

"It's hard to keep the house clean with a sick baby."

"I didn't notice," I said.

"Liar," said Jared before an extended coughing fit. When he

caught his breath, he said, "I've had a really spectacular week. The housekeeper is out of town, and last week, Mare got an upper respiratory infection, and now I have it. She's napping, so don't expect me to wake her." He slumped in a kitchen chair, elbows resting on the table, his fingertips massaging his temples. Still handsome, I had to admit, even in this state. Bedhead gave him a boyish quality. A cowlick sprung from the side of his head like an antenna. I fought an urge to lick my fingers and smooth it down.

"I'm going to make a cup of tea. Do you want some?" I filled the kettle and ignited the Viking stove.

"Oh, now you want to take care of me?" he said. "Thanks, Wynn, but guess what? I don't need a hero."

"I'm making one for myself. In the meantime, I think it'll help your congestion."

I wondered who Jared had become. For the years we were together, he'd never let a dish go unwashed, always grabbing my plate mid-bite to fill the dishwasher. I almost liked the house better this way. It felt more like a home.

"Your stuff is in the dining room," he said.

"How long have you been sick?"

"I don't know, a week or more. I think I'm through the worst of it."

"If it makes you feel better, a homeless man spit on me today."

"You probably deserved it." He smiled for a moment, a glint in his eyes.

"How are things otherwise?" I stalled. I wasn't ready to grab my things and leave yet. There was something incredibly comforting and familiar about being back at the house.

"Good," he said, making direct eye contact with me for the first time. "I have a boyfriend now. He's amazing."

"That's great," I said in an extra-chipper tone. I had no right to be saddened by the news.

"He's very family oriented."

"What's his name—?" The kettle's whistle saved me. I poured the hot water into two mugs. The tea seeped; reddish-brown swirls bloomed in the water. After a silence, I cleared my throat. I said, "So one of the reasons I wanted to come over— well, I never formally apologized for—."

"Don't bother," said Jared. "I'm too tired to be angry. It's why I'm being civil. But I'll never forgive you."

"That's OK. I'm still sorry," I said, trying to meet his gaze. I wanted to show him I wasn't a coward, but he turned away.

"Since you're here, though, tell me one thing. When did you know you wanted to leave?"

"I never intended to leave," I said, which was the truth. "I tried talking myself into staying right up until the end. God, Jared, I went through all the stages: denial, guilt, bargaining. I bargained with myself for so long. When you started getting all gung-ho about surrogacy and choosing eggs and agencies, I was so depressed between my dad dying and my job. Honestly, anything you suggested would've seemed like a good idea. You could've turned our house into a petting zoo, and I would've barely noticed, let alone stopped you from doing it. And then after I started dancing and quit Synergy, I thought it would be enough. Once I had a break and could just dance for a while and wanting this relationship, and this child, your beautiful child—I thought I would change over time."

"But you didn't," said Jared, looking down at his feet. I wondered if he was crying now, but he looked up, and his face was dry and vacant. "Then why didn't you tell me earlier? Why did you wait so long?"

"I did try and tell you, but it was too late. She was already a fetus. Meryl isn't a couch or a sweater. You can't return her. And . . ." I hesitated, searching for the courage to say what needed to be said, " . . . when you decide on something, Jared, there's no stopping you. You obsess like a broken record. You wore me down. You pushed the baby on me right after my dad died."

"That's not fair," he said. "I waited at least six months. You were already in dance obsession mode; you were already checked out."

"Aha, so you admit it was premeditated, that you'd planned around it. It's almost pathological," I said.

"I didn't say that—" he snapped back in a whisper, signaling that we should quiet down so as not to wake the baby. "Is it so bad to want a child? To want a family?"

"No, it isn't. But Jared, your wants—they are so big, so all-encompassing, there was never room for what I wanted in this relationship, and you know it—"

"Stop!" yelled Jared. "Just stop. I can't hear it. I thought I could, but—"

"We don't have to talk about it," I said softly. Arguing was never our strong suit. It felt weird to be doing it now after we'd broken up. Capitulating, I said: "I didn't come here to fight. Just to apologize."

Jared hunched over, his elbows on his lap, fingertips digging into his eyeballs. It had become abundantly clear that our relationship had been doomed. We'd only put off the inevitable. No couples' counselor or therapist could have saved us. The silence between us made me want to hurl myself into the ceiling. I racked my brain for an excuse to leave when a muffled cry crackled through the baby monitor on the counter.

"I'll be right back." Jared sighed. He sailed out of the kitchen, his bathrobe tail floating behind him. A minute later, he returned with the baby. Her face nuzzled in his armpit. "Mare, do you want to meet an old friend of mine? His name is Wynn," he said, an octave higher than his usual voice. "He's leaving on a plane tomorrow to see his friend, Nicole, who lives far away."

"She's beautiful," I said, though all I could see was the back of her head.

"Do you want to hold her?"

I didn't want to hold her. I was afraid, and Jared knew it, so he passed her to me before I could refuse.

When I finally saw her up close, I thought there had to have been a hospital mix-up. This baby looked full-on Asian. Once my surprise wore off, I had to admit she was pretty darn cute—all jowly-cheeked with her eyes and nose subsumed in skin folds.

Mare squirmed and let out a howl before Jared plucked her back. "Hmm, she's usually good with strangers." Her crying stopped immediately. Jared kissed her on the top of her head and said, "You're the one who gave me this horrible illness, didn't you, my little dumpling." He blew a raspberry on her belly, and she gurgled accordingly.

"Did you hear that? She's only three months and talking already. Aren't you a little genius?"

"Wow, she's very advanced," I said, confused since nothing she'd said resembled a word or phrase.

"It's time to eat, princess. We need to feed your growing brain," said Jared in his baby voice. She took her bottle, and her cheeks pumped while Jared looked down on her adoringly. It hurt to see him so in love with her. It hurt to see he'd moved on.

His phone rang, and he pulled it out of his bathrobe pocket. "It's work. It must be important if they're calling while I'm on paternity leave." He hastily passed Mare back to me. "Keep her at a forty-five degree angle, and don't forget to burp her after."

Before I could protest, he barreled down the hall with his phone pinned between his ear and shoulder. Once in my arms, she turned her face away from the half-empty bottle and wailed. Fat tears rolled down her tomato cheeks. I tried to poke the bottle back into her gummy mouth, but she squirmed and cried harder.

I gently bounced on the balls of my feet, which helped a little, but when I felt a tightness in my heel, I sat down on the couch. She howled louder, and I checked my phone. Jared had only been gone for three minutes, and I grew more annoyed by the second. I'd only come to pick up a few things, not babysit.

I held her against my shoulder for the next few minutes, and her drool and tears drenched my T-shirt. I waited for Jared to storm out of the bedroom and relieve me, but he didn't. I remembered to burp her, finally getting her to stop crying. Her inky eyes opened, and spit bubbles oozed and popped on her lips. I rubbed my thumb along the constellation of tiny pimples across her cheek, and then she turned her head toward my thumb. I let her suck on it. With my other hand, I caressed her wiry black hair swirling in every direction. Like me, I wondered if she would one day suffer the injustice of the ubiquitous rice bowl haircut, crooked bangs and all. Then I remembered Jared would probably take her to some overpriced kids' salon in Noe Valley, sparing her this rite of passage.

We sat on the sofa for a while. I couldn't remember the last time I'd remained so still, no phone, no TV, just sitting. I nodded off momentarily, only to be awoken by a sting on my chest. I looked down to find Mare nursing through my T-shirt. When I reached down to unlatch her, I couldn't go through with it. Instead, I caressed her back and kissed her head.

She eventually stopped nursing and fell asleep in my arms. By that point, it had been almost an hour. There was no way Jared could still be on the phone. I carried her toward the bedroom when I became distracted by our reflection in the hall mirror. We looked so much alike: same hair, same dark brown eyes, similar skin tone. We could walk out this door, and anyone would think we were father and daughter.

I looked down at her again and thought: If I don't leave now, I will stay, and I can't stay. The thought of turning into my dad was too scary. Like him, I was selfish and obsessive—him with manufacturing helicopters, me with dance—and once the novelty of having a newborn wore off, I would grow bored and constantly wish to be elsewhere. Eventually, I would become a resentful zombie who always wondered, "What if?"

. . . I had left them to visit Nicole in Kenya?

. . . I had pursued dance full-time?

. . . I had slept with other men?

Would I have become a world traveler with forty stamps in his passport, jet-setting to exotic locations every other month?

Would I have become a dancer who made a good living teaching online classes on RevTube?

Would I have missed out on giving my body to a bevy of handsome and horny men committed to giving and receiving pleasure?

Would I have ended up with the progressive man of color of my dreams who "got me," "saw me," and shared the same dreams?

These questions cut so deep that I walked straight into Mare's room to put her down. The fact that I didn't know when I would see her again made my heart ache. Mare would probably be walking by then, maybe even speaking in complete sentences. So, I savored my last few minutes with her and watched her belly expand and contract silently. My resting heart rate eventually matched hers. I tiptoed out of the room before opening the master bedroom door to find Jared face-down on the bed, his phone still clutched in his left hand. Small piles of crumpled tissues surrounded him like a wreath.

"Jared," I said in a low voice. "Wake up." There was no response, not even when I lightly shook him.

I draped a gray cashmere throw over him. The airflow blew some of the tissue balls onto the floor. Every part of me wanted to crawl underneath the blanket and nuzzle into the crook of his neck and go back to a time before everything got complicated, like when we'd first met in Boston or even when we'd moved to San Francisco. A time when we were young, and everything was new and full of promise.

It was too late for this, of course. I'd done this to myself, for myself. I'd gotten what I wanted. Jared was with someone else now—a family man—someone I wasn't. We both needed to move on, yet I knew I needed to see the baby again. I hoped one day to be welcomed as a trusted visitor, the cool uncle who returned from exotic trips bearing trinkets and stories of monkeys stealing my sunglasses. I scribbled a note and left it on the nightstand.

Dear Jared,

I didn't want to wake you up.
Thank you for having me over and
allowing me to pick up the rest
of my things. It was wonderful
meeting Meryl. She's beautiful.
I fed and burped her, and she's
down in her crib. I would love to
see you both when I'm back in
town. Get well soon!

Love always,

Wynn

Chapter 19

Jared
Coram, NY
Summer/Fall 1995

OVER TV DINNERS in the living room, Mom had told me about her upcoming date. Jenny had been out with her friends, and it was just the two of us. These were my favorite moments, just me and her when I wasn't her son but a friend. *Friends* played on the TV on the kitchen counter. It was a rerun, but Mom still waited until the commercial break to give me the scoop. She'd met Barry at work. He was a walk-in, and she didn't usually cut men's hair or take unscheduled clients, but her regular blowout had canceled. Barry said he didn't see a husband in any of the Polaroids tacked on her mirror and took a chance. At the end of the cut, he asked her to dinner. She agreed, and they had scheduled a date for the following weekend.

When Barry arrived at our apartment, I answered the door. She shouted from the bathroom about needing more time, so he sat on the tweed pullout in our living room, which also served as her bedroom. He looked a little like the dad from *Growing Pains* with his friendly face, broad shoulders, and freshly shorn head of dark hair parted deeply to the side with flecks of gray at the temples. We sat in silence. I was unnerved but thrilled by having a strange man in our living room. I blurted a monologue about myself out of nowhere. I told Barry my age, I was thirteen; my favorite subject in school, biology; my future career aspirations, doctor or astronaut; my birthday, April 14th, which had fallen on Easter two years earlier; and what I played in band, tenor saxophone. I confessed that I didn't take good care of the instrument. The mouthpiece and reed often got moldy from lack of cleaning, and Mom was pissed about it since she had recently bought it after renting it for the past two years. It didn't matter anyway since I planned on quitting marching band to try out for the junior varsity lacrosse team.

"I played lacrosse at my alma mater," said Barry.

"What's an elmer matter?"

"Alma mater is Latin for college," he explained.

"Where's Alma Mater College?"

"It's not a college. It's just a term. I went to Boston College," he said.

"Have you ever been to Boston?" When Barry explained things, he didn't look down on me for not knowing stuff. My sister rolled her eyes and snorted whenever I asked questions. On the other hand, Barry made the kindest eye contact, like he was about to cry and laugh at once. It felt like he was listening to me with every cell in his body. Barry stood up and dug into his pocket.

"I almost forgot." He held a miniature New York Mets baseball bat attached to a keychain and placed it in my hand. "Because of last year's strike, they were practically giving away tickets. I'm more of a Yankees fan anyway, and the Mets aren't doing so hot this season. Do you follow baseball?"

I shook my head, holding the keychain in my hand, examining the blue and orange logo. "Thank you," I said.

"No need to thank me. It was a giveaway. Maybe I can take you to a game sometime?" Before I could answer, Mom walked into the living room and announced she was ready, and they left for dinner. I was old enough to stay home alone and fell asleep before she got back.

When I asked her the following morning how it went, she smiled widely in a way I'd never seen her smile before and said they had another date planned. Also, Barry wanted to help me prepare for my lacrosse tryout "if I was open to it."

The following three weekends, we practiced scooping, passing, catching, cradling, and shooting at the high school soccer field using Barry's old sticks. After practices, Barry showered at the apartment before taking Mom to dinner on their weekly date. On the fourth weekend, Barry exited our bathroom, freshly showered and smelling of Old Spice and Barbasol shaving cream. I worked up the courage to ask why we never went to his house.

"Don't be rude," Mom said, though I could tell she was wondering the same thing.

"No, no, it's fine. I should have you, your mother, and your sister over for Labor Day. Celebrate the end of summer with a barbeque." Barry high-fived me and tousled my hair, which made me feel like a little kid but in a good way.

A few weeks later, when Barry opened the door to his gigantic house perched on the marina, I pushed past him and ran up the stairs, soaking the central air conditioning into my sweaty skin and digging the arches of my feet into the plush carpet. Each of the five bedrooms was spare and unlived-in, holding only a neatly made bed and a dresser or empty bookshelf. When I entered the smallest bedroom facing the marina, I froze in front of the bay window. I clutched the bottom of the window's frame and gazed at the dozens of white boats docked in the shimmering water.

"I want this room!" I squealed in a high-pitched voice, embarrassed since it hadn't yet dropped. It might have been the happiest moment of my life. Less than a minute passed before

I was knocked back into reality by the sting of my sister's palm against the back of my head.

"What is wrong with you, you greedy little bitch? It isn't your fucking house," she said. Her spit sprayed my face. The safety pin that pierced her black lips trembled.

After barbeque ribs and burgers in the backyard, Barry took us out on the boat. Soon after we left the dock, Jenny asked Barry how he had gotten all his money. Mom slapped the back of Jenny's head and told her to stop being rude. Barry laughed, and with one hand on the boat's chrome steering wheel, he said he started on Wall Street, where he often ran around a trading floor. Then ten years ago, his father had died, and he quit his job to take over the family's asbestos removal business. I didn't know where Wall Street was or what asbestos did, but I was sure I wanted everything he had: central air conditioning, a big house, a boat, and an alma mater. Instead of asking Barry more questions and risking Mom's temper, I looked out onto the Great South Bay, letting the wind lick my sweaty face. A much larger boat, a yacht really, sailed toward us. The driver, a young man in a white baseball cap, waved at us. Barry waved back with one hand, the other gripping the wheel.

"My neighbor," he said to me. "Nice guy. Works in computers. He's very successful for his age. That could be you in ten or fifteen years."

I made a pact that I would have all of this when I grew up. I would work hard and do what I had to: run the floors on Wall Street, make asbestos, work with computers, cut open sick people, or do whatever men did to have gobs of money. An unfamiliar surge of energy rushed through me. It was thrilling but also a little scary since I wasn't sure what it meant to not let anything or anyone get in my way.

The relationship didn't last past Halloween. Mom listed all the reasons over Kraft macaroni and cheese: he wanted her to quit smoking, she wasn't ready; he wanted more kids, she was done with all that; he wanted us to all go to Mass with him, she was a proud, lapsed Catholic; they didn't have enough in common; they didn't have anything to talk about; he was an old bachelor and stuck in his ways. I traced grid lines in my mac. Mom squeezed my arm. "I'm sorry, sweetie. I know you really liked him. It's better to end it now. It'll only get harder."

"He was a fucking douchebag. You could do better," said Jenny.

"Language," Mom said before half smiling. She turned to me. "Barry was a good guy, and he liked you a lot, too. He thought you had a lot of potential. I think the word he used was 'ambitious.'"

"More like a greedy little bitch," Jenny said. "I'm glad you weren't going to become some Stepford wife," she said, her mouth full of neon orange mush.

I excused myself from the table, telling Mom I was headed to a friend's house to compare earth science notes. Along the Sunrise Highway, I rode my bike on the sidewalk as cars whizzed by and, later, pedaled through a maze of side streets. The dim streetlamps guided the way, and the fall air chilled my face. Goosebumps covered my arms.

"Hey, what are you doing here?" Barry said, opening the front door of the blue-shingled mansion. He wore a Yankees cap and a plush bathrobe. I had never seen him in his pajamas before, which somehow made me feel closer to him. For some strange reason, I wanted to open his robe and curl up inside. "You must be freezing. Come in." The house was warm. He offered me apple juice, and I drank it in one gulp.

"What about that Mets game you said you would take me to?" I said, wiping my mouth with the back of my hand. My voice cracked, and I was shaking. I knew I was about to cry but didn't want to. It was in the back of my throat, and I swallowed as hard as possible to stop it.

"Buddy, me and your mom talked about it. She didn't

think it was a good idea." At this point, I stopped listening fully. Something about not getting too attached. Barry was getting busy at work. Everything in his sparsely furnished living room seemed to float farther away from my periphery: the TV playing football on mute, the French doors leading to the deck overlooking the marina, and Barry himself. Perched on a leather recliner, he continued to explain why we couldn't stay friends. The next thing I knew, he offered me one of his lacrosse sticks.

"It's a small gift. Please take it."

"I can't carry it on my bicycle."

"I can drive you home," he said, almost begging. "We can put your bike in the back of my truck."

I said no. He insisted on giving me a sweatshirt for the ride home, and I bolted out of the house and rode off. Instead of heading home, I pedaled slowly along the marina. At the pier, I dropped my bike and fell to my knees. I teared up but didn't cry. Everything felt empty inside, and I was too exhausted from the bike ride. Hunger eventually got to me, and even the overcooked mac and cheese I'd only picked at earlier started sounding pretty good.

When I arrived home, the pullout was open, and my mom sat on the edge of the bed, facing the front door, smoking a cigarette. She usually only smoked in the kitchen, so I knew she was probably angry.

"Where have you been?" she asked before dropping her lit cigarette into an ashtray. She looked genuinely worried, but I didn't care.

Jenny heard me come in and came out of her room. "Damn, I was hoping you were kidnapped."

"Cut it out. This is serious. I was worried sick," Mom said, walking toward me for a hug. I pushed her away. "What's wrong, baby? I was about to call the police. Is this about Barry?"

"He went to go try and seduce him," said Jenny, after which I picked up one of the glass ashtrays on the coffee table and hurled it at her. I missed by a lot, and it smashed against the wall, leaving a dent.

"What the fuck?" Jenny covered her head. She was in shock because I never stuck up for myself.

"Jarey, what the fuck are you doing?" said Mom. "You could have really hurt her. Who are you, and what have you done with my son?"

"I went to see Barry to find out why he dumped you, and he told me it's because both of you are trash." My sister lunged at me, but Mom held her back.

"And what does that make you?" Jenny spat at me. "Princess Diana, you little twat?"

"I'm not a twat. I'm ambitious."

Mom looked pissed; her arms were crossed, and her face scrunched into a red ball. "He didn't say that because he would never say something that awful," she said.

"He didn't have to," I said. I'd had it with them, so I stomped to my room. As I opened the door, Mom screamed, "For the record, I dumped him! I didn't want another kid. Can you blame me?"

"I hate you! I wish you had aborted me," I screamed before slamming the door.

Maybe an hour later, Mom knocked on my door to apologize, but I told her to leave me alone. She said that she was ready to talk whenever I was ready and that my being born was one of the best things that ever happened to her. Even though I believed her, I couldn't deal right then and needed to be alone.

For the rest of the night, I was sleepless and still hungry but too lazy to get food. I rubbed my privates to distract myself, keeping a clean sock handy so I didn't make a mess. Lying on my side, I conjured the scent of his aftershave. I imagined burying my face in the crevice where his stubbly neck and collarbones met. My tongue stuck out, and I could almost taste his prominent Adam's apple, the hardness of it against my lips.

I massaged my butt with my other hand, eventually licking my forefinger so it dipped in and out freely. I'd never done this before and wondered what had taken me so long to discover this. Then I realized I was getting close, so I stopped. During the break, I noticed the keychain on top of the nightstand. I paused, unclipped the baseball bat, and left the ring of keys before squirting two pumps of lotion on the tip.

At first, it hurt a little, but then I breathed deeper, and it felt so good I thought I would finish before I even started touching myself again. My hands slowly teased it in and out. My jaw clenched, and my teeth bared down so I didn't call out and wake anyone. I pushed it in deeper, playing with myself until I sweated through my sheets and writhed in a jumble of pillows. The sensation grew so intense I forgot to aim inside the sock and instead used it to wipe down the comforter. Once I removed the evidence, I reached in for the bat but accidentally tapped it farther in. I dug inside for the next five minutes, trying to fetch it but I couldn't reach it. It was too deep.

I moved to the floor so I could maneuver better. I tried crouching on all fours, then laid on my back with my legs over my head, but nothing helped. I started to panic. Though it didn't hurt much, the mini baseball bat didn't feel good anymore and made walking difficult. I threw on boxers and a bathrobe and hobbled to the bathroom to try to push it into the toilet. My face burned red and hot from pushing. After a few minutes, I started crying softly so as not to wake Mom in the living room. I wondered if I could just go through life with this thing up inside of me. I pleaded with God, whispering, "Hail Mary, Mother of God..." with my head in my hands, straining to get it out. If He could get me out of this bind, I promised never to touch myself or go back there again.

Out of desperation, I did the unthinkable. I double-washed my hands, wrapped my robe, and knocked on Jenny's door. She was always up late because she was a senior and didn't start school until fourth period. When the door opened, I almost didn't recognize her without her heavy eyeliner and black lipstick. Even the safety pin in her lip was gone. She whispered to get out but then saw on my face that something was wrong.

"It's an emergency," I whispered. "Please." I pushed my way in and shut her door. Her room looked like a wreck, mostly piles of clothes and vinyl records.

"I had an accident," I say. "I can't tell Mom. It's really, really, bad." I started crying again.

"What?" she said, like I was wasting her time.

"You know that keychain, the Mets baseball bat I got as a present," I stammered. "Well, it's stuck inside of me." I pointed to my behind.

Jenny covered her mouth and collapsed into a pile of plaid flannel and black denim on the floor, laughing. "You're kidding me."

In between shushing her, I told her I wasn't joking.

"You need to wake up Mom so she can take you to the fucking emergency room, you little twerp."

That's when I slowly crawled onto the floor and grabbed her socked feet. I begged, offering her all my lawn-mowing money from last summer and next summer. She didn't say anything at first, probably enjoying the view from up there, me on the carpet, begging for mercy. A wry smile eventually turned into an almost silent cackle. She wheezed through her open mouth and held her chest as if it hurt from the hilarity of my situation. Finally, Jenny agreed, not because of the money or out of sisterly duty, but because she liked dirty jobs and loved having power over me most of all. Also, I wondered if hurling that ashtray at her had won me some respect.

"I know what to do," said Jenny. "Something similar happened when Deidre got her tampon stuck, and I was able to get it out." Unlike Mom and me, Jenny lived for gore. She didn't gag at the sight of blood or vomit, had seen almost every horror movie ever made, and used to dissect insects and dead squirrels in the park with takeout cutlery when we were younger.

While she grabbed supplies, I cleared a space on her carpet and placed a towel on the floor. She returned with dishwashing gloves and a jar of Albolene, which Mom used to take off her makeup.

She told me to put my bare legs on her shoulders while I covered my privates with the towel. The situation was horrifying but way preferable to going to the ER with Mom.

"Don't push. If you shit on me, I will kill you," she said. "Take deep breaths."

She then dipped her rubber finger into the Albolene jar. It felt like she was tearing me in half so far up that she could pull my stomach out. The deeper I breathed, the farther she dug to get inside. Eventually, her finger touched the handle of the baseball bat.

"Don't push it in further!" I said, panicked.

"It's really deep, and these gloves are too thick." After a few minutes, she pulled off the yellow glove in surrender. "You're going to have to tell Mom. It's too far in."

"No, no, no," I whimpered. My feet carefully lowered off her shoulders and onto the shag carpet. I turned my face and bawled into the towel, not wanting her to see me.

"I have one more idea. But it will cost you five hundred bucks on top of the lawn-mowing money."

"What? I'll give it to you if you can get it out, but if you can't, I'm not giving you anything."

She rose and said calmly, "I'll wake Mom up, then."

"OK, OK, five hundred." I didn't know how to get this money, nor could I imagine how many lawns I would have to mow the following year.

Jenny rummaged through a makeup drawer. "Where are my eyebrow tweezers?" She found them and dipped her bare fingers and the tiny forceps into the jelly. "I'm going in. Remember to breathe," she said to me with authority, as if she were suddenly a doctor.

When she pushed in, it felt like she was scraping me with a knife, and I wanted to cry out but bore down and winced, sucking my teeth as quietly as I could. After a few attempts, the tweezers finally tapped the end of the bat. She finally grabbed it for a moment, but it slipped.

"Owww."

"One more try. Hold still," she said. "Got it!' And like I was going number two, I felt it pass through me until it was out.

"Gross, I should've asked for a thousand," she said before running to the bathroom. She left the door open so I could hear the sink running and Mom's snoring in the living room—thankfully, she was a heavy sleeper. Relieved it was over, I ignored the residual pain, pulled up my boxers, and retied my robe belt. After I wrapped the mess in the towel, I tiptoed outside to hide the evidence in the dumpster.

When I returned, Jenny was already waiting at my bedroom door for the money. I opened my nightstand drawer and handed her the wad of cash. I promised the next installment before Christmas.

"It's good we don't have a pet gerbil." She laughed at her own joke as she pocketed the cash.

I could have smacked her, but I was too relieved.

"Thank you," I finally said. "For helping me."

Before she opened the door to leave, she said in the nicest voice I had ever heard coming out of her mouth, "You really liked him, didn't you?"

Chapter 20

Jared
San Francisco, CA
Winter 2016

THE NEW AU PAIR scrubbed her hands in the kitchen sink. Jo, short for Josie, fresh off the plane from Marseille, should've lathered the crevice between her thumb and index finger. But Mare wailed and thrashed in her chair, so I decided not to bring up proper hand hygiene. Then, right as I handed Mare off to Jo, one of her chubby legs kicked me in the face.

There would be days when it would be hard to leave my daughter behind, and that day wasn't one of them. It was my last week of paternity leave, and I planned on making the most of it. So I waved goodbye, shut the front door behind me, and inhaled the crisp fall air. During my stroll to the MUNI, I was giddy at the prospect of a night of freedom.

When I arrived at the LGBTQ+ Community and Support Center on Market Street, excitement flickered in my gut—the same feeling I had the night I met Wynn at the Boston nightclub—sans the anxiety. Back then, I was a different person—closeted and ashamed. Fast-forward twelve years later, and I was out and proud: a tech executive and a new father.

In the center's "community room," clusters of middle-aged men in fleece vests and button-down shirts huddled around folding tables. They noshed on crudité and hummus and sipped wine from red and blue Solo cups. Many sets of eyes lasered in, making me feel self-conscious. It had been a while since I'd been surrounded by other gay men. Then I reminded myself to enjoy the attention while I could. Besides, I had a singular goal for the evening: to find a boyfriend. I needed to get noticed. If only Wynn hadn't come by the week before, I wouldn't have to be there. Why had I lied about having a new boyfriend? The reasons were obvious in retrospect: the house was a wreck, and I looked like hell.

Meanwhile, Wynn had seemed so refreshed and carefree. On top of looking amazing, he had the nerve to leave that condescending note. In no parallel universe were we ever going to be friends.

I heard my name and turned around and spotted the group leader, a dowdy man whose name I couldn't remember. Out of politeness, I returned his hug until a hand slid from my shoulders down the neck of my ass.

"We haven't seen you in a while. You look terrific," he said. "I saw on RevSo, you have a baby girl now."

"Yes," I said, taking another step back. "Meryl's at home with my new nanny. Uh, au pair. She's French."

"Ha, I know it's hard to leave the little ones at home, but daddies need playtime, too," he said with a wink. "The twins are three, and this little helper got me through the terrible twos."

He toasted me with his red Solo cup. I looked behind him to see if I recognized anyone else in the room.

"You may not know this," he said, "but my husband and I"— he whispered— "we've decided to open things up." He raised his eyebrows suggestively.

While averting my gaze, I spotted a striking Black man with

a lush beard and tortoiseshell glasses behind him. Unlike the other dads in the room, he actually had a child with him. A lock of curly black hair peeked out the top of the Bjorn strapped to the man's muscular frame.

"How's your little one?" the group leader asked.

"I'm sorry, what?" I said, continuing to gape at my target. He turned before swiveling back to me.

"I don't know why he brought his kid. Everyone knows this is supposed to be about making time for ourselves to support each other."

He marched off in a huff. The group leader then grabbed the mic and announced the program's start while everyone took their seats. I stood in the back. The guest speaker, a child psychologist, flipped through her slideshow titled *Women: How to Cultivate Maternal Figures in Your Child's Life*. None of her talking points seemed particularly salient since Mare was barely sentient. Her waking hours consisted of five activities: cry, poop, pee, eat, sleep. I watched the clock until the Q&A finished, after which I weaved through the crowd toward the bearded man, my hand already extended.

"I'm Jared," I said with my most winning smile, reaching for a handshake. "What's your little one's name?"

"He's Oliver, and I'm Landon."

The sensation of Landon's callused palm against mine triggered flutters in my chest.

"My daughter, Meryl, was the same way," I said. "About sleeping, I mean. When she actually slept, she could sleep through anything. But when she's hungry, she lets the entire neighborhood know. She's with my new nanny. Who's French. My nanny, not my daughter." I babbled when I was nervous. I hoped it wasn't too noticeable.

"I didn't know we weren't supposed to bring our kids," said Landon apologetically. "They did say it was a gay dads' meetup, so I assumed children were welcome."

My phone buzzed. It was a text from Wynn. I looked up at Landon, trying to find a subtle way to determine if he was attached.

"Where's your partner?" Landon asked as if reading my mind.

"I'm single," I said. "Funny enough, that was a text from my ex." Why did I say that? I reminded myself to bring the conversation back to him. "And your status?" I asked. "Relationship, I mean, not disease—"

"I'm single, too." He smiled, then looked down at his sleeping baby.

"Well, it's nice to know there are other single dads raising kids alone," I said. Oliver interrupted with a stir and whimper.

"Sorry," said Landon. "I should really get him home. It's way past his bedtime. Really nice meeting you, though."

As I was about to ask for Landon's number, my phone buzzed again. I was on the verge of silencing it when it slipped from my hand. Landon and Oliver were gone by the time I picked it up. I had also missed a call from the nanny and dialed her back immediately.

"Hi Jo, is everything OK?" A few men with Solo cups shot me dirty looks, so I scurried out of the room and down the stairs. "No, Jo, the Wi-Fi password is on the fridge. Oh yeah, I forgot I changed it. The new one is *marescastle*, all one word and lowercase."

Outside on the sidewalk, Jo gave me the update: Mare had pooped twice, taken most of her bottle, and was sleeping. A shiny BMW station wagon pulled up to the curb. The driver's side window rolled down. It was Landon.

"Fancy seeing you here," he said, "I've been circling, trying to find a garbage can, to toss in a dirty diaper stinking up my car."

"I feel like I've been in a similar situation before." I smiled coyly at him through the open window. The heat emanating from the car was inviting, even if it was noxious with diaper fumes. Knowing I wasn't the only one mired in crap all day was comforting.

"Were you just talking to your ex on the phone?" asked Landon.

"No, thankfully," I said. "It was the nanny."

"Your French nanny?"

"Yes." I laughed. "Thanks for pointing out how pretentious I sound."

"Anytime." He paused momentarily, then added: "You know, I've been through a recent breakup myself. Messy, very messy. But I adopted this one right after we ended things." His bass voice resonated warm and throaty. A total turn-on.

"Did adopting him help?" I asked. "With the breakup?"

"Definitely," Landon said. "What about you?"

"We were together eleven years and agreed we would build a family," I said. "He changed his mind."

Landon whistled. "Wow, that sounds rough, but maybe you dodged a bullet. Parenting is hard, and you need to be all in. The only reason I haven't gone crazy is that I've wanted to be a dad as far back as I can remember."

"Same with me. I always knew I wanted kids. At least two. A girl and a boy."

"I used to think I wanted four, but now that I know how much work it is—" Landon paused. "Hey, why don't you get in? It's getting chilly. I'll drive you to your car. Excuse the smell. Sorry about earlier. I thought I had to rush to get this one home," he said apologetically. "He's still out, though, so I don't want to wake him up."

By the time I strapped the seatbelt on, I was already so turned on, I could've unbuckled his pants then and there, but his son was in the car, and I wasn't even sure he liked me in that way. We drove off and talked more. Landon lived in the Oakland Hills and worked in marketing and communications at a pharmaceutical company. A nice, Midwestern boy—born and raised in Michigan—he had moved to San Francisco from Ann Arbor with his ex. I immediately started imagining our future together. Landon and Oliver would move in so we could share child-rearing responsibilities. Mare and Oliver would become brother and sister—best friends, too—and attend The French American International School together. Afterward, Landon and I would decide to have more kids together—some by surrogacy, others by adoption, a total mix, and by the end of my tale, I was basically Angelina Jolie with a brood of multiracial children. Eventually, we spotted a bin in which to dispose of the diaper, and he asked where I'd parked. When I admitted to taking the MUNI, he offered me a ride home.

During the drive, the topic shifted back to breakups, and he started telling me about his ex's drug problem, which started with weed, and soon moved on to the harder stuff. Though I was excited to spend more time with this handsome man and his son, I was also getting more anxious. After planning our lives together just a few moments earlier, I wondered if I was ready to jump back into the dating pool, especially with a kid. Before I could ruminate more, Landon asked me about my breakup. "Well," I said, "Wynn changed his mind about wanting kids only a few weeks before Meryl was born. I was devastated, but I had to keep it together since there was someone else to think about."

"I'm sorry," Landon said, his eyes widening in shock—and he had only heard a tidbit of my nightmare. "That doesn't sound easy. Your ex sounds very immature. Was he a lot younger?"

I chuckled. "He's actually older than me. He's thirty-six. But immature, for sure."

Landon touched my shoulder, and I thought I might pass out. He asked, "What was his reason for not wanting kids?"

"Get this," I said. "He wants to be a hip-hop dancer."

His hand retreated, and he asked, "Wait, quick question. Do you only date Black guys?"

"What? No, he isn't Black," I replied hastily.

"Good," said Landon, "'cause I've been down that road. Sorry, I just thought he was Black. Because, you know, hip-hop."

"No, he's Asian," I said. "Korean American, to be exact." I assured Landon that I didn't have a fetish or even "a preference." My years with Wynn had trained me well. Prospective romantic partners didn't like to be perceived or treated like a faceless "type." They wanted to be seen as individuals. Whatever I said seemed to have assuaged Landon's concerns because his hand rested on my knee.

When we pulled into my driveway, the lights in the nursery window were off. Only the ones in the great room were on, and through the front window, Josie sat at the dining room table, texting on her phone.

"It's been great meeting someone going through the same thing," I said. "There isn't a playbook for single gay dads."

"Yes, we're all just making it up as we go along," he replied. "I don't want to go home, but it's late and a school night."

He leaned in, and we kissed. His delicious beard smelled of expensive cologne. We made out hungrily until Oliver woke up and fussed.

"I know it's old-fashioned, but I want to give you this so we can stay in touch," I said, passing my business card. I could tell that he was impressed with my company and title from how his gorgeous brown eyes widened.

He backed out of the driveway, and I waved. Images from the future flashed before me: double strollers, Sunday dinners, and family vacations in Hawaii. No more sleeping alone. No more wondering how I would swing parenting solo once I returned to the office the following week.

Before opening the front door, I checked my phone. A slew of texts from Wynn plastered the screen.

So good reconnecting last week and

meeting Mare.

how ru? feeling better? how is mare?

Nairobi is good, not too hot. Nicole says
hi.

Btw did you get my note?

I deleted his texts and turned off my phone.

Chapter 21

Wynn
Nairobi, Kenya
Winter 2016

ON MY FIRST weekend in Nairobi, Nicole and I decided to have a "quit party" to celebrate her last night of smoking. We were stuck in traffic on the way to the club when she lit her third cigarette of the drive. She exhaled, reapplied eyeliner and mascara, and adjusted her hoop earrings in the rearview mirror. Lauren Hill's forceful voice blasted on the car stereo. It was always 2004 in Nicole's world—the year she had left Boston to join USAID in East Africa. I opened the window and fake coughed.

"All part of expat life. Live fast, die young," she said. I reminded her that my mom had died from lung cancer. "She never smoked, though," Nicole replied from the driver's seat of her Toyota SUV. "Besides, it's one of the reasons I wanted you to come. To guilt me into quitting."

At a busy intersection, she lowered her window to buy two packs of Marlboro Lights from a plump woman in a tailored, gold and teal kitenge dress holding a straw basket full of tissue packets, condoms, aspirin, fresh coconuts, and cigarettes. The narrow street teemed with cars, new and old, trucks, shiny and dusted. Ancient minivans stuffed with people hanging out the windows surrounded us. It was a virtual parking lot.

Nicole lit another cigarette. "I'm going to smoke my brains out tonight to get it out of my system. But tomorrow, I'm done."

An entire pack later, we valet parked at Oasis, a hotel bar in the center of town. We sat at a window table overlooking the rooftop pool and sipped gin and tonics. Nicole exhaled a series of smoke rings under the bar's dim lights. She looked more glamorous and relaxed than I'd ever seen her.

"Tell me, do you love it here? Do you feel free?" I asked. "I know I do."

She snickered and said, "Well, I'm exhausted, to be honest. But it does suit me here. Remember, you're not working. And besides, you're in *Africa* for the first time and single now." She said "Africa" in a mock accent that was probably supposed to be Kenyan but didn't sound like it was from anywhere. "I think you're just happy to be free from your controlling, narcissistic husband."

"Ex-*partner*. We never married," I corrected her. "Also, Jared is controlling AF, but he isn't a narcissist. He just needs a wife." She shot me a look that said that I was fooling myself.

"Name an attractive man, no, an attractive man or woman from a coastal city in the US with a great job who isn't at least slightly narcissistic?" I asked.

"Touché. It's one of the many reasons I don't want to go back to America. The self-obsessed, neurotic, workaholic professional class, not to mention the school shootings and cops targeting Black drivers. Not in that order. At least here, when I'm pulled over by the police, it's for some other stupid reason."

"True that." I held up my glass for a toast. "A toast to escaping everything fucked up at home." We clinked glasses. "I could get used to this life abroad, though. No kid, no responsibility. It's why I did what I did," I said, mostly to convince myself that I'd made the right decision. "Though I still can't stop thinking about Mare on my nipple. Is that the craziest thing you've ever heard? A baby latching onto a man's nipple?"

"It's actually not that uncommon. I looked it up," said Nicole. "They have oral fixations. But it sounds like *you* got more attached than she did. Babies," she shook her head, "can be more addictive than cigarettes."

"Yeah, but you can't do anything or go anywhere with them," I said. "God, if I'd stayed, I wouldn't be here." My arm swung gracefully in front of me like a game show hostess.

"Hey, not to change the subject," she said, "but did you contact the HR lady from the embassy about that temporary position? It's super easy, just some Excel stuff. It might be nice to have some pocket money while you're here."

"I did, thank you," I said. "We had a call today, and I think it went okay," I lied. I'd dutifully emailed the briefest of cover letters with a two-year-old version of my CV the day before. The recruiter called me minutes after sending it and gushed how the embassy would love to have someone with my experience and mentioned a different job, more senior and better paid.

The position required extensive travel throughout East Africa and quarterly weeklong trips to headquarters in Washington. Her description of the job requirements made me think of the "Sex, Gender, and Society" class I'd taken sophomore year of college, where the professor had said the main reason corporate America embraced LGBTQ people was that we were less likely to have children and therefore more willing to work long hours and shoulder the burden of extensive business travel. Shortly after my call with the recruiter, I sent her a short email saying I needed to return to the States sooner than expected. My fib was a gift to myself, a tiny reparation for living in this body.

Besides, I wasn't ready to return to a desk job—the same life I'd run from in San Francisco. I didn't want to take a giant step backward, especially since something more professionally fulfilling awaited me on the horizon. That said, I didn't want to offend Nicole. It had been thoughtful of her to put in a good word for me, and she'd seemed to be able to find inspiration and meaning, as well as a fat paycheck through her own work.

"Are you really smoking another one?" I asked.

"Yup, I'm gagging between puffs and don't care. It's my last night." She tilted her hand and spoke to the cherry. "So long, little friend." She beamed, revealing the gap between her two front teeth that made her look sexy and mischievous. "Tomorrow, I promise."

"I cannot believe you work in public health," I said. "And I can't believe they let you smoke inside here."

"I work in sexual and reproductive health, not chronic disease or cancer prevention." She looked around the club, which had filled with people—a mix of well-heeled Kenyans in slim-cut suits, slinky cocktail dresses, and expats in threadbare T-shirts, ratty jeans, and dirty sneakers. "We need to find you someone," said Nicole. "How long has it been?"

"I got busy at dance camp with a barely legal kid, okay? There was also that time when I was laid up with my torn Achilles, remember? I Netflixed and chilled with the redheaded, mixed guy I told you about. My number is up to six, thank you very much."

"Wow, impressive, Winnie," she said with a deadpan expression.

I gave her a playful, rebuking tap on the shoulder. "You know I don't want to reinforce the gay promiscuity stereotype, which is why I've stayed so virginal all these years." I fluttered my eyelashes and pushed my hands together in prayer.

"Well, let's try making it seven tonight," she said.

"And get me arrested and thrown in a Kenyan jail?" I swatted at a plume of smoke in front of my face. "No, thank you."

"You know, no one enforces that."

"The law says fourteen years for gay sex, I read it online, so it must be true," I said.

"The State Department would bail you out," said Nicole. "Anyways, there are lots of guys on the DL. You need to get out there, show your moves."

I scanned the dance floor. No one seemed gay, not that I could tell for sure. "What about you?" I swayed in my chair to the catchy Kenyan pop music. "See anyone you like?" All our chatter about babies and dating had made me antsy.

"Oh no, I'm on a break. No more men." Her eyes glazed over. She'd never been lucky in love. Attractive to men, yes. But nothing ever seemed to turn into any kind of lasting healthy relationship.

Her last boyfriend had worked as a security guard at the embassy, a Maasai whose family had left the tribe for jobs in the city. She'd sent photos of him: over seven feet tall, skin the color of sable, and thin as a broomstick. Nicole explained what had happened over the phone. They dated on the sly for a few months last year until he started asking for money. First, it was for his sick mother, then his niece's private school, and later he wanted a car to drive for Uber. She said it wasn't the money as much as how his requests articulated their unequal power dynamic in ways she couldn't quite explain, ways that had nothing to do with them and everything to do with culture, politics, and society. Ultimately, Nicole had proudly announced she was too young to be a sugar momma before breaking up with him.

A Kenyan rap song I recognized from the radio came on, and I shot up from my seat and threw my arms up in the air. "Let's dance!"

"I'm not finished with my drink yet."

When I sat back down, I spotted a few white hairs springing from her crown, making me wonder if we'd fundamentally changed since college. In many ways, we were still the same fresh-faced kids from freshman year, give or take a few pounds, some laugh lines, and a few silver hairs. Except now, we were both a little sad and disappointed with how life had panned out. I called over the waiter and opened my wallet full of shillings. Nicole swatted my hand away and handed over her credit card.

"You're my guest."

"Thanks, love," I said. "If someone had told me freshman year that I would be thirty-six, openly gay, single, unemployed, and living with you in Nairobi getting drunk in a bar, I would've told that person they were smoking crack."

"Crack is whack," we yelled at the same time.

Nicole tilted her head. "Or that I would be single and another statistic. Black woman with a doctorate, childless, and no immediate romantic prospects." She guzzled the rest of her drink. "We were supposed to meet our significant others at Swarthmore. If not, we were bound to end up alone."

"We met each other," I said, trying to lighten the mood. I lifted my empty glass and toasted her.

Some ridiculously high percentage of Swarthmore graduates married each other—they called it the Quaker Matchbox for a reason. The alumni office often bragged about this statistic during prospective student tours. I always wondered what the results might look like if they cut the data by race and sexuality. There were so few students—fewer than 1,400—that there were very few choices for us gays to marry from. When I came out as "questioning" my junior year, my straight friends turned into zookeepers, and I became a rare panda they tried to mate with the other gay Asian on campus. And though I'd never asked Nicole explicitly if dating had been similarly tricky for her, I sensed it might've been worse. At the time, there were only a handful of Black women on-campus and even fewer Black men, whom she claimed only dated white women. And though she'd been open to interracial dating, she said the white guys weren't, though their liberal guilt would never allow them to admit it.

Years later, when she rehashed her experience to me, I took it personally, especially after reading a news article about online dating that concluded Black women and Asian men were the least likely to receive introductory messages and replies from potential matches of all races. Nicole and I huddled in the same lonely boat. Even the data confirmed that finding love would be harder for us.

The club grew busier, and folks spilled out from the dance floor. A new DJ with a thick beard replaced Kenyan pop music with American hip-hop at twice the volume. Nicole ordered another drink, while I refused. The alcohol wasn't making me light and happy like I'd hoped. Instead, my mood turned flat, and I felt even more hollowed out than before. I could only think about how Nicole and I had lost our Swarthmore shine. And though our intelligence, charm, and healthful good looks had remained over the years, these traits had only set our expectations higher. Since undergrad, our cohort of peers continued to want more and more: rewarding careers, elegant weddings, home ownership in coastal cities, and high-achieving children. We weren't prepared for life's mounting disappointments, be it divorces, infertility, career disillusionment, or the general malaise that met our ilk at the end of the achievement race. Maybe Jared *was* right: capitalism did always prevail.

"At least you have your career and a paycheck," I roared in her ear after a long silence.

"That's not true," she shouted back over the music. "You're going to dance full-time. Have you checked out some of those dance studios I emailed you?"

"I will," I said, and I meant it. I loved her again. Whether or not she truly believed in my potential as a dancer, I appreciated her willingness to indulge me. I flexed my foot and felt a dull ache. The physical therapist in town said I could dance again, but it would take a few months until it was one hundred percent, if ever.

The slow, tinny piano intro for Mary J.'s "No More Drama" came on. "Oh my god, we must do our routine to this!" I said before chugging the rest of my gin and tonic.

Nicole slapped her thigh and said, "Are you serious? No fucking way. I'm still in my work clothes."

"We're going." I pulled her out of her seat.

"But I'm so fat!"

I wouldn't hear any excuses or fall into the trap of flattering her. She'd thickened a little, yet in all the right places. We parted the crowd and found a spot next to the DJ booth.

Neither of us remembered the routine, so we swayed and improvised awkwardly. Nicole shrugged her shoulders and helicoptered her arms, the sleeves of her taffeta blouse billowing. After, she shimmied her hips in an A-line skirt. Meanwhile, I rolled my torso and added some cross-steps and turns, nothing that required even a tiny hop. There were few spins, fewer drops to our ankles, and zero backspins or splits. Our old choreography never registered in our muscle memory—too much time had passed, so instead, we made silly faces at each other and laughed a lot. Nicole's mouth opened wide, exposing her tonsils, and I mimicked her. After so much time off, it was as if I were relearning how to dance. Somehow, the injury had freed me. I no longer took myself as seriously and was only eager to experience the unbridled joy of being in my body. All the self-pity we'd entertained minutes earlier dissipated. And just like that, we were nineteen years old again and dancing in the Swarthmore rec room.

The next song blurred into the mix: Tribe Called Quest's "Electric Relaxation."

"Holy shit, it's old school tonight!" I was so excited that I even hopped a little. When I looked at Nicole for her reaction, she was speaking into the ear of a hunky Kenyan man in a bespoke suit. He wrapped his muscular arm around her waist.

Eventually, I edged my way in and introduced myself. His

name was Collins. He said his full name like it should mean something to me. Once he could tell it didn't register, Nicole recaptured his attention, and they twirled away swiftly, leaving me standing alone at the edge of the dance floor, hugging the bar. Nicole and her suitor danced intimately; he positioned himself behind her while she twerked to a Reggaetón number. His lips grazed her neck, and she arched her back and shut her eyes. I admired how she lived. No matter the previous heartbreak and how often she swore off men, she always snatched the next romantic opportunity that came her way.

I eventually caught the bartender's attention. I ordered the drink special, something bright blue that tasted like mango juice mixed with nail polish remover. When I took a big gulp, I spilled some. The cold liquid dribbled down my neck and under my white shirt. A droplet lingered on my nipple, which made me think of Meryl, then Jared. I wondered if he'd read my note. I had texted him yesterday and still hadn't heard back. Maybe the cleaning lady threw it out, or a breeze from an open window blew it under the bed?

"Hey, you were great out there," a voice interrupted. "You can bust a move, man." I looked up to find the DJ, in sunglasses even though the club was dimly lit. "Can I buy you a drink? I noticed you spilled most of the one you're holding."

We made introductions, and I asked most of the questions since I wasn't keen on describing my current situation. His name was Fayyaz. Born and raised in Nairobi, he had attended college in Boston for a year. "Dude, BU was too much fun, man. Flunked out." He later finished university in the UK and worked in finance in London for three months before packing his bags for home. "Dude, I spent fourteen hours a day in a cubicle. That's not a way to live, man. Plus, that place is too damn cold."

All his American colloquialisms sounded bizarre, filtered through his British-Kenyan accent. I hadn't spoken to many locals yet and wondered if all the young men in town peppered every sentence with "man" and "dude." Nonetheless, I found myself drawn to his thick, well-groomed eyebrows and strong jaw and enjoyed hearing about someone's life that wasn't Nicole's or my own.

Fayyaz split his time between DJing and managing his family's portfolio of businesses.

"Music, man, it's all about my music, which is why I wanted to talk to you," he said, removing his sunglasses and propping them on his head. "We own one of the largest dance studios in Nairobi. Mostly Bollywood stuff for the Indian folks, but we're looking for a hip-hop instructor, stat. Our old one went back to New York. Do you have any teaching experience?"

I couldn't believe my luck. We exchanged numbers, and I searched for Nicole to share my good news but couldn't find her. After asking a stranger to check the women's bathroom for her, I assumed she'd left with Collins and resumed drinking.

When I got home Nicole was sitting on the outdoor patio, wrapped in a blanket, and smoking a cigarette, her mane dented on one side, chunks of leaves woven into her tight ringlets. Streaks of eyeliner smeared across one cheek. She looked like she'd just woken up in a ditch.

"I don't want to hear about it," she said when she saw me. "New quit time is noon today."

"Are you okay?" I said, panicked.

"Fine, I'm fine," she said between puffs. "I left with Collins, and we did it in the back of his Range Rover and then against that tree over there. He just left a minute ago. Back to his wife and four kids."

I told her about Fayyaz and my new job.

"That's great. Your news is much more exciting," she said, staring blankly at the tree in the yard's far corner.

"It doesn't pay much, but it's a start," I said, sitting beside her. "So, how was the sex?"

"That man smelled delicious, Winnie. Like babies."

"That's your biological clock kicking in."

"Seriously, I almost reached back and ripped the condom off in the middle of him fucking me from behind and screamed, 'Breed me!'"

We cackled, and when we finally calmed, she said, "I want to discuss something serious. I want a baby."

"So go back and ask him to give you one. I'm sure he's up for round two." I still felt rowdy from the potential job prospect and drinks earlier that night. "Go to his house and yell, 'Breed me!'"

"He's an MP. He's too smart for that."

We sat side by side on the bench in silence. Then I realized what she meant. How could I be so dense? "It's why you invited me here, isn't it? You were so adamant that I visit—"

"Don't make that face," she said, stubbing her cigarette on the bottom of her pump's skinny heel. "You wouldn't have to support the child or anything. I make more than enough."

I stomped into the house, slamming the patio screen door behind me. Nicole followed me into the kitchen. To drown out her voice, I ground coffee. She unplugged the grinder.

"I can't," I said, my back turned to her.

"I didn't know my dad. It's something I think about every fucking day of my life. I don't want my child to go through the same thing. They need to know their biological father exists."

I poured the grounds and filtered water into the coffeemaker, questioning how badly I wanted this teaching job at Fayyaz's studio. More importantly, where did I have to go?

"You don't have to do anything, I promise. No responsibility, no work. You can go off and do whatever you want, whenever you want." She turned me around and squeezed both my shoulders lovingly.

I felt woozy and avoided eye contact. "I don't know." What would happen if I said no? Would it be awkward between us? I didn't have anyone else.

"Think of it as a gift," she said. "This baby, he or she could have our moves?" She swung her hips and did a little body roll. "How cute would that be?"

Hadn't I left Jared and the US for this exact reason? Except this time, I wouldn't have any responsibility, financial or otherwise, for the child. I could go on with my life unplanned, building my dance career, couldn't I? It was just sperm.

I ducked under her arm and opened the fridge for milk. The spout was open. When I reached for it, milk splashed on the front of my shirt. Cold wetness on my nipples released tingles throughout my body. It was becoming a habit, spilling things down my shirt.

Nicole laughed, and I did too.

And because I have incredible boundaries and wanted—no needed—this teaching job, I finally said, "I'll think about it on the following conditions,"

"And what's that?"

"You quit smoking, and I'm in charge of breastfeeding."

Chapter 22

Jared
San Francisco, CA
Spring 2016

WE TRIED TO establish boundaries. First, Landon and I agreed to see each other only once a week, just dinner, no kids, and separate babysitters. But when we met more days than not, we set a new rule: no overnights. And then Landon's sitter called in sick, and Jo offered to watch Oliver. When we arrived home extra late that night, the kids were already sleeping, so it only made sense for them to stay the night. Just one night. And then, since my house was closer to Landon's office, he and Oliver stayed over the following evening. This pattern extended the next few days until they basically moved in, spending only one night at their house in Oakland each week. Afterward, we decided to coordinate and merge our nannies' schedules: Mare's Jo on Mondays, Wednesdays, and Fridays and Oliver's Alma on Tuesdays, Thursdays, and Saturdays. Our final compromise was that we were on our own on Sundays with our respective kids, though much of our day apart was spent texting each other.

Soon after, we had "the talk" and decided we were in an

official relationship—not partners, but boyfriends. I couldn't have been more pleased, really. No more sleepless nights alone. Someone to make coffee for in the morning. Even Mare, who shared a room with Oliver, seemed happier, waking up only once per night instead of four or five times, as if trying to be considerate of her new roomie.

Then there was the sex, which could only be described using one word: Incredible. The kissing lasted for hours until my lips and chin stung from his beard. On one uncharacteristically quiet morning at the office, I sat at my desk, closed my eyes, and relished the burning sensation that seared my right nipple and the patch of skin above my pubic bone where his beard had chafed the night before.

I texted him: "Are you free for lunch?"

We met in the parking garage underneath his office.

Landon said, "I have forty-seven minutes until my next conference call."

"Let's get a hotel room next time," I said.

"Next time."

We lowered the back seats, giving us more room in the hatch. For the next few minutes, we kissed and grinded our bodies together. The fogging windows granted us privacy.

Eventually, a water bottle dug into my thigh, and a baby rattle poked me in the back. I did my best to try and ignore these minor nuisances since Landon seemed to be enjoying himself.

"Stop, stop, I'm getting close," he said. "Can we at least try? Give it a chance?" His eyes watered like a puppy's before he climbed over the passenger seat and unlatched the glove compartment to reveal a box of condoms and a bottle of lubricant.

I pressed my hand against the steamed window, leaving a print, and said, "I don't know." I'd told him I wasn't ready the previous times we'd messed around.

"What do you mean, you don't know? You were married to a man for over ten years."

"We weren't married," I said. "And we just preferred not to. I didn't like anything down there, and neither did he."

"OK," said Landon. "No need to shout."

"I wasn't shouting."

"How about the other way? You inside of me?"

"There are lots of germs and bacteria down there," I said.

"Whoa, are you calling me dirty?"

"No, I've read the book, *Everybody Poops*."

"So, if you don't have anal sex, what did you and your ex do?" he asked.

"Everything else." I was confused why penetration was so important to him, yet I couldn't ask him directly. My palm pushed harder against the back window. I tried to put some breeze into my voice when I said, "I guess I haven't been with that many guys. Only my ex and now you. Is that a problem?" I unlatched the hatch to let in the garage's stale air.

"No, it's just interesting," said Landon, buttoning his shirt.

I could tell he was disappointed, and I knew something had to give if I wanted to keep him.

After the babies fell asleep, we lay in bed naked and tried— Landon on his back, supported by a pair of geometric, mid-century pillows, his long, muscular legs on top of my shoulders.

After three thrusts, he said, "Stop, please stop. You look so unhappy." I lied and said it was fine.

"I feel like I'm assaulting you or something," he said.

The next blissful twenty minutes were spent on our sides, kissing as we finished each other off at precisely the same time. The synchronized timing was auspicious, compensating for the evening's rough start. Also, I always took longer to finish than Wynn. Over the years, he had often joked our sex life gave him carpal tunnel.

We cuddled, and I was euphoric. Even though I couldn't give Landon precisely what he wanted, we were clearly sexually compatible otherwise. We were much more professionally aligned, too. He was very successful for his age. I loved that Landon was even more ambitious than me and not the other way around, as in my previous relationship. Unlike Wynn, Landon spoke glowingly about his job as a communications executive for a pharmaceutical company that manufactured HIV and hepatitis drugs. On our second date, he said, "If I don't see the letters 'Sr.' before 'Vice President' in my email signature by the end of Q4, I'm out."

After lovemaking, it was time for bed. We needed our rest if we were going to achieve our long-term professional goals. We released our embrace and wiped down each other's stomachs with fresh washcloths that I kept stacked in my nightstand drawer. I turned off the lamp and said, "That was great." His eyes remained glued to his work phone, tapping out an email. After a long pause, I added: "The sex."

"Yeah, it was hot. I like jerking off with you," he said absentmindedly. His finger swiped north-south on the screen.

The following week, Landon texted to say he had gotten the promotion: "Senior" in the title, more stock, a twenty percent raise. We planned to celebrate with a home-cooked dinner that night. After putting the kids to bed, we prepared saffron risotto with peas and swordfish from Reverie's Apron and paired it with a bottle of sparkling wine. Landon encouraged me to have a sip with dinner. I reminded him I didn't drink due to my family history. He said, "To advance your career, you're going to have to attend more work functions. You don't want people to think you're some rigid teetotaler or, worse, an addict." He poured two glasses and then tipped his flute empty. "You don't have to finish it, just one or two micro sips."

I slurped off the rim of the glass. It tasted crisp and bubbly and left a sour film on my tongue. Each sip after the first was progressively sweeter, and when I finished it, my head already felt floaty. I started giggling uncontrollably for no reason.

"You're drunk already?" he asked.

"I haven't had any alcohol since college, more than ten years ago," I said.

"How cute," said Landon. "Well, we haven't even made a toast yet."

He refilled our glasses, and we clinked flutes to his promotion.

Things did work out for the better. When Wynn had left me earlier that year, I thought my life was over, but really, it was all part of a bigger plan that led me to this man, and his son, Oliver, who would soon be my son one day. We were going to be an unbelievably stunning, multiracial family.

"One more toast," I said. My cheeks flushed hot. "To meeting you," I said. "You and Oliver have made my life so much better."

"Cheers to us, Oliver and Mare," said Landon. "May we remain close for life."

He leaned in and kissed me, the sweet finish of his wine on my lips. I placed my hand on his and blurted, "Well, now that your promotion is settled, I want you and Oliver to move in."

"Too soon," said Landon, pulling his hand away. "We just met."

"But it feels so right. You're already here all the time."

"I know, but it's too soon to make it official," he said.

Even though his response stung, my foggy instincts told me to let it go. The alcohol made my eyelids heavy, and I blinked aggressively to stay alert.

"Well, let's at least go away this weekend," I said. "We can bring the kids someplace close like Calistoga or even Monterey. I want to celebrate."

"This weekend? We're trying a new church on Sunday. My

college friend, Nichelle, is taking us."

"We are?" I asked. "You never told me about it."

"No, I mean, it's for Oliver and me. It's a Black church."

"Well, I'm not religious. I don't know how I feel about going to church."

Landon put his hand on my thigh and squeezed too firmly. "I wasn't inviting you," he said with a tight grin. "It's just for Oliver and me."

"I see."

My heart sank. Sweat poured from my pits down the sides of my ribs and into the waistband of my boxer briefs. I leaped out of my chair, opened the dining room window, and watched the fog roll in.

We cleared the dishes and retired to bed quietly. Neither of us initiated sex. Landon said he had an early morning meeting, and I complained I was too drunk. Long after lights out, I lay awake with a dry mouth and worried that our honeymoon phase was over. My mind whirled with questions: Why was Landon so hesitant about moving in together? Why didn't he want to get closer? I was a catch. Everyone said so. I looked over at him, and he was sound asleep on his side, a crème-colored satin mask over his eyes. Such a feminine accessory on such a masculine face. It took all my willpower not to wake him and freak out.

In the morning, I sat at the kitchen table hungover with a baby in each arm, both squawking in morning bird voices. Oliver gurgled, spit bubbles oozing from his lips, while Mare shrieked, her gummy mouth open, threads of drool hanging from her chin.

Landon walked in, freshly showered and looking rested. "Thanks for letting me sleep in," he said. "Ooh—and there's coffee and eggs. I could get used to this." He leaned in for a kiss, but I turned away. "Let me guess, you're either mad about the church thing or the moving-in thing?"

The ibuprofen hadn't kicked in yet, so I said nothing, placed the babies in their highchairs, and mixed their formula.

"Good morning," he said formally. I grunted. "I cannot believe you're acting like this. Just so you know, it is way too soon to move in together. Period," he said. "You are just out of a relationship and still have issues with your ex. You aren't over him yet and need to forgive and let go. Not everyone wants the same things you do or at the same time. We need to slow things down until you get this sorted out." I was about to tell him he didn't understand Wynn and me, but he wasn't finished. "Oh, and this church thing, well, I need my son to have a community. Do you know anything about raising a Black boy in America?"

And when I didn't say anything, not out of spite this time, but because I didn't have an answer, he circled around the kitchen island, pulled Oliver out of his chair, and left. I followed him with Mare in my arms. She cried, and Oliver followed suit. The living room was a chorus of wailing babies.

"Where are you going?" I shouted over them.

"I'm leaving. I don't do silent treatments, Jared."

My cheeks burned hot, and my forehead pounded from last night's wine.

"We can give him community. Oliver will have a sister and two dads instead of just one. You need to get over all your silly rules because you're scared to get close."

"This isn't about moving in," he said. "You just don't get it, do you? I don't have the energy to teach you." He slapped the wall, making the newly hung photos of Mare vibrate. The babies cried even harder. "Do you read the news?" he asked. "Do you know Black boys are getting shot by police and crazy neighbors daily in this country?"

"What the hell does this have to do with Oliver and going to church?"

"The fact that you're even asking this question is telling," he said.

"Churches are homophobic. Is that why you don't want me there?"

"No, Jared." He sighed. "The church is in Berkeley, and it's super inclusive." He grabbed his bag and opened the door. Oliver banged his fists against Landon's shoulders. "One last question for you," he said. "What are you going to do about your own daughter?"

"What do you mean by that?" I asked.

"How are you going to give her community?" he said slowly, over-articulating each consonant. My pet peeve.

"You're changing the subject," I said, copying his tone and diction.

"No, Jared, this is the same subject. Are you blind? Look at your daughter carefully, and then look at yourself in the mirror."

"I want to talk about this church thing more," I said.

"Well, I don't." The door slammed behind him. I jumped at the sound of it, startled by how it shook the house.

After they left, I tried to feed Mare. She cried and cried and refused to take another bite. I accidentally dropped her spoon, and it landed on my lap. Mushy peas and carrots splattered everywhere, ruining my work outfit. My head felt like it was going to explode. I hurled the spoon at the sink, but it missed and ricocheted off the counter before skipping and clinking across the floor.

Rising from my seat, I leaped over streaks of green mush toward the foyer. I heaved open the front door and yelled at the empty space in the driveway where Landon had parked. "That was Wynn's job!" I screamed. "He was going to help with that part! He was supposed to give her community, and he left us!" With brute force, I beat my fists against my soiled pants and crumpled to the ground.

When Jo arrived, I was in the kitchen, mopping the floor.

She asked about Oliver. I ignored her question and passed her Mare, who had been crying and still hadn't eaten. I then locked myself in the bathroom and sat on the shower floor, hot water scalding me pink like a raw chicken breast. I didn't even care that I was late for work.

In front of the vanity mirror, I commanded my reflection to think positively. Fights happened in every relationship, though Wynn and I had never shouted like that in all our years together. I needed to stop acting like a drama queen and start being rational. I typed next steps on my phone:

- Give Landon some space
- Call him tomorrow
- Apologize to him before accepting his apology

After finishing my list, I imagined us in church together, the four of us dressed in our Sunday best, singing gospel music like in *Sister Act*. In a few days, we would laugh this off. By the end of my pep talk, I couldn't stop thinking about the makeup sex.

When I made it into the office in the afternoon, I received a text from Landon.

> Sorry, I can't do this.
> I thought I could, but I can't.
> We're just too different.

Chapter 23

Wynn
Nairobi, Kenya
Spring 2016

FOR THE NEXT few weeks, Nicole and I avoided the word "sperm." We needed to get "it" screened to make sure "it" was disease-free and viable. And when I finally did get "it" tested—paid for by Nicole—the lab proclaimed "it" free and clear of bugs and germs. And to our luck, there were over eleven million "its" per milliliter. Later, I found out "it" was way below average for my age.

I assumed these medical services were expensive, so I offered to pay Nicole's rent. She refused, reminding me that her furnished house was part of her compensation package. Then one day, I returned home from teaching at the studio and found a stack of white linen boxers neatly folded at the foot of my bed with a note:

These will let the boys breathe.

Love,

Nicole

A pit formed in my stomach: I was owned. I avoided the gift for the next few days until I ran out of clean clothes. I piled my dirty laundry in the hallway's corner, knowing the housekeeper would return it the following day. It arrived the following day, tightly-wrapped in a mesh bag and smelling of lavender. Just one of many ways my life was too comfortable in Nairobi. The boxers slipped on cool and silky against my freshly bathed skin.

Meanwhile, as the days ticked closer to the middle of Nicole's cycle, I justified "my gift" as living proof that my being gay wasn't a genetic error or some evolutionary means to control the world's population but that I, Wynn Kang, was a centrical force meant to help bring life into this world. Was I becoming Jared?

This thinking, this transformation into my ex, spurred me to sit buck naked on the toilet lid of Nicole's guest bathroom, load porn onto the iPad, and tug away into a sterilized jelly jar.

"Come in," said Nicole after I knocked on her bedroom door.

Her head peeked out from her mountain of covers. A foot-high pile of unread *New Yorkers* was stacked on the nightstand. The afternoon sun cast a shadow of the window's iron bars across her duvet. I held the jar up to the sunlight for her to see.

"Yummy, it's all fresh and warm," she said in her Yoda voice.

When I passed it to her, she inspected it as I had.

"Now get out of here," she said. "I need to squirt this up my dried-up old pussy."

On my taxi ride to the studio, the leafy streets of Gigiri whizzed by. Unending rows of towering hedges concealed stately homes and gentleman farms, legacies of the country's colonial history. After a few miles, the blur of lush green seamlessly melded into the crowded and dusty streets of Westlands with its hodgepodge of concrete block buildings and glass-front high-rises. Pastel buses and dust-covered SUVs surrounded me at a traffic standstill.

As usual, I was running a few minutes late for class, which usually bothered me, but punctuality seemed small and unimportant considering what I'd just done. I was now part of something monumental. Something that would result in a little boy or girl. A little boy or girl who might dance like me.

When I arrived, the studio wasn't packed but pleasantly full of regulars—a balanced mix of expats and Kenyans, primarily women of course, but some men, almost everyone in their twenties. Fayyaz spun in his makeshift DJ booth in the corner, already blasting music as my assistant led the warm-up.

Saturday's class was my favorite. It was designed to feel more like a daytime party than dance instruction. We kept the lights dim and the window shades down, and unlike most dance classes where a few counts are taught to a brief excerpt of a single song, I choreographed a routine that could be performed to a rotation of songs curated by Fayyaz. I prohibited questions and side chatter, keeping the momentum and energy level high throughout the hour. While the music blared, I performed the routine in slow-motion. My students watched, then imitated me, gaining sharpness and mastery with each repetition. After about a half-hour, most students memorized the choreography, and I switched on a strobe light. The room's energy buzzed, and in between takes my students hollered, clapped, and whooped—which I permitted as long as they didn't use words. When I turned the overhead lights on at the end of the hour, the students groaned in unison. I cut the music and asked everyone to sit.

"Big announcement," I said as they stretched on the floor. "In light of Prince's tragic death, I'm planning to lead a flash mob in his honor, and I wanted to gauge folks' interest in—"

Hands shot up in the air. Applause echoed throughout the

studio, then a scatter of whistles. Goosebumps burst along my arms. I couldn't have imagined a more enthusiastic reaction, which was almost enough to affirm the tough decisions I'd made over the past year.

Once the room quieted down, I shared the flash mob details. We would hold eight weeks of rehearsals every Saturday to prepare for a ten-minute performance. Given the level of interest, I considered holding off on the location but couldn't help myself. I said, "I'm hoping we will perform someplace with historical significance. Like Uhuru Gardens Memorial Park." Fayyaz shot me a look from his booth as if to say *don't make promises you can't keep.*

After high-fiving the students as they left, I swept and mopped the studio floor while Fayyaz packed his DJ equipment. When I opened the studio's blinds to reveal the dusk of early evening, I said, "You haven't said anything about my flash mob idea." I hadn't run it by him, hoping that student interest might override any of his concerns.

"Bro, that's some cheesy ass, mzungu shit," he said. He then clapped me on the shoulder. "But if it brings in more customers." His head lolled to one side, making him appear boyish and sweet.

The comment stung. I hated that he'd used that word, *mzungu,* against me. It meant "white foreigner," and though I was technically a foreigner, I wasn't white. Besides, I considered myself somewhat superior, more of a global traveler and citizen.

"Flash mobs are kind of kitschy now," I admitted. "But, it'll be fun. So, are you in for making the music mix?"

"Sure. Which songs are you thinking, man?"

I pretended to mull it over even though I knew exactly what I wanted. "'When Doves Cry,' 'Thieves in the Temple,' 'Kiss,' definitely 'Raspberry Beret.'"

"What?" asked Fayyaz. "No 'Little Red Corvette' or 'Purple Rain'?"

"They're cliché," I said.

"—Says the mzungu, who wants to throw a Prince-themed flash mob. And what are you going to do about permits?"

"Permits?" I asked. "The whole point of a flash mob is to be spontaneous."

"Dude, this isn't America. Life here isn't a Lionel Ritchie music video. You can't just blast music and dance in the streets. It might be easier to do it in a mall, like Two Rivers, or even Westgate, since the management there probably wants to bring cheer to that place."

I didn't want to put in all the work required to have the results showcased in a mall best known for a bloody terrorist attack. "No, let's do it someplace outdoors and in public. How do you suppose we get a permit?"

"I'll tell you what, my cousin knows people. He's an event planner and has the numbers of everyone in the Ministry. I'll have him get it for us."

"That would be great, thanks," I said. My face started to flush. Here he was, this quirky, funny, and talented guy standing right before me, my biggest supporter and fan. Why hadn't I seen it before—the undeniable tension between us?

"Hey man, I'd do anything for you." He touched my shoulder, and I took it as an overt signal. I hadn't been touched in so long. So, I gazed into his eyes and leaned in. Whiskers from his soft beard grazed my chin.

"Whoa, what are you doing, boy?" His hand moved to my throat, about to choke me, before pushing me away. "I'm not like that. What would give you that impression?"

"I don't know. I am so sorry." I took a step back, feeling dizzy. How had I miscalculated his interest? It didn't make any sense, the facts didn't add up, and I no longer trusted myself.

"You're thirty-two and live at home. You don't have a girlfriend. You never mention girls. I thought maybe—"

"Well, you thought wrong." He lifted his laptop case and portable speaker by their handles and scurried toward the door.

I called his name. "Can we forget this ever happened?"

At the studio's exit, he turned around. "You're not in San Francisco anymore, bro. You better watch out."

Chapter 24

Jared
New York, NY
Spring 2016

"THIS MOVE WILL be good for you," said Nigel, his cockney accent singing into my earbuds. "New York will get you closer to your true calling."

I liked the sound of this and happily RevPayed him his fee. Because we talked weekly, he'd given me a "frequent flyer" discount, so it wasn't like I was handing over my life savings. Besides, there had been a lot of upheaval in my life. First, the breakup with Landon, then Mare, who was teething, and finally, this new role that entailed moving to the East Coast. I needed support.

Before my psychic consultation, I had already leaned toward taking the new job within the Reverie Corporation since there wasn't anything left for me in San Francisco. I would miss the temperate climate and coastline, but who had time to enjoy it? Besides, my priorities had changed, and my focus was on raising my daughter and advancing my career. More importantly, if I lived in New York, Mare could spend more time with Grandma

Lois, which might give me some much-needed free time.

The Reverie corporate machine took over as soon as I agreed to the new job. A real estate team sold the house the same day they listed it. They immediately secured me a three-bedroom rental on the Upper West Side, a ten-minute subway commute from the company's offices in Chelsea. My lawyer then talked to Wynn, and she struck a deal with little fanfare or drama. We split the house fifty-fifty, which was more than fair. His inheritance had covered the down payment, but he abandoned me at the worst possible moment. And you know, it was funny because I barely even thought about Wynn anymore. No part of me wanted him back. It was as if Landon had cured me of Wynn, and both had cured me of men. Not that I was no longer attracted to men, because I was. But I no longer felt the pull to be in a relationship. Whenever I tried to think about dating again, I realized I was dead inside.

The upside of switching coasts and taking the new job was that I no longer had time to ruminate on Landon. Whenever he did creep back into my mind, I usually remembered his lively, baritone voice, the broad smile, and the pair of beautiful hands with thick veins that meandered up his wrists and into his muscular forearms. But mostly, I missed talking to Landon every day and the little things: waking up together, negotiating who got the shower first while the other checked on the babies, and the chaste kiss before bed. Of course, I also missed little Oliver, his chubby cheeks, and how he drooled bubbles all over his Thomas the Train bib.

I was 0-2 in the relationship department. I should've probably reflected on what I had done wrong or learned from it, or whatever. Newsflash: I could be controlling. I liked things the way I liked them. Of course, I should've probably educated myself on interracial adoption for Mare's sake and learned how to be a better parent to a child of color. I even considered texting Wynn and asking for his advice. Maybe I needed a parenting book? Maybe I also needed a book on how to date men of color? Better yet, I needed a book explaining why I was primarily attracted to non-white men. Would I have had any of these problems if I had dated my clone? I didn't know why I was this way, but I suspected it would be my downfall. If put on the spot, I imagined that part of me wanted to be them, to fuse our identities together so we could set ourselves apart and confirm our "specialness." Or that I had always wanted to be "cool," even though I wasn't and never would be, and dating "cool" might be the closest I would ever get to it. Thinking about this, let alone talking about dating anyone, made me anxious. The last thing I needed was another person accusing me of being racist.

None of this analysis-paralysis would bring Landon and Oliver back. I'd already asked, and London had ignored my texts. A lingering question kept me up at night: why didn't either of these men want to work it out with me? Wynn had run away. He didn't want to do the work. Now Landon had stormed off and ghosted me, just like his predecessor. What was wrong with me? Was I that unfixable? These questions made my head spin, and I couldn't be a good single dad and do my job without my head on straight, which was why I should probably avoid introspection. As I mentioned, I had my priorities: Mare and my career. In that order.

Within a few weeks of accepting the position, I sat in my new corner office with floor-to-ceiling windows overlooking the West Side Highway and the Hudson River. And unlike my workday in San Francisco, where my schedule was packed with back-to-backs, I woke up to an almost empty calendar. The former Director of Ad Sales, who'd been slated to transfer to London, had decided at the last minute to keep his job. Since I had already been relocated, the higher-ups promised me a new department in a top-secret, not yet launched division dubbed Reverie XTE. Feeling stuck in limbo and without a role was unnerving, but I was still getting paid. I tried to make the most of my downtime until they were ready to move me.

So I tried to enjoy my corner office. I stared out the window for hours, and periodically checked in with the nanny or Lois, who babysat once a week. Even Jenny had offered to babysit, and I hadn't decided if it was a good idea since she had just left rehab again. I didn't want to stress her out, nor did I need the help. I checked off most of the tasks on my to-do list: arranged the nanny's schedule, spoke to Nigel, and even scheduled my annual checkup. Everything in my life seemed under control, and I could finally take a breath for the first time in ages.

Which really meant I wasn't only depressed but also really bored. Bored of rehashing the past and looking for answers that would never emerge. Bored of walking the High Line with its tiny plants and swarms of European tourists, bored of calling and texting the nanny to check if Mare had pooped, bored of the sparkling Hudson River and the growing skyline of New Jersey. Bored of photographing images and uploading them to RevSo. I was bored and randy and could no longer deny it. A tingling in my crotch pushed me to download the app, the one with all the squares, telling you which horny man was standing outside the door. I groped the outside of my fly.

My erection poked through selvedge jeans. This past weekend, my now-sober sister, needing something to do, had taken me shopping and pushed me to buy an entirely new wardrobe. Jenny insisted I replace all my khakis and polo shirts with slim-cut designer jeans and bespoke Oxford shirts, and I agreed. New York was not San Francisco, and my old uniform made me feel like a suburban tourist. But I was done thinking about clothes. What I really wanted was to grope clammy skin, for a man to grunt and pant hot breath into my neck. Something messy beckoned. Something transactional with a stranger, where we met each other's needs, no names exchanged, then immediately went our separate ways because we both knew that relationships were the messiest encounters, expectations that ultimately led to disappointment. May I make a toast to the Wynns and the Landons of the world who were more trouble than they were worth?

Messages popped up on my phone screen, after which I discarded them. None of them matched what I was looking for, not that I knew what I wanted exactly. Then I read a message from a young couple, both early twenties, NYU students looking for a third. They wrote, *wassup?* I kept calm and wrote back, *I'm good. It's very nice to meet you both.* They could be brothers if they weren't of different ethnicities. Both wore their dark wavy hair floppy in front and tight across the sides and back. I zoomed into the photo. The more Latino-looking one had a beauty mark below his eye. At the same time, the white one revealed a touch of vitiligo in the shape of some mysterious island on the side of his neck. I decided they were too young and was about to move on when they said I was the hottest guy they'd seen on the app in a long time.

Flattery will get you everywhere, I typed. And then I thought, how much longer would guys this young find me attractive? Last month, in the shower, I found my first gray pubic hair. They asked if they could come over and play, and I wrote back, *How about I come to you?* And just like that, I was tired of being good and being me. NYU_hungry_ twinks texted a location pin to their apartment. I told the receptionist that I had to step out for an emergency dental appointment and headed toward the elevators, passing the snack and espresso bar, the pool table, the video game room, the music practice room, and the kombucha keg next to the elevator bank. A short cab ride later, I stood before a white brick building at Union Square. I had a bad feeling about heading upstairs and considered turning back. What was I thinking? This was so unlike me, and it was also unsafe. What if they were kidnappers or worse—cannibal murderers catfishing as college boys? I pulled out my phone to text them that something had come up with work when I saw their message.

we see u.

I looked up, and a hand waved out an open window. They buzzed me in, and the door was already cracked open when I reached their apartment. The tiny living room was empty except for a half-deflated air mattress, an empty pizza box, and a few textbooks scattered on the parquet floor.

"Come in," a voice beckoned from an open door. The two almost identical young men were lying on their sides on the bed. Their matching white briefs hugged their pert backsides, and their slim legs braided each other. They kissed as if I wasn't in the room observing them. Though it was undoubtedly a performance, I didn't think I had ever witnessed anything more beautiful. They were straight out of mythology, like young centaurs wrestling in a nest of sheets.

"You started without me," I mumbled. Unbuttoning my shirt, I took a whiff of the room, which smelled of warm bodies, deodorant, and fabric softener.

"We're working from home today," the Latin one said.

"I thought you were students?"

"We have internships we need to finish before we graduate," the white one said, his eyes a bit glassy. I wondered if he was stoned. I hung my shirt neatly on the back of the desk chair. The young men pawed at me and unbuckled my belt. My jeans fell, then my boxer briefs. I kissed the darker one, then the fairer one with vitiligo, attempting to pay equal attention to both so no one felt left out. Soon I found myself counting backward from twenty with each one, then losing focus and starting again. They gradually stopped alternating with me before making out only with each other. I watched them intently before kissing the delicate crevice between their shoulder blades. Again, for

214

equity's sake, I kissed the second set longer to make up for choosing the other one first.

"I love you," one said. I was initially taken aback until I realized he wasn't talking to me.

"I love you, too," the other replied. They kissed passionately. I felt like an interloper and wilted in their hands. Eventually, I suggested we return to the bed so they could sit back and relax while I took care of them. Minutes later, I said in a high-pitched voice, "All done." It was the voice I used with Mare after she swallowed her last bite. I totally creeped myself out. Using a crumpled T-shirt from the floor, I cleaned them up and said, "Thank you for a lovely afternoon. I should get back to work."

"Yeah, it was hot," they said in flat unison.

"I'll be less nervous next time," I said. "I usually don't do this type of thing."

"No worries," said one.

"These things happen with guys your age," said the other.

Later that evening, when in bed, a series of messages lit up my phone. One contained a link from NYU_hungry_twinks.

I hope u don't mind.

It was a fourteen-second video of me sitting in a desk chair. The camera shot me from behind. All I could see was my bald spot magnified. The breathing and moans sounded effeminate and fake. I turned up the volume and realized they were coming from me.

Delete this, please. I beg you, I never said this was okay. I never consented to this. I felt sick, but I also thought, *Chillout, no one can see your face.* Hastily, I deleted the app and swore off all men: no more relationships or sex. I leaped out of bed and checked on

215

Mare, who was sound asleep, her bow-shaped upper lip curled, exposing a baby tooth's nub. The hall light illuminated her face just enough so that I could count her lashes. "If it wasn't for you," I whispered, "I don't know what I would do."

Chapter 25

Wynn
Nairobi, Kenya
Summer 2016

ON THE HOTTEST day of the year, I hid behind a bush in Uhuru Gardens Memorial Park wearing a purple crushed velvet blazer and a ruffled shirt. Sweat dripped down the front of my curly mullet wig into my mouth. My makeup had taken two hours, so I didn't dare wipe it away. Sweat and face powder seeped into my eyes. I aggressively blinked to flush it out. With blurred vision, I somehow tapped out a group text to my forty students in their cars, waiting in a nearby parking lot for their cue.

Any minute now. Stay put, please.

Fayyaz should have made an appearance already, rolling a giant battery-powered speaker strapped to a dolly behind him. This would've cued my dancers to march in formation from the parking lot to the memorial. But that was over an hour ago, so we all waited with nothing to do, dressed in Prince-inspired costumes representing varying stages of his career.

Like me, most of the dancers chose the early years: cheetah-print bodysuits, ruffles, chunky crosses hanging off chains, and tight bell-bottom pants. The remaining performers donned costumes from later in his career—tilted hats, oversized jackets with mandarin collars, and skin-tight turtlenecks. I thought we looked pretty amazing.

Once my vision cleared, I peeked over the hedge again, looking for Fayyaz. Yet, all I could see was a sprinkling of tourists milling about the memorial, a miniaturized, Eiffel Tower-like structure with a pair of giant praying hands at the base. A flurry of texts buzzed, interrupting my search. The dancers, bored with sitting in their cars, announced they were coming out. *No, no, no,* I furiously texted with both thumbs. *Please, wait a little longer.* What was the rush? I was the one sweating my balls off, crouching behind a bush like some pervert while they waited in the comfort of their air-conditioned cars.

No one listened. They trickled in, their garish outfits wearing them. Some took selfies, others staged photo shoots. Tourists pointed at them, some even asking to take selfies with the impersonators. We were supposed to enter in a V formation in tight rows, myself at the front tip, just like an old "I'd Like to Buy the World a Coke" commercial I'd found on RevTube.

A tourist within earshot asked one of the dancers about the occasion. She replied, "We're here for a Prince-themed flash mob, but the DJ's late, so we're just waiting around."

Facepalm. Flash mobs were supposed to be a surprise, hence the word "flash," but what could I do? I was hiding in the bushes. A voice chirped, "Where's Wynn?" My phone vibrated with another slew of texts from students asking for me and Fayyaz and what they should do next. Fayyaz finally wrote back.

Sorry on Kenya time. lololololol.
Just a few minutes, man.
Traffic is freaking horrible.

I wrote back.

Kenya time was an hour ago.

For a few weeks, things had been very awkward after the attempted kiss. Due to the intense planning and coordination required for our event, we had recently found our way back to an equilibrium. I had invested hundreds of hours into this precise moment: the choreography, the rehearsals, the costumes, the medley mix. And this wasn't even counting the money I had to pony up to cover the permit so we could use the grounds by the monument. I had penned the application myself, describing the event as a celebration of decolonization, a tribute to a recently deceased, Black-American cultural icon intersecting with the Black-African Independence Movement. A sociology degree from a liberal arts college plus a decade in brand and management consulting had made me an expert in bullshittery.

The sun lowered before my eyes, cooling the air, making it almost bearable. Shade covered the steps leading up to the monument itself. The idea was to kick the flash mob off at sunset so that the closing number, "I Would Die 4 U," would cast an array of dancing shadows onto the crowd.

What was the point anymore? I should've just gone home. No one was even coming to see me. Nicole was on a safari with her mother, who was visiting. They'd been estranged for years but had put their differences aside once Nicole told her she was trying for a baby. Soon after they made amends, her mother, who'd recently retired from the military in North Carolina, booked an impromptu trip. While Nicole wasn't pregnant, she and her mother had spent the last week shopping for baby clothes and furniture before leaving for the Serengeti.

When I checked my makeup on my phone's camera, I was heartbroken to see eyeliner and eyebrow pencil streaked vertically down my face. I closed the app. The sun dipped into the horizon, and the crowd of tourists had thinned. Just as I was about to text the group to call the whole thing off, Fayyaz rolled in, dragging the speaker on wheels, a sheepish grin wiped across his handsome face. My heart lifted, and I shot out of the bushes to greet him.

"Sorry, man, I suck," he said.

I sprinted toward the largest cluster of Princes and announced the show was still on and to hurry up and get into position.

When the bouncy disco intro of "I Wanna Be Your Lover" played, my stomach lurched, and a surge of adrenaline coursed through me. *Showtime.* I swaggered to the performance area, stopping front and center across from the sparse audience while the other dancers followed. When Prince howled in falsetto, I bounced on the balls of my feet before strutting across the stage, gesturing the audience to move closer and clap along. My students buzzed from behind, their energy feeding me. After the next wave of dancers joined me from the sides, muscle memory took over, and I spun with exacting velocity and performed the routine of my design.

Just as I was about to perform my second half-split, the music cut. Thinking it was a temporary malfunction, I continued with the routine until the other performers exited the stage, and I was alone. Over my shoulder, Fayyaz argued with a policeman.

"What's going on here?" I asked, short of breath, sweat and makeup dripping down my face. The rheumy-eyed cop shouted in a mix of Swahili and English. Fayyaz gazed pleadingly back at him, holding wads of crumpled permit papers as an offering.

"You do not have the right permit. This is a noise permit. You are required to have a secondary permit for a public event," said the policeman in English.

"We paid for that already, right?" I said, looking at Fayyaz.

"I did pay for it. The clerk never gave me that sheet of paper," he said.

I turned around to look for my students. They sat on the steps, smoking or gazing into their phones which glowed in the early dusk. As the leader, I had to fix this, but I didn't know what to do. My temper flared. I pulled my wallet out of my pocket and opened it, flashing a thick stack of bills.

"Is this what you want? Some kitu kidogo?"

Fayyaz grabbed my wallet and said, "What are you doing?"

"Do you know I can send both of you to jail for bribery?" The policeman bared his teeth.

I took a step back. I was a little scared but decided to call his bluff. "Try me. My best friend works at the US Embassy. Maybe I should call her now?"

"No need." The policeman spat on the ground. A yellow wad landed next to my patent leather shoe. He called the group, "All of you need to go home. The park is closed now."

"What? This is unfair. This is unjust," I said, my fists punching the air above me.

"I'm unjust? You should be ashamed of yourself," the policeman said, pointing to the monument. "Hosting your silly dance party in front of our national symbol of freedom. Look at those hands and that dove. Thousands of Kenyans died for this. You make a mockery of it for the benefit of your RevTube or RevSocial, whatever."

He was right. I hadn't noticed the dove perched on top of the hands before.

The officer then asked, "How long have you lived here? Two weeks, a few months, maybe a year? You probably don't know more than a few words of Kiswahili." Perspiration spread through the front of his crisp blue shirt.

After he left, Fayyaz hurled my wallet at my chest. "You trying to get us thrown in jail?" he asked. "If you ever do that again, I will beat the shit out of you, faggot. Oh, and you're fired."

Ignoring him, I walked off to make a few calls.

After I arrived home, I immediately drank half a bottle of vodka and passed out in bed. I woke up the following morning in a hungover stupor, hoping it was all a bad dream. I didn't even remember how I'd gotten home. Later, when Nicole and her mother returned from their trip, I pulled the covers over myself and tried to sleep more, hoping I'd wake up a different person. Within a few minutes, I heard a knock at my door.

"I'm sick, don't come in," I said.

Nicole barged in and slammed the door behind her. "Should I call the doctor?" she asked with a sharp bite in her voice.

"I was trained as a medic in the army," Mrs. Bradley chirped through the door.

"No, Mom, he's fine. Crazy, but fine," said Nicole. "I don't think modern medicine has found a cure for narcissistic personality disorder."

I didn't move under the covers. I was too ashamed and hoped that if I played dead long enough, it might happen.

"I know you can hear me under there. My mom is going to Lamu on her own tomorrow. When I get home from work, we need to talk."

By the following evening, I'd written out and practiced an apology. When I heard the garage door open, I trudged down the hallway and stairs to meet Nicole, typing away on her laptop in the dining room. She glanced up at me, then frowned before clamping her computer shut.

"How are you feeling?" she asked flatly.

"Much better, must've been a forty-eight-hour bug or something—"

"So, I don't appreciate you calling the embassy and using my name to file a complaint with the Legal Affairs Department. Do you know how bad that makes me look? My roommate, calling the emergency line at the embassy to complain about his little dance show getting shut down?"

I scratched my head. "I was upset. The officer totally made up some permit we didn't need."

"Oh, you don't have to tell me the entire story. I heard it already since they recorded your call and played it over the phone while I was on safari. We left our trip a day early. Or are you so self-involved that you didn't even notice?"

"What I did was really shitty," I said. "I'm sorry."

"Why, though? What were you thinking?"

"I don't know. I was upset. It might have seemed like a silly event, but it meant a lot to me. Maybe too much," I said. "Do you want me to leave? Because I would if I had anywhere to go. I don't have anyone else."

"Oh, spare me," said Nicole. Her hand clutched some of her hair by the root, and she tugged twice. "Forget about Al Qaeda and the refugee crisis. Wynn Kang and his expat friends didn't get to perform their dance."

"I can go pack now," I said.

"No, don't go. I would never kick you out." Her voice softened. "But you do need to find a new place in a few months. I wasn't going to tell you until it was final, but I'm moving to Addis at the end of the year. I put in for a transfer a few weeks ago and found out today it went through."

"Addis? As in Addis Ababa in Ethiopia? But you love Nairobi."

She looked down at the table. "I need to live in Ethiopia for a few months if I'm going to adopt there."

"Adopt? What about the turkey baster?"

"Just got back my gyno results. My tubes are fried."

I had to sit down. When I pulled out the chair beside her,

she flinched as if I repulsed her.

"What about surgery?" I asked.

"I can do surgery for the fibroids, but it won't help with the amount of scar tissue I have. Between that and the fact that you're shooting blanks, my chances for a successful pregnancy are slim to none," she said, rubbing her scalp before putting on a fake smile. "So, it turns out I can't be a reproductive narcissist like your ex. Hey, wait. Hey?" She moved to the seat next to me and grabbed my arm. "I thought you'd be relieved."

"I'm not." My elbows rested on the tabletop, and my hands shaded my face. I was floored. I'd already pinned my hopes on this dancing child.

I reached across the table and clutched her hand. "What if I came to Ethiopia and helped you with the baby?"

Nicole snorted. "You're joking, right?"

I squeezed her hand twice and looked her straight in the eye. "I'm totally serious."

"My mom has already offered."

"But you guys don't get along," I said.

Nicole pulled her hand away. "Can we be real?" she said. "That is *not* your thing. You don't cook or clean. You haven't gone grocery shopping once since you've been here. And might I add, you dumped your partner right before—"

"But I give it three more weeks until you and your mom . . ." I trailed off, unwilling to finish the thought.

Nicole stood up and said, "Yes, but at least she's useful." She breezed out of the dining room, her laptop under her arm.

Chapter 26

Jared
New York, NY
Summer 2016

I HAD NIGEL on automatic bill pay. We spoke daily. The NYU video had pushed me over the edge, and nothing he said placated or comforted me.

"The cards tell me it's just a small bump in the road. You are only obsessing because work is slow." He sighed in frustration when I asked for the umpteenth time if they were going to fire me since I still wasn't staffed. "Probably not, but as I've told you many times before, why not find something new? Maybe a career you're more passionate about? You know, Meryl won't require all of your attention forever."

"What can I do?" I asked. "All I know is digital advertising, and it's about as exciting as it sounds." I hated the sound of my voice right then. There was nothing more unattractive than hearing a grown man whine.

"Have you thought about opening your own business?" he asked. This was something new. Nigel continued, "I see you outside of the city, working from home in the future. I see a kidney-shaped swimming pool, a circular driveway, and a house with lots of space for entertaining."

I admitted that a big house did sound appealing since I'd only been in Manhattan for a few weeks and already hated it: rats the size of small dogs, the crowds, the subway's screeching wheels, and the whole living on top of each other thing. I especially hated that Mare and I had to take an elevator down fourteen floors to go outside and play in the park.

Call waiting beeped, and Nigel said, "Oh, my next appointment is trying to get through. I have to run. Cheers!"

After he hung up, I didn't have the luxury of feeling sorry for myself because I had to go to work. I bid my goodbyes to Mare and the French au pair and started the sixty-three-block commute to the office. The stroll downtown was especially lovely, the first spring-like day of the year. A gentle breeze caressed my cheeks, and the hazy sunshine warmed my neck. The hour-long walk underneath blue skies cleared my head, and I felt almost normal when I reached the office. I even smiled at the new receptionist on the way in.

As soon as I sat down and booted up my computer, I heard a brisk knock at the door. The Senior VP of Human Resources, Emily, a prim woman with an icy-blonde pixie cut, poked her head in and asked, "Can we talk?" When the door opened, a nebbishy man with close-set eyes followed her in and shut the door. I assumed they were there to tell me my new assignment, so I welcomed them, sat up straight, and smoothed the front of my new linen shirt. They sat, and Emily said, "This is Daniel Corbett, our new Chief Legal Counsel." We shook hands. I wasn't expecting anyone from legal.

"What is this about?" I asked.

Neither of them answered my question. Emily propped a tablet on my desk. On the screen, a video played an image of a bald spot amid a thatch of wavy blonde hair. My hair. She turned up the volume, and I heard myself moaning. I shut my eyes. "Do you know that the men who made this video were interns at Reverie?" asked Daniel.

"They work here?" I popped out of my chair and knocked over the tablet.

"Please sit down, Mr. Cahill," he said. "They don't work here anymore. According to our records, they finished their internships the day after you startedm at this location."

"I suspected you might not be acquainted," said Emily.

At least she was giving me the benefit of the doubt. My first day in the New York office had been a whirlwind. During my tour, I had met all fifty or so executive staff—shook their hands at a special lunch in my honor. Emily had briefly introduced me to everyone else—the underlings—in large groups. They sat motionless at their workstations like cattle. I said hello and goodbye in the same sentence before being shuttled off to more important meetings.

"This is bad," Daniel said to Emily as if I were no longer in the room.

"I just said I didn't know they were interns," I said. "This is only a small misunderstanding."

"This is a huge liability for the company," said Emily. "The young men in question were quite disappointed they weren't offered full-time jobs and are threatening to sue."

"And now I'm being blackmailed," I said.

"No, you aren't being blackmailed. The company is," said the attorney.

"We highly recommend you do not reach out to them," added Emily.

"I won't, but what does all of this mean?" I asked. "I hope you'll see my side of things. I've given my life to this company, and I would never do anything to jeopardize my standing."

"We understand and have already discussed this situation at some length, and frankly we think it is best if you transition," Daniel said. Emily slid a thick manila envelope across my desk.

I opened it to find a nondisclosure agreement on top.

"As you can see," he said, "it is a very generous package. You get to keep your Reverie stock options, one year's salary, your estimated annual bonus pro-rated, and even your health benefits for six months."

"You're firing me? I moved across the country for this job," I said.

"No, Jared," said Emily. "We're helping you transition."

"You're making me sign an NDA. You're offering a severance package. It sounds like I'm being fired," I said, snot dripping onto my lips.

Emily handed me a tissue, but I batted it away. I used my shirt cuff, which somehow seemed more manly. I sniffed up the rest, which trickled down my throat.

"Just so you're aware," said Daniel, "these papers weren't drawn up today. They've been in process for a few weeks. Management wants to go in a new direction for Reverie XTE. They're bringing someone in from the outside. They want fresh blood."

The word "fresh" punched me in the gut. As if I'd gone stale, like old bread. I told them I wanted my lawyer to read it over.

"Just leave your computer and work phone. We won't call security if you leave quietly and professionally. You can get your personal belongings another time."

"Security? And you're not firing me? This company is so full of crap. You're so full of crap."

"We'll be in touch with your lawyer," Emily said coolly.

I grabbed my jacket and rushed out of the office, taking a different route so I didn't run into as many people—past the pool table, the newly installed cereal bar, and the row of flat-screen TVs, around the corner to the elevator bank.

Outside, a rush of warm air hit my tear-soaked face. My skin tingled. I immediately called Nigel and told his voicemail that he was a charlatan and a liar. And then I was alone, completely lost on an Eighth Avenue sidewalk.

Chapter 27

Wynn
Nairobi, Kenya
Summer 2016

NOT ONLY DID I take a taxi to six different grocery stores to find Nicole's favorite brand and flavor, Haagen Dazs Black Cherry Amaretto, but I tidied the kitchen, ordered Indian takeout, and stocked enough groceries to last a month. When Nicole returned from the office and entered the dining room—food plated, candles lit—she jumped up and down and clapped her hands, her gold hoops dancing in her curls.

After dinner, I showed her the two pints in the freezer, and she said, "Winnie, where did you find it? Tuskys and Shoprite have been out for months."

We ate straight from the carton and perused profiles of expecting mothers on an Ethiopian adoption website.

"I have to get started on this now," she said. "There are rumors they're going to ban foreign adoption." She scraped the bottom of the pint and held up a liquid spoonful in the air. "You want it?"

"No, it's your favorite," I said. "Kill it."

"You know, you can always join me in Addis. It'll be a full house between my mom and the baby, but we'll make it work."

"Thanks, but I need to go home for a while," I said.

"Back to San Francisco?"

"I'm thinking New York. I've been dying to take these Alvin Ailey Extension classes."

"And this has nothing to do with Jared living there?"

I laughed nervously. "Wait, how did you know that?"

"He only announced it three times on RevSo," said Nicole.

I cleared the table without saying more. We moved to the patio to sip wine and watch the red sun dip into the violet- and orange-swirled horizon. Nicole lit a cigarette, and before I could complain, she said, "I'm going to quit once the adoption—"

"Give me a drag," I said.

"What? No?"

I pulled the cigarette out of her hand, pinching it between my thumb and index finger. My mouth wrapped around the lipstick-stained paper and sucked hard until I choked. I hacked into the crook of my arm and gagged. "This shit is so gross."

Nicole laughed. "You're getting kind of reckless. Smoking, moving to New York City. I'm excited to see the next version of you." She took back her cigarette and blew three elegant smoke rings in a row.

My head floated from the nicotine, lowering my inhibitions. Peering into the darkness, I said, "I booked an early flight to JFK for tomorrow morning."

"What?" A speck of ash landed on her chin. "Why the rush?"

I rubbed the ash off with my thumb. "We both know I've stayed too long," I said. "I no longer have the teaching job, so it's time."

"To get back together with your ex."

"No; maybe," I said. "But fair enough."

She scraped the cigarette's cherry on the patio's cement and asked, "Do you think he's going to take you back?"

"No," I said. "He has a new boyfriend. I'm just hoping we can be friends or, at least, try."

"If you say so," she said, sounding skeptical.

"What?" I laughed. "God, I can never pull a fast one on you, can I?"

"I know you too well." She smiled wide. The outside edges of her eyes crinkled, and I didn't think I'd ever seen her look more beautiful. "This is good, Winnie," she put her arm around me and pulled me close. Her breath smelled like tobacco and sweet cherries. "You really could be a great dad. Parenthood is a chance to heal your childhood. You don't have to be anything like your parents."

"My parents weren't bad," my voice croaked. "I would do anything to have them back."

"Of course, they loved you and you them. But your mom was an overeducated housewife who managed you like a Fortune 500 company—not that different from how Jared treated you, for the record. And your dad, well, he was checked out. You're afraid of becoming them. But you won't. I know you will love that baby girl. You'll learn from their mistakes."

"Oh, Nicole." I started tearing up. "Fuck! You got me all emotional over here. Why do you always have to be right?"

"Who knew the Freud class I hated junior year would be useful?"

We hugged, and I squeezed like my life depended on it before burying my face into her neck. "Thanks for everything. I mean it. I don't know what I would've done without you. And I'm sorry I acted like an entitled, neocolonial asshole and got you in trouble at work."

"Apology accepted." She was crying now too. A clear booger peeked out of one of her nostrils. I wiped it with the corner of my sweatshirt sleeve. "You see! You're going to be a great dad."

I wiped my tears with the same sleeve before asking, "Now, can I give you some fatherly advice?"

"Maybe." She looked away from me.

"Can you please stop dating unavailable men?"

"But I'm so good at it." She turned back to me, fluttering her eyelashes, which were now clumpy from crying. "I haven't finished with you, though. There's also nothing wrong with being a househusband, by the way. Why were you so freaked out by it? It's more than a little misogynistic, no? Work that has been traditionally seen as women's work is still work."

"I know, you're right. Nicole knows best!" I said sarcastically. She *was* right, and I was also too tired to argue.

She smiled again, and the crinkles returned. "I love you, Winnie."

"Love you, too."

Nicole kissed my forehead before announcing that she was tired. We hugged, and right before she slid open the patio door, she said, "Fly safe. Text me when you land in New York."

For the next few hours, I packed. I was worried about oversleeping and missing my flight, so I stayed up and did what I'd put off. I wrote a long email to the Managing Partner of Synergy Consulting's New York office, asking for a job, any job. When I pushed send, a lump as sharp as a splintered chicken bone formed in my throat. I wasn't looking forward to sitting in a cubicle, spending the rest of my days typing and clicking on a computer, doing meaningless "make-work" for corporate America. Still, it was a small price to pay to make amends for all my wrongdoings. Besides, didn't most people hate their jobs? My father hadn't, but he had also been fortunate enough to have a talent that the marketplace rewarded. For one reason or another, I had not been blessed in the same way. The market never ceased to hold my passion accountable, reminding me that I would have to use my own resources to keep it alive. With my credit card in hand and the click of a touchpad, I booked a closet-sized studio on Airbnb, a few blocks away from The Ailey Studios near Lincoln Center.

Afterward, I logged into the investment account where I'd stashed the money I'd gotten from my share of the house. It didn't feel like it belonged to just me anymore, so I opened a 529 college account in Nicole's name and transferred a large sum. I jotted down the account number, login, and password on a blank sheet of paper. Below the account information, I scribbled a note to her future child:

> Dear Best-Loved and Most
> Wanted Child,
>
> I haven't met you yet, but I love
> you already. Study hard and be
> good to Mommy. She loves you
> more than you can possibly know.
> This little gift is so you can follow
> your heart's dreams. The world
> awaits.
>
> Love always,
>
> Uncle Winnie

I folded the note and taped it to her door.

To fight an oncoming wave of drowsiness, I turned on all the lights and blasted hip-hop through my headphones. I thrashed without caring about form or choreography. When I got tired, I pulled off my sweaty clothes and sat naked in a lotus position. My skin glistened, my chest heaved. All I could hear was my heart pounding.

Nicole was right. I'd become someone different. Someone trustworthy and dependable—the type of person who did right by his best friend and her child. By his *own* child. Someone who accepted his reality. Someone who begged for his old job back.

Hanging my head in the space between my crossed legs, I prayed for the first time in my life. Prayed that fate would be merciful.

And though I was despondent about giving up my dream, I was also relieved. Relieved to put others first, whether it be Mare, Nicole, her soon-to-be adopted child, Jared, or someone new if he didn't take me back. Wasn't this what adulthood was about? Live for others; work a soul-sucking job to support others, all while trying to sneak in a tidbit of personal joy, whether it be a weekend dance class or a pint of ice cream to get through the long days?

More than anything, I wanted a life, and more specifically, my old life. What had seemed overly practical and mundane— private health insurance, an 8-to-8 job, my own home—now all seemed pretty enticing.

And sure, Jared drove me nuts. He wasn't my dream man, and sure, he had his blind spots but didn't I, as well? Ultimately, he was a good man who had been devoted to me once upon a time. Not only had he loved me once, but I was also falling in love with his baby, and soon, she might love me one day. There was also his oniony scent and the hugs; I yearned for it all. Besides, there was nothing wrong with a man with a good job.

I surrendered. Jared had been right all along: capitalism and the free market had won. The Chinese, Russians, and Eastern Europeans had all figured it out. Only the Cubans and my distant cousins in North Korea were left behind and look how they turned out. Now that I was finally ready to raise my white flag, one question lingered: would he take me back? I didn't know, but I, too, had checked Jared's RevSo profile and noticed his tag "In a Relationship with Landon Woodruff" had disappeared. I'd immediately booked the one-way flight, not knowing what I would say when I saw him.

I sat naked for a little longer before deciding to test the waters with a text. I thought I could casually mention a job interview in Manhattan. A little lie, but not really, since I'd just emailed Synergy's New York office about a job. I then thought a text might be too easy for Jared to ignore. And since it was late afternoon in NYC, I hoped to catch him between work meetings.

His phone rang until it sent me to voicemail.

"Hey, this is Wynn," I said, feigning a casualness I didn't feel. "It's been a while since we've talked, and I just wanted to let you know that I'm flying to New York for a job interview. I know you're probably busy, but it would be great to see you and Mare . . ."

Chapter 28

Jared
New York, NY
Summer 2016

I WALKED TOWARD the apartment, but slowly, so slowly that people zigzagged around me, sometimes even bumping into my shoulder or hip. A woman in a pantsuit snickered as she rushed by me. A boy on a skateboard muttered under his breath, "Will you fucking move?" None of it bothered me. I didn't give a crap anymore.

When I strolled past the FIT building, Nigel returned my call, but I no longer wanted to talk to him, so I sent him to voicemail. Texts from him popped up immediately.

> Jared, this is the universe sending you a message.
>
> It's telling you to make a change in your life.
>
> Be more open to the possibilities.
>
> Call me when you're ready.

I deleted the texts and returned the phone to my pocket. I continued to sleepwalk up Eighth Avenue, one foot in front of the other, following the crowd.

It was all too jarring to process. One minute, I was a Senior Director at one of the largest digital advertising departments in the world, and the next, nothing. I had never been without a job. Even in middle school, I'd had a paper route and mowed lawns. Throughout high school, I worked at Baskin Robbins, and in college, I answered phones and filed papers for the school's alumni office. After graduation, I worked at an investment firm in Boston. I started at Reverie as a temp, then a contractor, until they switched me to full-time only four years ago. I'd missed the big IPO and the two landmark stock splits that made many of my colleagues filthy rich. As a result, I had to settle for being "house poor," which also meant hiring an international surrogate—a hostile one, at that—rather than a woman based in California.

Ten years and five title changes and promotions in total. All gone. Poof. And with it, who I was.

With unemployment came the looming issue of money. I had some savings, and if I had to I could cash out my remaining shares. I imagined the right attorney could probably negotiate a better settlement. But who was I without this job? How would I spend my days? At that moment, I decided I needed to let Jo go since I would be home. The thought of spending all day with a toddler made me want to kill myself. Just kidding.

I needed Lois. I needed her to make things better and was about to call but couldn't bring myself to pull her name up on my phone. I needed a story before I faced her—and the rest of the world, for that matter. It was all about the framing, and like HR and legal counsel had said, I wasn't fired. I was transitioning.

I quickened my pace, and by the time I reached Penn Station, I was speed-walking. The ideas came at me fast. Maybe I could freelance, eventually starting my own digital agency or consultancy, tapping the network of Reverie alums I'd met throughout the years? I then realized I could do this from anywhere, and Mare was the first thing that came to mind. She needed her grandmother. I had to move home. I hated to admit that Nigel was right, but we needed more space. We needed a house. It struck me that I'd spent my entire adult life running away from Long Island, only to find myself wishing to be back there, where it was safe, the schools were excellent, and I had family. And if Lois wanted her own salon, I could open one for her, which meant that I might have two businesses: a high-end salon *and* a digital agency. The new Jared was going to be an entrepreneur!

The crosswalk signaled red, and I waited in front of the Hilton Garden Inn for the line of cars to turn right from Forty-Ninth Street onto Eighth Avenue. I looked up and spotted a billboard advertising the revival of *Rent*, which made me think of Wynn. I wondered if he was still dancing. I pulled up his RevSo profile and streamed a video clip of him wearing an awful wig, lacy black leggings, and a purple velvet blazer. The caption read, *Prince dress rehearsal today. So proud of my students.* I chuckled at first, then laughed harder and harder until I couldn't stop. I could barely breathe. The costume was just awful and made Wynn look like an idiot. But wait! Something tugged at my heart. Once I stopped laughing, a lump formed in my throat. I missed him. I missed his stupid dancing. I missed Wynn lecturing about microaggressions and telling me to be more politically correct. I missed his body, where everything was tight and trim and how it was supposed to be. I decided I would call Wynn, but later. I needed to finish designing my new life.

The light changed, and I started running. The exertion brought focus, and I reiterated the plan in my head and then mumbled it aloud: entrepreneurship, Long Island, a McMansion with a circular driveway and kidney-shaped pool, and an SUV. How I couldn't wait to drive an SUV again! The thought excited me so much that I ran faster. Then I got too hot, so there went my jacket. Four hundred dollars of linen slithered to the ground. A woman's voice called out, "Sir, you dropped your blazer." I ignored her and kept running. I really didn't give a shit anymore.

At the next crosswalk, I slowed to a brisk walk and decided to launch my plan on social media. It was all about the framing, and I didn't want anyone to think I'd left the company in any way but by my own accord. I tapped out a typo-filled announcement on RevSo. When a red light forced me to stop walking, I edited and posted it.

> It is with a heavy heart that I
> announce my last day at Reverie.
> Over the past ten years, I've met
> the most incredible bunch of
> people, all committed, gifted,
> and capable. I can't imagine
> working anyplace better, which is
> why I've decided to strike out on
> my own and follow my dream of
> becoming a solo entrepreneur.
> More details to come . . .

I was too sweaty to take an accompanying selfie, but it would have to do. I rebroadcast the same message on a different platform. Then the likes and thumbs-ups rolled in. I felt good. So good that when the light changed, I sprinted again, my arms and legs pumping with all my might. When I passed the Seventy-Second Street subway station, my phone buzzed, and I pulled it out to find a text from an unknown number:

> For a small sum, we can
> drop our complaint with Reverie.

Is this who I think
this is?

How did you get my
number?

Company staff directory

I slowed to a jog. Why would they want money from me when they could get far more from Reverie? A lawsuit took months, sometimes years, and would smear their reputations, undoubtedly affecting future job prospects. My mood switched from elation to rage. Emily from HR had told me not to contact them, but they had contacted me. I couldn't help myself and dialed them. When the line picked up, I ranted about how I didn't need their amnesty. Sure, they could recant their accusation, but I'd already lost my job. They couldn't change anything. They had ruined my reputation, my life. The crosswalk signaled red, but I didn't see any cars so continued speed walking. Everyone in New York jaywalked and besides, I couldn't stop moving.

When I was done screaming, I was greeted by silence until their cackles rang in my ear.

"How dare you laugh? Do you think this is funny? I have a young daughter to support."

"Buddy, watch out!" a voice from behind said, interrupting my train of thought.

When I turned to see who had said it, I found myself in the middle of a busy intersection. The blur of a white bus charged toward me.

Chapter 29

Wynn
San Rafael, CA
Fall 2036

IN ANTICIPATION OF Mare's arrival, I scrubbed and cleaned my tiny house. In truth, it wasn't really a tiny house but actually an old school bus spray-painted matte black and mounted on cement blocks. The previous year, I'd bought it for almost nothing and had it moved to a mobile home community in Marin County designated for low-income working artists fifty-five and over. I literally won a lottery sponsored by the county to distribute affordable housing—and lucky me, I drew a number that entitled me to a lifetime lease on a patch of land overlooking the San Francisco Bay. Even my students were tired of hearing me brag about how I slept a thousand feet from the beach.

Over the past few months, I had gutted the seats myself, insulated and sheet-rocked the interior, and installed an IKEA kitchen and Murphy bed with the help of a local carpenter. The only outstanding issue was the bathroom, which to my relief the contractor had finished the day before. My sleek outhouse stood a few feet from the bus, and had a sliding barn door, a solar shower, and an incinerating toilet. I would've held out on this big-ticket item until I was eligible for the next bump in my basic income allowance, but, once I got word Mare was coming, I borrowed the money from good ole Freddie (some friends had a lot of gold and, thankfully, stayed gold). Kyle, my on-again, off-again boyfriend, called it the most bourgeois outhouse in Northern California, but then again, he worked as a forest ranger and lived in a tent, by choice, even in the winter. He had just left that morning for his new post at Big Basin, and we agreed to exchange letters—yes, the old-fashioned, handwritten kind—until he could visit at the end of the season.

A cool breeze rushed through one of the bus's open windows. It blew a napkin off the kitchen counter onto the metal floor. I'd told Meryl to pack warmer clothes, hadn't I? I checked my phone, and yes, I'd texted her twice. Despite global warming, the Bay Area still got foggy in July. I typed:

> Pack for midwinter in New York.

Soon after, I drove to the outdoor equipment co-op to rent four sleeping bags and two tents and returned home. While stacking the gear against my bus home, they texted me:

> Change of plans. Bandmates want
> 2 stay in San Fran.
> Marin too far. Can you
> meet us 2morrow near our
> hostel?

> No problem, Meryl.
> Text me a meeting spot.

> Would you mind spelling it Merrill?

It reads less gender binary.

> Got it. I'm he/him/
> his btw.

Looking forward to seeing you.
I'm they/them/their.

I tossed the sleeping bags and tents into the back of the pickup truck, switched off my hearing aid, and blasted the hip-hop station with guilt-free abandon. Why did they want to stay in a smelly hostel when they could sleep on the beach in one of only three places in the state where you didn't need an air filtration system or a face mask? I needed to let it go. They were young, and young people liked the city. At the co-op, the manager, a friend of Kyle's to my good luck, refunded me in full.

The cafe was located on the ground floor of their hostel and stunk of burnt coffee and unwashed feet. A young woman came to my table, and at first I assumed she worked there until I took a closer look and realized they were Merrill. I had expected them to look like their social media profile: fresh-faced with long raven hair, wearing a burgundy Vassar hoodie, but they'd had a dramatic makeover. They wore raccoon eye makeup and a septum ring through their freckle-dusted, button nose. Their hair was shorn to a crew cut and dyed fuchsia. Filigree tattoos in navy and red covered every inch of their slim hairless arms. I apologized for not recognizing them. They didn't reach for a hug, so I didn't initiate one.

"So great to finally meet you, Merrill. Please sit down." Ugh, I sounded totally phony.

"I'm actually Jae now," they said. "With an 'e' at the end."

"You changed it?"

"Yes, I chose it yesterday. I no longer want to be named after a hyper-privileged, cis-gender, straight white woman. I'm attempting to decolonize my body."

They sat down, and we read the menu in silence. They asked for an unsweetened iced tea, and I ordered a Turkish coffee and an organic fruit and cashew cheese platter for the table.

I asked about school, and they said it was cool, but "Poughkeepsie was in the middle of nowhere." They wanted to be in a big city like San Francisco, so they had taken the past semester off to tour with their gender-queer, Asian-American punk band, Rice Kweens. The group performed English translation covers of K-Punk and J-Punk songs. Jae invited me to a show later in the week in Oakland. This perked me up. I said I would be there and made a mental note to find a sub for my class that evening. I couldn't hear their reply when I asked Jae if they sang. I adjusted my hearing aid on my phone and leaned over the table until they hollered, "I just play bass, I can't sing, I don't even do backup."

My hearing aid continued to malfunction. I repeatedly asked them to speak up until we ended up frustrated. A new device would have to wait since I had just built the outhouse. All those years blasting music through headphones and speakers had finally caught up to me a decade ago, and I was getting deafer by the week. Jae talked about the band to fill the silence, though I could only hear every third or fourth word. I eventually gave up and focused on their face. At first, I didn't see much of a resemblance. After staring longer, I could've kicked myself for missing it. My throat tightened while familiar shapes came into focus: the square of Jared's chin, the deep curl of his lashes, the high apple of his cheeks. After so many years, all his beauty in front of me was so overwhelming that I excused myself and pretended to use the restroom.

When I returned, I said, "Hey, you know what? You should come to one of my hip-hop dance classes. I teach at a studio a few blocks from here on Tuesday nights. I could comp you and your friends."

"I don't know," they said. "I have two left feet." My hearing aid finally kicked in, and the word "feet" rang so loudly in my ear that I writhed in my seat.

"Are you okay?" they asked.

"It's a beginner class. Anyone can do it," I said, probably too loudly. Jae looked down at the menu. I didn't push it. Our waiter brought our food, and we made small talk with him, which saved us from further awkwardness. They sucked their iced tea down in one long sip. I picked up a square of honeydew with a toothpick and nibbled on it. I asked where else they had been on tour.

"We were in Portland last week."

"Has it recovered from the big fire?" I asked.

"More or less. There aren't any trees anymore, but they're rebuilding like crazy. I pushed for it because my bio-mom lives there."

"Bio-mom?"

"My egg donor. Yuna Maldonado."

"Oh," I said, feeling more disappointed than I should have.

Jae had met Yuna for the first time right after their eighteenth birthday. Yuna was a sculptor turned interior architect who lived in Eugene but commuted to Portland for the rebuild. Her Venezuelan husband made a living as a semi-famous world music percussionist. They had ten-year-old twin boys. When Jae talked about her, their voice rang louder and brighter, their eyes widened, and their posture straightened. They would never talk about me with this much enthusiasm. I was a bit part in their life story, as inconsequential as an extra.

"So I have a question," Jae asked. "Do you know anything about my surrogate? I know you and my dad were together when you picked her. I thought you might know something."

"I don't. I'm sorry," I said. "Your father and I were on a break when you were born."

245

"I can't find her. The Cambodian government has no record of her. It's really frustrating. I'm thinking of moving out there to do research so I can get some answers."

"That sounds great," I said. "You'll never regret traveling."

"It's so bizarre. In this day and age, I thought I could find at least something online." They dug into their messenger bag and placed a stack of newspaper printouts on the table. A front-page story declared a winner in the Cambodian presidential runoff. In the adjoining photo, a handsome woman named Chariya Voan lifted a victorious fist over her head. Underneath this headline was a story about a mysterious fire that had destroyed the country's surrogacy archives.

"Look at all this research I've done. Nothing."

"Maybe some people don't want to be found," I replied.

It was clear that Jae was on some kind of a quest, and my letter to them had just happened to coincide. I stifled an urge to bombard them with information. It would have been a feeble attempt to prove I was more than an ancillary character on their journey. I had so many questions, though. Did Jae know that Lois had asked me to leave Jared's funeral when I showed up drunk? Aunt Jenny had held baby Mare in her tattooed arms and escorted me to the parking lot. She had told me to get sober and called me a cab.

Had Lois ever told Jae that I popped by unannounced at her apartment a week after the funeral to make amends? Lois opened the door, and I could tell she was close to accepting my apology until I offered to share custody. She then proceeded to chase me into the street. Who could've blamed her? We were both heartbroken and in deep denial that Jared was gone. To this day, I still don't believe he committed suicide. It was just too out of character.

My knee braces dug into my skin, forcing me to adjust them again. All these memories made me dizzy, triggering more than I anticipated. I couldn't help but be disappointed by our reunion.

What did I expect? For Jared's spirit to show up and exonerate me? Although he would've liked his earthly return to emulate the second coming of Christ.

I reminded myself that Jae was young, only twenty-one years old. How could they possibly understand what I'd been through? After Jared died, I wasn't allowed near them, which brought me to a very dark place. I thought a job might help, but I was hired and fired from Synergy within weeks— it turned out I couldn't return to that life—and soon after, I stopped dancing and started drinking full-time. A few years later, in AA, I ran into Kyle, the redhead, and we dated for a year before breaking up. To heal a broken heart, I moved to Addis with Nicole and her son, Kofi. The kid couldn't dance, but he more than made up for it with his sense of humor and the most infectious high-pitched giggle. I followed them to Jo'berg, then Bangkok, playing manny and teaching dance classes to expats—though I never did make it to Angkor Wat. Then Nicole met another USAID staff person, a handsome and kind man with two adopted kids from a previous relationship, and they married. Of course, I wanted to give their blended family some space. Still, I had also run out of money, so I hightailed it back to the Bay Area, where I got a job working for a youth development nonprofit and started dancing again, then teaching. Soon after, I quit the nonprofit job to teach dance full-time, and then Kyle and I got back together, too. Life was finally good. Why had I stirred the pot and revisited all my missteps and bad decisions?

One of Jae's bandmates joined us: shaved head, South Asian, gender nonconforming. A Ganesh neck tattoo spanned from their chin to their breastbone. Two of them giggled and touched until they suddenly became reticent when they remembered my presence.

"This is Parveeta," Jae said. "They play drums."

They looked at each other again and giggled. They were in love. Anyone could've seen it. Part of me wanted to interrupt their lovefest to tell them they were brave and that I admired them for taking a break from school to follow the path of an artist. It was an option unavailable to me growing up. My family had assumed I would take a safer and more linear path, and it had never occurred to me as a young person to question it. Even though I eventually veered off course, there was something to be said about figuring out one's calling earlier. I was glad the younger generations didn't struggle as much with this issue. Maybe it was because safe and linear paths were no longer an option.

I wanted to impart to these lovely young people a snappy one-liner full of original wisdom. But only a cliché came to mind: "With courage comes sacrifice." I wanted them to know that the pathless path was far from easy, but it was worth it.

After some hesitation, I finally decided what to say: "Kids, the world is on fire, and the 'winner take all' economy isn't going away anytime soon. Everything in our immediate surroundings is out of our control. We all feel helpless and inert every day, and the only thing left to do is precisely what we feel called to do."

I was about to say all this when Jae interrupted. "Sorry, we have rehearsal, so we gotta run."

"Work first." I was relieved I hadn't ruined our pleasant meetup with a diatribe. I liked these young people. They were bolder and more daring than I had ever been—so little ambivalence about their needs and wants. They didn't need my so-called wisdom.

I paid the bill, and we stood on the sidewalk, our carbon filter masks over our faces.

"Nine p.m. this Thursday." I spoke loudly so they could hear me through the mask. "I can't wait to see your band play."

"Wear earplugs," Jae said. "We're very loud."

"My hearing is already shot. I can't do any more damage."

"We're the opening act," Parveeta said. "You should be in bed before 11 p.m."

"I don't mind staying up," I said, removing my mask. I wanted them to remember my face without it. "Well, it was wonderful meeting you, Jae, after all these years. And you too, Parveeta."

"Likewise."

I leaned in and embraced Jae. They were sturdier than I imagined and had a familiar scent—a little oniony like their father. A tear tickled my nose, and I slipped my mask back on to wipe it away without them noticing. I waved goodbye and headed to the ferry terminal.

Once aboard, I pulled my mask off entirely. The state surgeon general said we should wear them everywhere to protect our lungs from pollution. But the air was cleaner on the water, and besides, I felt reckless—invincible, really. I looked out where the Golden Gate Bridge used to be and then at the expanse of green waters surrounded by dry hills, the relics of a once stunning bridge and monument, a pile of cement blocks and rusty steel pillars. And yes, I could have been sad about it, sad about how it had been lost, sad all the time about everything. But I wasn't. I could have also mourned my former jewel of a city. I could have mourned the loss of the country, the imminent death of the world. But I didn't. I leaned over the ferry's railing. The bay breeze misted my face, and I opened my mouth. Drops of brackish water sprayed over the railing to touch my tongue. I felt compelled to dance at once—my shoulders rocked, hips swayed, and sweaty knees throbbed under tight braces. But then, the bad heel seized. I sucked my teeth and continued dancing anyway. The irony wasn't lost on me. Only when everything inside me was broken did I realize I wasn't. Nor was I empty. Quite the contrary, I was full. I was whole.

Acknowledgements

THERE'S NO WAY to acknowledge all the family, friends, teachers, writers, mentors, workshops, and programs that helped make this book possible. If I've overlooked you, please forgive me.

Jim, this book is as much yours as it is mine. I'm indebted to you for going above and beyond and being my surrogate book daddy. Special thanks to Tori for reminding me to focus more on the sentence level. I also greatly thank Lisa for publishing my first chapter in *Joyland*. Natashia, thank you for reminding me to keep going.

Thank you to my teachers at the San Francisco Writers Grotto. To Glenn, thank you for making workshopping fun and low stakes. Faith, this adventure began in your travel writing class at The Writers Grotto. Let's keep being the African girl in Asia/Asian boy in Africa duo.

Thank you, Micaya and David, for teaching beginner-friendly hip-hop classes that brought me so much unbridled joy that I was delulu enough to write a book about it.

I would also like to extend a special thanks to the friends whose stories inspired scenes in the book. Hector, please don't call me the diva. Michaela, while I loved your stories about dancing in Switzerland, watching you dance is even better. And yes, I know I'm "brave" to dance in front of an audience. There's a reason I've stuck with writing.

Daniel/Steven and Jonathan/John, I am grateful for the gracious invitation to your homes and surrogacy stories. To your credit, the happiness of your households made poor fodder for the juicy novel I so desperately wanted to write.

Tess, I will always appreciate your belief in me and this book. You deserve the client Rolodex of your dreams. Special hat tip to my early editor, Paula. You immediately understood what I was trying to do and helped bring out my voice.

Eric, I appreciate you pushing me to make the manuscript the best possible. To Salem and the rest of the staff at Bywater Books and Amble Press, thank you for giving this little book about the gays a chance. I dream of making you rich.

To my cheerleading squad, Mark, Adam, and Ramzi, I hope I always do the same for you. Hugh, I am grateful for your gifts and the many reminders that this wasn't a fool's dream. Much gratitude to Rafael for being my biggest fan and keeping me somewhat sane for the past decade. To my parents for supporting my education and encouraging me to read and write. When you read the book in Heaven, please skip the dirty parts, especially Chapter 19. To Brett, Joe, James, Michelle, Travis, Wilda, Jeanie, Cathy, Betty, my fellow travelers, friends, and family—the pandemic may have scattered many of us around the country. Still, your texts and phone calls help me remember who I am and where I come from. I'm the luckiest guy alive.

About the Author

Tom Pyun is a novelist and a writer of creative nonfiction. He earned his MFA at Antioch University Los Angeles and has been awarded fellowships at Vermont Studio Center, VONA, and Tin House. His writing has appeared in *The Rumpus* and *Joyland*.

Tom didn't begin writing creatively until the age of thirty-five. He studied sociology at Vassar College and public health epidemiology at Columbia University. After an almost two-decade-long career in the philanthropic, nonprofit, and governmental sectors, he has finally accepted his calling as a storyteller, artist, and healer.

AMBLE
P R E S S

Amble Press, an imprint of Bywater Books, publishes fiction and narrative nonfiction by LGBTQ writers, with a primary, though not exclusive, focus on LGBTQ writers of color.

For more information on our titles, authors, and mission, please visit our website.

www.amblepressbooks.com

Printed in the USA
CPSIA information can be obtained
at www.ICGtesting.com
JSHW080830061024
71184JS00002B/24